THE
WILDEST SUN

Also by Asha Lemmie

Fifty Words for Rain

THE WILDEST SUN

A Novel

ASHA LEMMIE

Dutton

Lemmie

DUTTON

An imprint of Penguin Random House LLC
penguinrandomhouse.com

LIBRARY OF CONGRESS CATALOGING-IN-PUBLICATION DATA
has been applied for.

ISBN 9780593185711 (hardcover)
ISBN 9780593185728 (ebook)

Printed in the United States of America
1st Printing

BOOK DESIGN BY ELKE SIGAL

This is a work of fiction. Names, characters, places, events, and
incidents are either the product of the author's imagination or are used fictitiously.
The author's use of names of historical figures, places, or events is not intended
to change the entirely fictional character of the work. In all other respects,
any resemblance to persons living or dead is entirely coincidental.

For Oliver

No one can make you feel inadequate
without your consent.

—ELEANOR ROOSEVELT

CONTENTS

THE WILDEST SUN

Prelude

~~~~~~~~~~~~~~~

Delphine

Paris, France
September 1945

The heat from the hundred flames washes over me, and in this moment I am purified like true gold. I keep my eyes tightly closed and my head bowed. Here, in this little chapel, I kneel before the altar covered in candles. It is one of the long gray hours between midnight and dawn, and Paris is sleeping peacefully, her lights shining once more, now that the war is won.

I would be asleep too if I had not killed a woman.

Mother Bernadette—formerly known as Louise de Valence—says that only passionate prayer and true repentance can save my soul. She urges humility. Easy for her to say—this is a woman who was born with notable beauty and wealth, and threw both into the gutter to become a bride of Christ. But humility is not something that comes to me naturally. I am the daughter of a proud father and a delightfully vain mother. I am a girl who has always known that her destiny must lead to greatness, and that I must achieve it whatever it costs me.

I fiddle with the borrowed rosary in my hands. Maman wanted me to have a good education, and so she entrusted me at a young age to the care of the nuns at the Académie de Sainte Geneviève, under the watchful eye of their Mother Superior, her dearest childhood friend, Louise. It did not matter that we could not afford the fees, that all of Maman's family money had trickled away over the years, that all we had was the roof over our heads, heirlooms she was too proud to sell, and a good name tarnished by the rumors about my begetting.

Louise insisted that I be given an opportunity to learn. Christian charity, she called it. She was kind, patient, and attentive towards me, and I hated her nearly as much as I loved her. It was childish of me, but I did. My pride could not bear it. My temper, quick and lethal, simmered every time she fixed her serene smile on me.

I dig the sharp edge of the rosary's ivory crucifix into my palm, and I know without a doubt that my rage has finally destroyed me.

There is no possibility of forgiveness for what I have done. Not this time.

I cannot look into Maman's cornflower blue eyes and tell her that I am sorry. I cannot go to school in the coming weeks to doze through Latin and mingle with my classmates who don't like me much but are too polite to say so. I cannot walk on the Left Bank of the Seine and buy books from the peddlers and then read them on the very same day with my feet dangling above the water.

My native city is more alive than ever before, delirious with joy, bursting through the ashes like a phoenix taking flight, but she is lost to me forever. I have had her all my life, and even through these harsh, joyless years of war, I was grateful. I don't know who I will be without Paris.

When I rise from the floor, I will leave the girl that I was behind.

I lay my head on the cold floor and I whisper my final confession.

"Mon Dieu," I say piteously. My voice is full of tears, but my eyes have run dry. "I was jealous. I was foolish, and prideful, and I hated her for her weakness, and for her beauty, and for being so unceasingly charming." I dig the crucifix deeper. "I wanted so much," I whisper, dropping my voice so low that I can barely hear myself. "I wanted people to love me as they always loved her, no matter her failings. I wanted her to love me."

The darkness swims before me. I can feel my face burning with the last remnants of my shame.

"I didn't want to be second," I whimper. "Eternally silver."

I shove my fist into my mouth to muffle my desperate cries. I can't unravel. Not again. I spent more than a week bedridden, sobbing as if I would tear myself in two, refusing food, refusing water, refusing even sleep because it was a respite from grief.

I have no right to do that again.

I will have to move forward now with only enough confidence to get me from one day to the next. I must keep moving forward. I am damned, but I am free now too, and I have to find him.

I rise slowly from the floor, my limbs aching, my head heavy. I light a candle for her soul, and I hope that the God I have never given much thought to at all is indeed real, so that she may find the peace that so cruelly escaped her on earth.

I drop the rosary, and I turn my back on the dancing lights and walk slowly back to my room.

In a few hours, the sisters will awaken for morning prayers. I gather my few belongings, and then I sit down at the small desk to write a note.

My hand shakes, though I have known for days now what I must say. Even as I write, my mind has already flown away, slipped through the cracked window like a freewheeling sparrow. I can see the ocean that I will cross, shimmering beneath the moonlight, and the towering buildings of America. I can see his warm brown eyes, and his laughing mouth. If I try very hard, I can just barely imagine the spark of recognition that will pass between us, and I feel, once more, the fleeting joy of a fool flying too close to the sun.

Dearest Mother Bernadette,

Or Louise, as I know my darling mother would call you. I am so sorry to leave you like this, but I didn't have the courage to do it any other way. Thank you for everything you have done for me. I'm so sorry to fail you, but there is something I must do.

You need not trouble yourself with worry for my soul. It is past your power.

I will write to you, but I can never come back. You know why. I love you, and I wish I could stay, but that is not my destiny. I took the money Maman entrusted you with from your room. You told me that she gave it to you for safekeeping when I was a baby, the last of her inheritance, so that she could never squander it and leave me destitute. I know you didn't want me to have it yet, but I need it now.

You said once that you thought God had a great plan for me, but I cannot trust His ways, and so I have made a great plan for myself.

I'm going to find Papa.

All my love,

Delphine Violette Auber Hemingway

PART I

Chapter One

~~~~~~~~~~~~~~~~

Virgo Terrae

Harlem, New York
October 1945

When I was five years old, I learned how to roll my mother onto her side so that she would not choke on her own vomit. I learned how to press a cool, damp rag against her flushed cheeks and coax her to drink some water. I learned that a little chilled white wine could bring her down gently, not the terrifying crash that would leave her shaking and writhing on the floor. At nine I could make a perfect dry martini, and I was always so pleased to see Maman's eyes light up. If I waited until the right mood struck her, she would let me sit between her legs, and she would braid my hair and sing. If I begged, she would laugh like a little tinkling bell and tell me stories about when she was young and one of the most promising young socialites in all of France. She was friends with anyone important, and she wanted to be a famous poet whose words would make her immortal. Her parents wanted her to marry well, and God knows she could have—her creamy complexion, thick auburn ringlets, trim figure, and luminous blue eyes were a painter's dream—but she had her head turned by an American writer, and he was her savior and her doom.

I know the story by heart, I know it backwards and forwards. I know more about my mother's past than I do about myself.

When Maman met Hemingway, she loved him instantly.

She met him at a bar called the Dingo, where they were introduced by her favorite of the Americans who flocked to Paris twenty years ago, a writer she called "dearest Fitzy." For two years she was Papa's mistress, and he called her his *tournesol*, his sunflower. He called her poetry trite, and they had terrible rows, but she could refuse him nothing.

He kept his promise to leave his wife, but he did not leave his wife for her.

"I could have almost lived with it had he stayed with the dull one," she'd bemoan, her cheeks flushed, her eyes mournful. "After all, she was there first, and they had that adorable little boy. One could say she had a right to him. But to be abandoned for that *awful* drowning terrier . . . the shame of it. To have him turn from me and place a ring on the finger of that gaudy slut." She'd brush the invisible tears from her cheeks. "But at least I have you," she'd sigh. "Ma belle Delphine. Mon ange."

I was born on the eleventh of January 1929. By the time I entered my mother's life, he had already left it—retreated back to America with his second wife.

Louise told me that the drinking escalated when he left, and that the persistent melancholia set in after Maman's parents disowned her for falling pregnant. But I didn't need Louise to tell me that.

It was something I've always known but never let myself dwell on. I was never one for self-pity or for wishing things were different. My mother needed me; there was no room for those indulgent feelings.

But now that I am alone, here in this chaotic foreign city, I have all the time in the world for thinking. And I think it is a great shame that by the time I inherited my mother, the best of her had gone.

The scent of chicken frying wafts through the floorboards below me. It's a smell that is new to me, but one that I am finding rapidly addicting.

I live in a little room above a restaurant called Blue's. It's owned by one of Maman's old friends, a colored man named Joseph LaBere, who everyone calls Blue, and his wife Delia.

I had only met him four or five times before coming to stay here, on his infrequent trips back to Paris. I have always thought him very handsome—tall, bronze skinned, with wavy hair that he gels back, and flashing, mischievous dark eyes. He is from Louisiana originally, and speaks quite good French from his time in Paris in the twenties. His wife is fluent. Even though our shared language is the reason I chose to write to him weeks ago, to beg for refuge in America, I also happen to prefer him above the others in Maman's remaining circle of confidants. If I had to grind my pride to dust and throw myself at the feet of any one of them, I am glad that it is him.

I think he and my mother were almost lovers, but she told me that he was chasing after every skirt in the jazz clubs until he met his wife, and she was waiting for an epic love that I'm still not sure she found.

"Delphine!" Delia hollers up the rickety staircase. "Come on and get some dinner."

I almost respond that I need a moment to make myself presentable.

My dress is wrinkled, and my hair is unwashed and uncurled. I've spent the entire day at the desk in front of the lone window, scribbling the nonsense I am trying to forge into a real book.

I think about changing my clothes, but then I remember that I have abandoned vanity, and I settle for washing the ink off my hands and heading down. I take my life into my hands every time I descend this staircase.

The restaurant is closed—it closes early every Thursday night—and the empty dining room looks eerie. It's a crowded, noisy, joyful place that is always full when it's open.

Delia decorated it herself, with clean, simple decor and a white magnolia in a vase on every table. The windows are wide and arching, so the space doesn't feel cramped even though it is tiny. She's put her own sketches up on the wall, landscape scenes from her childhood: willow trees, steamboats, and people picnicking in their Sunday best on the promenade.

Blue and Delia's brownstone is just across the street. They offered me space in it, but I opted to take the small apartment above the restaurant's kitchen that the cook used to occupy. I like my privacy, and more importantly, I don't forget that I am meant to be in exile. How could I? My skin is itchy with shame, and I spend half my time glancing over my shoulder. I don't imagine that the deep waters of the ocean I crossed have washed the blood from my hands.

Delia smiles when she sees me, and I hold out my hands to take the heaping platter of shrimp and grits. She's holding a pot of something green—okra, I think, which tastes quite ghastly—in her blue checkered oven mitts.

"I already took the rest over," she says, in her genteel Southern drawl. "This is the last of it." She's a tall, striking woman with a light complexion; long, loose curls; and hazel eyes. She's something called Creole, and she went to a women's college in Quebec to study art when she was in her twenties. She still looks like she's in her twenties, which I told her when we first met, and she giggled and told me I could have all the dessert I wanted for the duration of my stay.

She's very warm, and it is not easy for me to carefully walk the line of showing my gratitude for her hospitality and keeping my distance. She has the kind of eyes that make you want to tell her the truth.

We walk across the street to their home. Their dog, a Jack Russell called Babette, sniffs my ankles as I walk in.

Blue is sitting at the beautifully set dining room table, reading his newspaper. The crumbs on his plate tell us he didn't wait for us to start eating the biscuits.

"Joseph!" Delia fusses, and at the use of his Christian name he looks up and grins. He is openly vain in a way that is oddly endearing.

"Don't be mad, wife. You're too darn pretty to frown."

"I told you to wait on us!"

I duck my head to hide my smile and slide into my seat. I start to play my game with myself: noting the objects all around the room and trying to make myself think of their names in English, not in French. My English is improving. I can understand some, but I am shy with my speech, which means I don't practice as much as I should.

Maman taught me some of the English she learned from all of

her American and British confidants from the old days. One of the few useful things she ever managed. She said it would help me get a good job one day.

"You could be a teacher," she said. "Or a travel agent. You're going to have more opportunities than I did, I'm going to make sure of it. You can't depend on a man, my love. God didn't make them that way."

She told me that Papa never really bothered to learn French beyond a cursory level, he just gestured a lot and expected people to take his meaning. "He figured that people could learn to speak to him if they had something important to say," Maman told me. His first wife was fluent, and he relied on her, and later, on my mother. "I shouldn't have enabled him," she'd sigh.

I can see her rueful smile floating before me, and I blink it away.

Delia is still fussing even as she puts food onto my plate. Last night it was gumbo so spicy it made my throat hurt, and then I had two slices of blackberry cobbler.

My skirts are fitting tighter than they did before. Delia is a masterful cook, and I have never eaten this well. Maman rarely touched our stove unless it was to light her cigarettes—we ate at cafés when she came up with the money, or I'd make stew from whatever I could find—and there wasn't much to be found during the war years. Canned anchovies were common, served with a side of stale bread.

We never once used the fancy dining table Maman inherited from her own mother. She avoided it like it was a relic from a mummy's tomb. Maman didn't like to talk about her parents. Whenever I asked, she would look ashamed.

"I just don't see why you can't wait," Delia goes on, smoothing out the tablecloth before taking her own seat across from her husband. "Did you even say grace?"

He shrugs. "God knows how I feel 'bout Him."

She mumbles something in English that I don't understand. They usually speak French around me so that I don't feel left out.

"If you would fix the stove in our own kitchen, I wouldn't have to cook our meals at the restaurant."

He chuckles. "Next weekend."

I raise my eyebrows. He sounds just like my mother swearing she would do the laundry, or buy me new clothes for school, or take me to Antibes—as if our family's beautiful chateau had not been sold years ago to pay off the debts. I see why they got on so well. Both of them could charm the scales off a snake.

Delia is clearly as unconvinced as I am, but she lets it go. She turns to me and shakes her head, as if lamenting how much she loves him.

I want to tell her that at least he married her, and is here, and did not leave her alone with a disappointing daughter and a broken spirit. He's a man who keeps his promises. He built that restaurant because it was her dream, even if he did name it after himself. I want to tell her she could do worse than his vanity, because he clearly has eyes for no one but her.

But I take a bite of dinner and say nothing.

Blue chats about the happenings in the neighborhood for a while: marriages and scandals, births and deaths. He says that the preacher's daughter was spotted with a white boy, and that she won't be able to sit correctly for a week now that her father is through with her. I know that in America, the races aren't meant to mix—Maman told me they have a special streak of foolishness when it comes to the color of one's skin—and Blue warned me when I got here to keep far away from the boys in the neighborhood unless I wanted trouble.

The old me would have taken it as a challenge. Now I think that I have enough problems without searching for new ones.

His eyes fall on me. "Do you have a sweetheart back in France, my dear?"

I conjure the image of a shy smile in my mind's eye before I can help it, though he was never anything to me but capricious hope.

I pinch the inside of my palm underneath the table to stop myself from sliding into the past. I will get mired in it like quicksand, and I will never get out. My lungs spasm, the air in the room grows thin. "No."

Delia interjects. "Don't ask a young lady things like that. You'll embarrass her."

He tuts. "I've known her since she was a baby. Her mother is family. There's no shame to be had between us."

My ears burn, but not because I'm ashamed. It's because I know what he's going to ask me, and I am preparing myself to lie. I am an excellent liar, something that used to give me great satisfaction, but now I view it with grim disdain. It is a necessary skill, and one I will use without hesitation or guilt—but I don't take pleasure in it anymore.

"So how is your mother? Have you heard anything lately?"

Amazingly, I smile without any strain at all. I have good teeth, one of my better features, and I let them sparkle.

"She's well. She's in Cannes, I think I mentioned before? She's staying with her cousin. She says she's writing poetry again."

I pull the folded letter from my pocket like a magician brandishing a rabbit from a hat. "I have another letter from her, for you."

It's a forgery, of course.

I have been forging my mother's signature, and later all of her handwriting, for years. How else could I have written that initial letter to Blue, with her name on it, urging him to take good care of her daughter while she recovers from cirrhosis? When I sent a letter in my own hand, it was nothing more than a finishing touch. I knew he wouldn't refuse my mother. My father is the only one I know of who ever has.

Blue takes it and opens it right there.

Delia leans forward in her seat. She's too confident for jealousy; there is only curiosity on her face. "Well?"

He scans it in one quick glance. I kept it brief. Short lies are much easier to remember.

"She seems better," he says, and he sounds relieved. "She says the fresh air is doing her good."

Delia nods and looks at me. "Well, make sure your mama knows we're feeding you well. And that I'll let out your clothes before I stop cooking."

"I'll tell her," I swear, false as any sinner. "Of course."

. . .

Later that night, I kneel on the wooden floorboards and face the lone window. This is not a cathedral, and there is no exquisite stained glass portraying the lives of the saints. The orange light that streams down on me is from the streetlamps. A cat is yowling, and I wish that I had a balcony like I did back home, so that I could step out onto it and howl too.

I am not praying, but I find that I can think very clearly when I am like this. For a brief time, I can gather my errant thoughts together and hold them still in my hands.

I have Louise's reply to the note I left her spread out before me.

Dear Delphine,

I cannot sanction what you have done. You are far too young to be on your own. I would ask how you managed it, but I am sure that you would not tell me the truth. I know that your mother's hands were in many pots once, and I am sure that you found a way to capitalize on the questionable company that she kept, and her endless need to be beloved. I must tell you to come home, though I doubt you will heed me. You should be here, with me, in the care of the sisters. We spoke about this. We prayed about this, did we not? I thought we had agreed that you would stay here and complete your education. You say you want to be a writer, but how can you write if you have not learned to be the master of your own thoughts?

I urge you to give up this foolishness of chasing a man who may or may not be anything to you. I know what your mother has always told you, but God bless her, she was unwell.

I do not blame you for believing it—you were a child clinging to a fairy story for comfort, and for an escape from a hard world.

But you are a young woman now. You must ask
yourself what it is all worth. Humble yourself with
prayer, and God will guide you.
    I too followed a path that no one else understood.
I cannot sit in judgment of you, Delphine.
    I will pray for your health in body and soul—
which is not now, and will never be, beyond saving.
    Louise

I crumple the paper up into a ball and toss it into the waste-basket. I don't want to think deeply about the state of my soul now; I don't want to be tormented with introspection. More than any-thing, I cannot entertain the possibility that I might be wrong.

I stand up and cross to the full-length mirror. Gently, I slide my nightgown from my shoulders and let it fall around my feet. As I peer at my own nakedness, I am filled with the usual disap-pointment.

I am of average height, but as gangly as someone much taller, with skinny arms and legs that don't seem to fit my frame. So far at least, I am flat as a washboard. I am olive skinned, with large eyes, a pinched mouth, and a small, straight nose that is one of my only favorable features. My eyes are the world's most uninspiring shade of brown, and my hair matches them exactly. I despise my hair most of all, because it is ludicrously thin. All the product in the world will only help me for a few hours. Right now I have it cropped so that it falls just below my chin. I try to pin curl it, but it's mostly hopeless.

Maman had thick, wavy hair, auburn like a lion's mane, that

cascaded all down her back. She would never cut it—only curl it and put it into a net—even when it was the fashion in the twenties to have hair as short as a boy's. She says it's one of the reasons Papa noticed her. She was exceptionally tall for a woman, and slender but exquisitely proportioned. She had all of the Parisian charm oozing out of her pores like a sweet perfume.

When she came to school to fetch me, on those rare days when she was feeling well enough, the other girls would always stop and stare at us. Their faces were animated, all screaming the same question: *That's* your mother?

And this is how I learned that I am not beautiful.

When she was well, she would read Perrault's fairy tales to me, or some Greek myth in which a nymph was turned into a tree to escape the clutches of Apollo. I always pictured her as one of the nymphs, and myself as the tree.

I have given up lamenting my lack of resemblance to her long ago; now it is simply a fact. There is no use wallowing in it. It's merely another thing that I should have inherited but did not.

I have my father's features: dark eyes and hair, a firm chin. And, I hope, I have his vision. I hope that when he looks at me, he will see his daughter, and when he reads what I have written, he will see something better still: his equal.

I cover myself up again.

If I go to Papa now, he will see nothing but a foreigner who cannot even speak English, who looks as common as a dandelion. He will have no reason to believe a word I say. Maman never told him I existed.

Who knows how many women he has bedded? He's on his third wife now, not even the woman he left my mother for but another woman entirely. I imagine all of his women like dominoes, each one falling seamlessly into the next. Maman told me that he had a heart as wide as the sea but as shallow as a puddle. His love was most generous where it was most hurtful.

I lie on the bed and fix my eyes on the cracks in the ceiling. Sleep creeps towards me but scatters away every time.

My determination to find him is the only thing tethering me to the material world. It blazes inside me like my very own sun. As long as I have it, I cannot die—even if I am heartless, bloodless, soulless. I cannot die.

It has kept me safe for all my childhood. It has given me the stomach to beg, steal, abandon.

And so I do not even entertain the possibility that he will not want me.

I tell myself that Papa has been waiting for me his entire life, even if he does not know it. He has three boys, three sons. I have no doubt they are clever and handsome, I have no doubt that he adores them and they worship him. Perhaps they are talented and ambitious in their own right.

But I am his daughter. And I will be the greatest of them all.

For certainly, I have paid the greatest price.

Chapter Two

~~~~~~~~~~~~~~~~~~

Firefly

Harlem, New York
November 1945

Delia insists that I enroll in school, being a woman who is fiercely proud of her own education, which is uncommon among women, no matter their race. But I cannot speak enough English to enroll even if I wanted to, which I don't. Blue sets me to work as a waitress, and I take to it well. I know enough English to take orders, and my accent seems to please people. The other girls who work here are always quick to help me if I look around.

I am speaking better and better every day, and I am proud of my natural ability to memorize things. I always got good marks in school, and I know that I am not stupid. I will apply myself to the task and not stop until it is done. If I am to write in English, in a way that is beautiful, I will have to work very hard indeed.

"Why don't you take some night classes?" Delia asks me one morning as we sit in her bright, sunny living room. Her artwork is all over the walls, and the scarlet couches are elegant but comfortable. Duke Ellington is playing in the background, and I am momentarily transported back home. I grew up listening to this music. I can see my mother clear as day, dancing around the living room, pulling me with her. *You have two left feet, mon Dieu, Delphine! Attention. Watch me, like this.*

Delia smiles at the look on my face. "What are you thinking of?"

She has her needle and thread out and is stitching up a tear in one of my dresses.

"Nothing," I say quickly. "Just that I can't afford to pay for classes. Can't I learn English just by talking to you?"

She shrugs. "Well, you want to be a writer, don't you?"

"I *am* a writer," I say, a little more petulantly than I intended to. I write a few ideas for novels down at least monthly, and I sign my true name in bold letters: Delphine Hemingway. Someday the whole world will know it.

She is unperturbed. "Maybe there are some classes offered through some churches. They'd either be free or not very expensive."

I want to protest at the thought of taking charity, but then I remember where I am.

My education was charity. The bed I sleep in, the food I eat, even that faded, ugly dress Delia is mending because I can't afford to spend my money on new clothes. I have to guard my funds like an old miser.

I also cannot afford my pride. This is not a new lesson, but I still buck against it like a stubborn horse that will not be broken.

My ears burn. "Oh, well. Do they cater to French speakers? Isn't it what, mostly Italians who come here?"

"People come here from all over," she corrects me. "This is a great country for the white man. He can be anything that he wants to be."

I blink at her. "Only for them?"

She wrinkles her nose. "Well, in New York I'm able to have my own business, and the people in this community always support each other. This is a better place for us than anyplace else I can think of. Much as I love my home, you'd have to hog-tie me to make me go back down South, and Blue feels the same way. New York is probably the closest place to the American dream for us." Her little chuckle is humorless. "But it's still America. It's not built for everyone."

"I don't understand," I say frankly. "It seems like a terrible fuss to make over nothing."

She gives me the same look that Louise so often gave me: the gentle condescension of an older, wiser woman to a young fool. It is free of malice. If there is any anger, it is not directed at me.

"It's not nothing to a lot of folks. It's all they have to cling to. Everybody needs to feel better than somebody else."

"I understand that." Of course I do, I have been guilty of it myself many times. "I just don't understand the selection criteria. Maman always said if you want to judge a man, judge him on something he can choose. Like wearing cheap cologne."

She laughs, and this time her eyes light up. "Everybody thought like you two, it'd be a better world. I hear she's been heavily involved in women's suffrage, is that true?"

I nod. It never struck me as remarkable before. I realize that the things I have taken for granted as natural are in fact not, and I appreciate my mother now more than when she was with me.

"She was the leader of a local chapter for a time, but it was all for nothing until de Gaulle and the provisional government wanted to reward women for their service during the war." I feel shame curdle in my belly that it took another war for my country to recognize women as competent. "But it's not in the constitution yet."

She shakes her head. "I tried to register to vote back home. My family said it was foolish, they barely let white women vote, but I did it anyway. I'm sure I got every answer on that test right but they didn't pass me." A defiant smile flashes across her lips. "I'm registered in New York, though. I found a way. I sincerely hope they add that amendment to your constitution soon."

"My mother says that hope is like chivalry. Both sops to keep the meek from realizing what has been taken from them, and to lull them into such a false sense of complacency that they don't bother taking it back."

Delia hands me back my dress, clearly amused. "Tell her to come visit once she's convalesced. I think I'd like to meet her."

They would have gotten on wonderfully. I look down. I'm telling Delia too much. "So you'll look into those classes for me?"

Thankfully, she bites at my attempt to change the subject. "I can if you'd like me to. It would be good for you. You spend all your time cooped up here, it's not healthy. You're a young woman, your mind is still developing, and it's a terrible thing to let it sit idle."

"Merci, madame."

She pours herself a glass of lemonade from the silver tray beside her. "And it will be good for you to make some friends. It's got to be terribly lonely not being able to speak to anyone besides us."

I shift my body slightly away from hers so that I don't look into her sweet face and tell her the truth—which is that I have never had any friends and I doubt learning English will change that.

. . .

New York is a selfish place. It hogs all of your senses, it attacks you with light and color and sound and *people*, so many people who don't seem to notice that anything is amiss.

If Paris is a watercolor, an impressionist painting that radiates beauty, sophistication, and a storied history, then New York is cubism: lurid, pretentious, and widely overappreciated.

It has none of the grace of a proper European city. Everything looks and feels far too big: the cars, the buildings, the displays in the store windows. Almost nobody knows how to dress, though it is obvious from their expensive clothes that they think they do.

Times Square is the gaudiest place on God's earth, the kind of tactless monstrosity that only an American could come up with. If I see one more poster telling me to go see Marlene Dietrich tap-dance, or whatever it is that she actually does, I'm going to lose my mind.

The subways are like cattle cars; the city's homeless sleep down in the fetid tunnels and beg for coins from everyone who passes by.

When I was just a little girl, I used to see some of the men who fought in the Great War sleeping in the empty doorways of the Latin Quarter in Paris. I asked Maman if the poor were like locusts, thinking I sounded very clever, and she told me to stop reading the newspaper.

It is autumn, and the breeze has turned chilly, so that I have to pull my shawl around my shoulders when I walk down the sidewalk. I know I look out of place, but I also know that nobody is looking at me.

The class Delia found for me is located on the Upper East Side, where some of the wealthiest people in the city live. Blue tells me that colored people aren't generally welcome here unless they're staff. There's no signs saying so, not like in the South, but everybody knows.

I pass several strollers with blond-headed children being pushed by brown-complexioned women. I give one of them a shy smile, and she nods back at me.

I find the townhome that I'm looking for on East 73rd and Lexington. There's a signpost out front that says *Bienvenue* but nothing else.

I can see through the window what looks like a living room that has been rearranged into a makeshift classroom, with about half a dozen desks facing a chalkboard.

It's certainly not the Sorbonne, but it's twenty cents a class, and Delia was able to talk the woman down to fifteen. I have three hundred and forty-seven dollars to my name, hidden in an antique jewelry box underneath the bed. I wear the key around my neck. I don't take any tips from the restaurant but give them all back to Delia and Blue in exchange for my keep. They agreed to take it but insist they'll give it back to me whenever I ask.

I smooth my hair behind my ear and press the buzzer. A gray-haired woman answers the door, as wide as she is tall, wearing a bright orange dress. The skin underneath her blue eyes is wrinkled and stained brown, but her smile is friendly.

"You must be Delphine," she says in French. "I'm Madame Juliette."

I can tell from her accent she's from France, but not from Paris.

I offer her my hand. "I'm very happy to be here."

She shakes it and her palms are so sweaty that I instantly regret my choice. "I was born and raised in Brest, but I've lived here for twenty years now. I own a patisserie a few streets over—I could not stand what passed for pastry in this city—and I teach in the evenings. Only ladies, I don't want men in my house. Class is every weekday, from seven o'clock to nine o'clock. From now on we will speak only English, unless it's an emergency," she warns me. I blink at her, and she switches to English before I have a chance to respond. "Do you understand?"

"Yes," I say weakly. I hear how clumsy I sound compared to her, and it makes me flush. "Yes, I understand."

I give her the money and she beckons me inside. She has put up a curtain blocking off the classroom from the rest of the house. It's sparsely decorated, with plain walls and a neglected-looking potted plant in the corner.

Most of the other women look to be older than me, and I spot several wedding rings.

I take the only empty desk.

I pull out the notebook that I have brought with me, and my pen. It feels eerie, and the hair on my arms stands up. When I left school, I thought I was done with the feeling of learning something new, and the anxiety of wondering if I could be the best at it. Or at least not the worst.

The two hours go by quickly, and I do my best to keep up. At one point the teacher singles me out, and we have a simple conversation that feels easy. *Are you looking for the cinema? It is two streets over. It has a blue sign.*

She tells us all to go practice at home, and she hands out a worksheet to fill out. When the clock strikes nine, she shoos us all out as if we are cats who have invaded her kitchen.

I emerge onto the street, and the crisp night air is an immense relief. I dislike confined spaces. When I was home my favorite place to be was our balcony at nighttime. I would curl up with a blanket and play the game of lights: the city unfurled before me like a constellation, and every time one went off another would rise to take its place. On the nights when Maman went into her room and locked the door behind her, that vista was the only company I had.

I don't want to go back to Harlem yet. I don't want to answer Blue's inquiries about whether I've written to my mother, or have Delia grill me about whether I've made any friends.

I walk around the neighborhood feeling very plain and wishing that I had thought to put on a nicer dress and some heels. I have my hair braided like a country girl, not styled like a society lady, and I cringe a little as I catch my reflection in a shop window.

I stop in front of a grand building with a doorman out front who looks straight through me. It's obvious I'm no one whose name he needs to know.

A taxi stops on the street right beside me, and two men get out practically holding up a woman between them. She's wearing a white fur coat, and her platinum blonde pin curls are out of place. Her lipstick is smeared onto her cheek. She's fussing at them so fast I can only catch pieces of what she's saying. Then suddenly, the older of the two men slaps her across the face.

I jump as if he's hit me too, and as she crumples to the ground I have to press my hands to my mouth to stop my gasp.

No one else seems to be alarmed. The doorman is looking at his watch as if it's telling him something highly important, and the two men have already gone inside the gold-plated glass doors.

The woman is left alone.

She picks herself up on wobbly legs, stumbling on tall high heels, and then starts slowly across the street, without looking both ways.

I follow her without even thinking about it. My curiosity always has outpaced my sense of self-preservation, and even though I am committed to change, this woman is the most interesting thing I've seen in months.

She goes a few blocks with me trailing behind her before she notices me. She stops beneath an awning, and I stop with her.

The face she gives me is ugly, though I can still tell that she is not.

"Do I know you?"

I realize now what I must look like to her. I take a tiny step back, preparing to run off. "No."

"So why are you following me?"

I have to think of the right words to reply, and she taps her foot impatiently.

"I . . . I saw what happened. I am . . . sorry."

She drops her scowl. I realize that I am not looking at a woman at all, but a girl not much older than me.

"Oh, that." And the way her voice goes up I can tell she is ashamed. I am very familiar with the look and sound of shame. "My friend just had a little too much to drink at the supper club."

Not much of a friend if he strikes her in the street in front of everyone. I nod. She looks like she's had a little too much to drink herself.

"I don't want to go home yet," she says, more to herself than to me. "I'll wait until he calms down. I think I'll go get some coffee." She eyes me. "You're not crazy, are you?"

I think I understand. "I'm Delphine," I volunteer. "I'm . . . new to the city. To America."

She picks up on my accent. "Oh, where are you from?"

"Paris."

She gasps. I see her color rise under her heavy blush. "Oh, really! Well then, you can *definitely* come have coffee with me."

She gestures for me to follow her and keeps walking. She seems very sure of herself, even as she wobbles.

She leads me a few more blocks, to a small café. It's only got a few tables, but the man behind the counter greets her warmly. There are no other patrons at the moment, and she goes to the left corner table as if she owns it and slides into a chair.

I sit across from her, and she studies my face.

"How old are you?"

"Almost seventeen."

She shakes her head in wonderment, as if she cannot imagine such a thing. "You're just a child."

"How old are you?" I retort, defensive now.

"Eighteen," she says proudly, as if there is a vast difference between us. "Though I tell people I am twenty-one. I'm Teddy. Teddy Dolan."

I bite back a laugh. What kind of name is that? "I'm Delphine."

"Delphine who?"

I look at her hands, folded on the table. The fingernails are carefully painted a dark red. She has a gold bangle on each wrist.

I want to say Papa's name, but I have not said it out loud since I was a little girl, and I faced laughter then. I remember the way the sound washed over me like a cold tidal wave. I hear it echoing in my mind even now, and know I will remember it until the day I die.

"Only Delphine," I say weakly.

Her eyes are a similar shade of brown to mine but somehow far more interesting. Though her nose is slightly large for her face, she's still a very pretty girl, and I feel a twinge of annoyance that I have nothing to be proud of as I sit before her. I can't even bring myself to tell her my name.

"I speak some French," she volunteers. "I took it in school. I was *très bien*."

I smile at her ludicrously overdone accent. "I am trying to learn English. Ce n'est pas facile."

"You speak well," she says encouragingly. "It can't be easy. I moved here from Ohio."

I frown. "Where is that?"

"Nowhere," she says bitterly. "I couldn't wait to get out of there."

I don't understand exactly what she means, but I hear the scorn in her voice. "You live with . . . your friend?"

She starts to answer me but then breaks off and looks around. "Where's my coffee?" she shouts. "And one for my friend!"

My ears prick up. Not just at her audacity, or in truth her rudeness. But at the word "friend."

I barely know her. There is no reason I should care that she likes me. But I find that I do.

Teddy shrugs her shoulder, revealing a low-cut turquoise party dress beneath her coat.

"I come here all the time," she says. "I expect better service."

"Oh."

The man bustles over and puts two steaming mugs before us. I take a sip and it takes everything I have not to spit it back out. It tastes like hot tar. Worse than the ersatz coffee I used to offer Maman to sober her up.

Teddy makes no move to drink hers. "Sometimes you have to be bold if you expect to get what you want. Harlan wouldn't stand for not being helped immediately. Most men don't, you know."

"Oh."

She slides a piece of paper across the table at me. "That's my phone number. You can call on me, if you like. I go out every night, almost. Harlan knows everyone, and we get into all the supper clubs and shows. You could come." She looks me up and down. "If they'll let you in, as young as you look."

"You want me to come?" I am sure that I must be misunderstanding her. "Why?"

Teddy giggles. "I've never met anyone from Paris. You can tell me stories. And I can introduce you to New York. But you'll need new clothes."

"I can get them," I say hurriedly. I will have to work even harder on my English now.

She stands up. "I've got to go. It's late and I'm expected."

She bends over and kisses me on both cheeks, and I blush from the tips of my toes to the crown of my head. My jealousy is replaced with intense fascination; I feel it take hold of me like a straitjacket. I will not be satisfied until I understand this girl, until I have learned to mimic her radiance. I will not try to steal it, as I have done before, so disastrously—I am better now.

But I can sense that this girl will also open up chaos before me, and I know, I just know that I will fly straight into it like a firefly into a jar.

Teddy beams at me. "Enchanté, Delphine. Good night."

She puts down some bills and leaves without touching her coffee.

Chapter Three

~~~~~~~~~~~~~~~~

Mirage

Harlem, New York
December 1945

Christmas morning, I wake early and go to the window, pressing my nose against the frosty glass. I don't put much stock into holidays. Christmases were bleak in the war years, and even before, it was just Maman and me most of the time. Usually she could dig out an old friend to borrow money from and we would go to a restaurant, or I'd get a new dress or a new pair of shoes with shiny buckles. Sometimes she would give me one of her old pieces of jewelry, given to her by one of a dozen admirers from the days before, and I would go to my room and dance around in the mirror.

Delia taps on the door as the sun rises. She is wearing sprigs of holly in her hair and a red dress that I suspect she made herself. She is an excellent seamstress.

"Merry Christmas," she says with a bright smile, drawing me into her arms as if she's known me all her life. I catch a whiff of her signature perfume, a dark, musky smell that I quite enjoy.

I reply with considerably less enthusiasm, but she is undeterred. She turns her back to the door while I get dressed.

"I got up early to make dough for biscuits," she explains. "I just *love* Christmas, even when I was a little girl and we hardly had two nickels to rub together. It was the only time of year we got store-bought penny candy and a book each. My daddy tried not to shop at those white stores if he could help it. He didn't take to them waiting on every white man, woman, and child in the store before us. Sometimes if they wanted a laugh they'd make us stand out in the rain to wait for our orders."

Once again, I am aware of my skin in a way that I have never been before as I pull my dress over my head and run a brush through my limp hair. Until the Germans came to steal what was left of my childhood, I never really thought of people as being white, or colored, or Jewish. One was either blessed enough to be a Parisian or they were not.

Maman didn't see people as categories, and I took it for granted that she spoke for everyone.

"I'm sorry," I say awkwardly, because I feel somehow responsible for these people.

Delia tuts. "Don't apologize for those fools. Lord knows they'd never have enough sense to apologize for themselves. But you're a sweet child for thinking of it."

I frown at this. "I'm not a child."

"You are," she says cheerfully. "And once your innocence is gone it's gone, so try to appreciate it more and don't be in such a hurry all the time. Now, come on, breakfast is ready."

She leads me downstairs and across the street, whistling all the way. I try to let her joy infect me. I'm just grateful no one has mentioned going to church. Besides, it's the first Christmas since the war ended, and I am not looking for reasons to be glum.

Blue is waiting for us in the living room listening to Bing Crosby on the radio. Delia has decorated every inch of the house with garlands and bells, ribbons, and holly. The sharp scent of pine leaves from the Christmas tree fills the air and makes me slightly queasy. She has put enough lights on it to fill Times Square. Delia goes to him, and he wraps his arm around her shoulder.

They both turn to look at me, beaming, and I take an involuntary step back.

"What is it?" I ask. Could they have discovered my ruse? Do they know that the letters I pass on to them are as counterfeit as I am?

"We have something for you," Delia says. She points to underneath the tree, where I had not even thought to look. Maman never got us a tree.

But underneath this tree there is indeed a large box wrapped in shiny red wrapping paper adorned with a golden bow.

I blink.

"For me?"

Blue rolls his eyes. "It says 'Delphine,' doesn't it? Go on and open it."

I hesitate for a split second before kneeling down and drawing the gift towards me. It's heavy.

I tear open the paper and find what looks like a hat box inside. But when I take off the lid, it is not a hat at all, and I have to bury my face in my sleeve.

It is a typewriter. A gorgeous, brand-new typewriter.

I look up at them in wonderment. "This is really mine? *Vraiment?* To keep, you mean?"

Delia giggles and pats my hair. "Do you like it?"

I run my fingers over the bold lettering. *Remington. Model Seventeen.*

Something as fine as anything that any real writer in the world may have. Perhaps Papa has one just like it, sitting on his desk, waiting for him to visit at the end of each day like a trusted friend.

I am one step closer.

This is mine now. Because of them.

I am humbled to dust, but for the first time, it doesn't hurt.

"It's the nicest thing anyone has ever done for me. *Thank you.*"

Blue nods at the two of us. "It was an easy decision. Now you don't have any excuses. Promise me you'll work hard now."

"I will," I swear. "I really will."

Delia claps her hands together. "There are more gifts for you, of course, but the rest can wait. Let's eat."

. . .

Dearest Louise,

I send you the warm greetings of the season. I am sorry I have not written for some time. I have much to confess.

I experienced my first American Christmas, and I liked it very much. Blue got me a typewriter! It is the most beautiful thing in the world. He asks only that I remember him when I am famous. He is a good, kind man, and my mother chose wisely to count him as a friend. Delia made me twelve new dresses, one each for the twelve days of Christmas, and she made a feast the likes of which I have never seen. I had far more fun than I deserve, and I have to confess to the sins of indulgence and vanity. I have never known anything like this house. The parlor smelled of roasting chestnuts for the entire month, and Delia played the piano and we all sang carols together.

I have met someone. Her name is Teddy, and she is only a couple years older than me. I think we are becoming friends. I have been out with her a dozen times now, and she takes me to the most wonderful places—all the best clubs and shows, and her boyfriend pays for it all and tolerates my presence because it makes her happy. That is the only nice thing I can say about him. He is ancient, at least forty, and he drinks far too much and is short with her. She says that it is a small price to pay, for he is a director and will make her a famous actress one day. I am not sure how to advise her, or if it is even my place to advise her? After all, if I was meant to be a writer, and you were meant to be a bride of Christ, then who is to say she was not meant to be an actress? Anyway, she is older than me, and probably wiser too.

I am keeping up with my English lessons, and I speak much better now. Teddy wants me to teach her French. She swears that one day she will have a house in Paris,

*and all of the other celebrities will come and visit her.
She pesters me constantly for stories of Maman's youth,
how she knew all of the dancers and writers and painters.
Teddy is dazzled by it all, as I was, but I have not told
her about Papa.*

*I have made a little progress on my novel. At least it
has a title now. I am calling it "The House of Pristine
Sorrows." I still do not have the slightest clue what it will
be about, but I know that the inspiration will come to me
soon. Now that I have my typewriter, I feel like I am one
step closer.*

I have not forgotten I am here to find Papa.

*He has a home in a place called Florida, so I'll look
there next.*

*Your loving daughter in Christ,
Delphine*

. . .

Long Island, New York
December 31, 1945

Teddy's lover, Harlan, throws a massive party on New Year's Eve
at his house on Long Island and I am invited. The house is huge, a
relic from the Gilded Age with twelve rooms, and he tells us all
loudly that it's been in his family for generations. Teddy is glowing,
her creamy skin radiant against the dark green sequins of her gown.
Harlan insists on making a toast to his family's great legacy, which
I unfortunately understand every word of, and Teddy rolls her eyes
at me during his speech and winks.

She will make a good actress. Every time his gaze falls on her, she adopts this doe-eyed expression and smiles coyly, as if she is overcome with desire for him but is afraid to show it. She does not flinch when he fondles her in public, when he slides his hand up the inside of her thigh in plain view of everyone. She lights a cigarette and looks around for someone to chat with as if she has not even noticed. She talks to him when he likes, and scurries away quickly when he is in a temper, which usually coincides with how much scotch he's consumed. Watching him, I appreciate that my mother was never a mean drunk.

I cannot pretend to like him, but I bite my tongue and settle for speaking to him as little as possible. Not that he cares. He clearly has a type—blonde and pretty—and I am neither. We tolerate each other by ignoring one another, and that is fine by me.

He is unbearably arrogant for being so physically unappealing— he is paunchy, balding, and has a face like a scheming ferret—and it reminds me of my mother saying a man never lacks for confidence. "A woman has one hair out of place and she despairs," she told me. "She will hate herself, and the world will join her. But a man? A man can have the face of a gargoyle and will think himself the handsomest person in the room. They don't lack self-confidence, Delphine. Only self-awareness."

I wish I could take Teddy away from him. If I had the power, I would give her everything that she wanted. I would not see her debase herself at the feet of such a man.

But she explains to me quite calmly that this is the way of the world, and that if she must sell herself, she will make sure that she fetches a high price.

"You sound like you are in a meat market," I say distastefully.

We are sitting out on one of the many balconies. The stench of smoke inside was starting to make me ill.

She hiccups. I've seen her drink three glasses of champagne. When we are alone together, she never drinks at all. "Of course it is. What else could it be? We are all buyers and sellers. The only difference is what we happen to want."

I can't argue with her. I would sell everything I have ever owned for my father's love and acknowledgment. I would burn cities to the ground. And once I have it, whatever I have done will be worth it, and there will be nothing left to haunt me.

"Are you a romantic, my love?" she teases. "Do you wish for a great love story?"

"No," I say bluntly. "I have seen how that goes. I don't have any interest."

She nods. "That's smart."

"How did you meet him anyway? Harlan?"

Her mouth goes hard. "My first week here, I stayed at a ladies' hotel, but I didn't have money to stay for long. I met a woman who asked me if I wanted a more permanent solution to my troubles. She introduced me to a few different men before I met Harlan, and I moved in with him a little while later." She tries to smile, but it's frail. "And now look at me. Living on the Upper East Side of New York in a gorgeous apartment, wearing new clothes every month. It's perfect."

She straightens up a little in her seat. "It's perfect," she says again. I don't think she's talking to me.

"So are you ever going to tell me why you came here?"

I am suddenly alert, like a deer who hears a twig snap in the deep forest. "I have told you before. I want to be a writer."

"Hm, yes. I know. But you could have been a writer in Paris. You're not like me, you don't come from a place with no opportunity. And from what you tell me, your mother knew everyone, and she could have helped you."

She has cornered me. I feel the old instinct to deflect, to lash out and say something cruel, but I suppress it. "Perhaps. But things were different with her in her later years. She was melancholy. She lost touch with most of her old friends. And now she is not in Paris at all, she is in the country, recovering."

Teddy is diverted. "Recovering from what?"

"A long illness," I say quietly, hoping that she will sense my discomfort and leave it be. "But she is on the mend now."

"And will you go back to Paris when she's better?"

"Why are you so curious tonight?" I snap at her, the thin thread of my patience finally worn through. "What is it you want me to say? That my mother is a drunk? That I left the city I love more than anything because I had no choice? That my home and my family are lost to me forever?"

I bite off what I want to say next. My temper feasts upon itself; I cannot allow it to go any further. I try to remember Louise's voice. I visualize the chapel: the whitewashed stone, the powerful smell of incense. The light pouring in through the stained glass windows, Louise's gentle hands clutching mine as we kneel together, a sinner and saint. I hear her quiet words in my mind, and I put my face in my hands and take a long breath.

I will not feed the bitter seed.
I will not nurse it like a babe in arms.
I will not burn to cinders in my own fire.
I will not feed the bitter seed.

I feel hands on mine, and for a moment I think that I really am transported. That God has seen fit to pluck me from my purgatory and put me back in time. I am home, I am restored, Maman is with me.

But then the tug grows more insistent, and I look up into Teddy's tearstained face. She is kneeling before me.

"I'm sorry. I'm sorry, Delphine, forgive me."

"It's all right," I hear a voice that sounds like mine say.

Her eyes are large and pitiful. "I'm the most horrible girl in the world."

"You're not." I touch her dyed blonde hair. I can see the tiniest bit of light brown at the root. "You're not, Teddy. I'm just upset with myself. I came here to find my father, and I've made no progress at all."

She rubs her mouth with the back of her hand as if she's tasted something foul. "I came here to get away from mine."

I'm hardly listening to her. "Mine's a writer, like me. I'm his bastard, and he's got no idea, and I came here to . . ." I trail off. It sounds so ridiculous. And I really don't think I can bear to have her laugh at me. Not Teddy. Not my friend, my first real friend.

She doesn't laugh.

"Well, I must help you, then," she says with concern, as if it's the most natural thing in the world. "Because it's love."

"It's destiny," I correct her. I can smell the sharp scent of blood in my nostrils, I can feel the body going cold in my arms. "For me to meet him, and for him to admire me, and for me to become a writer greater than him. It's my destiny. I have given up everything for it." I catch myself. "It's the only path for me. There's no other choice. I have to do this."

She smiles at me. Wordlessly, I reach out a hand and she takes it. Even with all the noise from downstairs, I feel a sense of calm flow through me, and by Teddy's sleepy smile, I know she does too.

"I have an audition next week."

I seize onto the change of subject, pushing back thoughts about my mother, or before. At once I can see Teddy on a stage, smiling into bright lights.

"Do you?"

"It's for some play. By somebody named after the state of Tennessee, if you can believe it. We'll see how it goes."

"You'll be fantastic," I insist, and she chuckles and squeezes my fingers.

"And what about you?" she asks. "How is writing now that you have that shiny new typewriter?"

"I'm not so good with it," I admit. "It's going to take some practice before I do anything but waste paper. For now, I write my ideas down with pen and paper."

"And what ideas are those?"

I hate that I don't have a more polished answer for her, and I curb the temptation to lie to make myself look better.

"I have very little," I confess. "I'm waiting for divine inspiration like my father must have. But I think I want to write a bildungsroman."

She frowns. "A what?"

"A story about someone growing up. They're usually about boys, but I want to write one about a girl."

She wrinkles her nose. "Oh, don't do that. Growing up is miserable."

"I think Papa will like this," I insist. "He has to like what I write or there is hardly any point. That's why I'm going to write it in English, even though it will take me twice as long."

She rolls her eyes. "So is he here or not? Your father?"

I look down at my lap. "I just assumed he'd be here, but he's not. I finally got up the courage to ask Blue, who told me that he has a home in Florida. Now I have to start over again."

"Don't run off just yet," she says quietly. She is using her real voice, with the slight twang in it, the unpolished speech of a farm girl. "I can't stand to lose you. Don't leave me on my own with these miserable people. I really will die of misery if the boredom doesn't kill me first."

"You have everything," I mumble. "You're beautiful, you have a wealthy man at your feet. You're talented. You don't need me."

She looks at me with wide brown eyes. "I want you, though."

And I have to look away from her and blink twice, because these are new words to me.

"You'll be happy when you're famous," I insist. "When you have your Oscar and I have my laurels, we won't even remember what misery feels like. We'd be happy all the time."

She closes her eyes. "A body can't be happy all the time, Delphine. Then it wouldn't mean anything."

From inside, we can hear a great roar, and we know that the New Year has come at last. It's officially 1946. The worst year of my life is over. Miracle of miracles, I have a friend. And a temporary home with Blue and Delia.

And now everything will be different.

. . .

The Wildest Sun

Harlem, New York
January 30, 1946

Louise's reply to my letter arrives a few weeks after my birthday. Blue hands it to me, and I tuck it into my pocket without so much as a glance. I don't want to be chided now. I don't want to be reflective now. Teddy is taking me to a new supper club to celebrate, and I will wear one of the dresses that Delia gave me. I have written ten whole pages of my novel—ten!—and Delia is making me an apple pie tomorrow. I don't want to be anything but glad, and if that means putting my blinders on like a horse, then that is what I will do.

Blue narrows his eyes at me, but his grin is friendly. "I'm not your mama."

I look at him, startled. "Sir?"

"I'm not your mama," he repeats. He always speaks so slowly, as if he has nowhere in particular to be. "But as long as you're under this roof, I have a duty to look after you. And it seems to me you've been keeping late hours."

I blanch.

His dark eyes are pinned on me. "Haven't you?"

"Yes," I say, rather sheepishly.

He nods. "There's only a few reasons for a girl your age to stay out that late at night. And none of them are particularly fitting."

"I've made a friend," I say quickly, too quickly. "We go to shows. I'm still going to my English lessons. I help in the restaurant, I help Delia around the house. I don't do anything bad. I promise." I sound like a child, but I can't take the words back.

He puts his hands up to stop my denials. "Now look," he says. "You don't seem like a dumb girl. You say you're doing right, I believe you. But you're young, and you're a long way from home. And if you run into any trouble, I expect you to tell me."

I hesitate. I know he's a good man, but his loyalty and love are with Maman, not me. There is a limit to how far I can trust him.

I force certainty into my voice. "I will."

I can't decide whether to sound assured and sophisticated, so that he'll respect me, or sweet and innocent, so that he'll trust me. Besides, if he has dealt with the many faces of my mother, then I doubt I can fool him anyway.

He nods and leaves the room. He seems like the kind of man who only says things one time. I imagine what it would have been like to have him as a father. I would have liked to have grown up with a mother who drank only when she was happy, and not when she was sad, and a father who sat me on his knee and read me stories. It would have been a happy, busy, musical childhood.

But there is no point in thinking like this.

I cross the street to the restaurant. I nod at an old woman sitting on her stoop next door, and she gives me a gummy, toothless smile. Most of the people in this neighborhood are comfortable with my presence now.

I mount the deathly staircase and go as fast as I dare. If I move quickly, the thoughts come slower. I'm going out tonight. All I care to ponder is what I'm going to wear.

I spend a full hour on my hair, but it fails me as usual. We're going to a place that just opened. Me, Harlan, Teddy, and the usual pack of sycophants whose names I don't try to learn. I identify them by their coats, their hairstyles. They are all flies to me, buzzing around Harlan and his money like a jam tart left to cool on the windowsill.

I don't like to wear as much makeup as Teddy, but I look far too young without it, so I halfheartedly plaster some on. I smile at my rouged reflection. I look like a tart. I have seen classier-looking women on the Paris street corners, and I take a tissue and wipe half of it off.

I practice my writer's expression: a teasing half smile, my head cocked to one side. I look ridiculous. I don't look like him at all. I have studied his face all my life; I have read every one of his books translated into French. When my English is a bit stronger, I hope to read them in their original language. I admire his simple, elegant prose, and his pithy dialogue. I don't mind that his characters don't often get what they want. Who does?

When I was five or six, Maman placed his photograph on my bedside table like a holy icon. It was one of the few things that I brought here with me. Since I came to New York I haven't been able to bring myself to look at it. I can't bear to have the frozen likeness of his honest brown gaze upon me. I know he will see straight to the heart of my failings, wherever he is tonight.

I adjust the belt on my dark green dress. I pull the neck down a little, but to no avail; I am still flat as a washboard.

I can feel my irritation turning to loathing, and I look away from the mirror before I feel the urge to shatter it.

Louise's letter—a lecture no doubt, it's always a lecture—sits on my desk beside my writing journal, which I have left shamefully empty this week. Again.

I have to get my coat and dash from the room before I succumb to the temptation to read the letter. Despite myself, I miss her. She's the only person in the world who sees me for what I am and hasn't turned away.

It was her I ran to that day, with the blood still on my hands. It was she who washed it off, and held me as I screamed.

When I respond to her letter, I will try to be humble, so that she will not feel her teachings have been entirely wasted on me. Perhaps she can advise me on how to ask God for inspiration, so that I can finish my novel.

Inspiration, and breasts.

·   ·   ·

Teddy is in a mood. I can tell the second I take my seat beside her around the round white table at dinner. She doesn't say a word to me; she doesn't even smile. She's wearing long sleeves, which she never does no matter how chilly it is, and she's got a sheen of sweat on her forehead. The entertainment hasn't started in earnest yet, but the band is playing softly in the background. The room is dark and smoky, which I take it I am meant to be enjoying, but really I can barely read the menu unless I hold it towards the glowing centerpiece in front of me. I am on her right; the girlfriend of one of Harlan's companions is on her left. I think I heard her say her name was Fiona. She's tall, leggy, and has very dark hair in contrast to her pale skin. Her gray-blue eyes are large in her heart-shaped face.

She's pretty, in a way that would irk me if I stood any chance of competing with her, and that I know will irk Teddy, who does.

There are eight of us tonight, five men and three women. I recognize the man from the first night I met Teddy, whose name is

Peter or Jacob or something boring and biblical. He doesn't say much, and he does whatever Harlan tells him to. I have started inwardly referring to him as the Greyhound.

I can't quite figure out what any of these people actually do for a living.

Harlan is supposed to be a director and a playwright, but all he does is spend his grandfather's money. He's written one play in three years, and nobody has ever heard of it. Some of the others are musicians, and I think one is supposed to be a painter. But none of them appear to be trying very hard. They are far from starving, in their minks and tailored suits, so perhaps there is no urgency behind it. Perhaps it simply makes for good conversation over a game of cards and a cold drink.

At first, I was flattered to think that I had fallen in with the artists' crowd, just like Maman. Twenty years ago, when everyone who was anyone came to Paris, Maman was at the center of it all. Her name was on every list; she sat for portraits and read now-acclaimed poems when they were still half formed, snippets written on bar napkins and whatever else was at hand. I used to wait until she had gone out, or nodded off on the couch, and then sneak into her room to look at her collection of photographs. She never wanted me to read her own poetry, though. She had volumes of poems written in leather-bound journals that she kept in a box beneath her bed. After Papa left, I think she gave up on showing them to anyone else.

Before then, it was all so gorgeous, and I tortured myself that I had been born too late to enjoy any of it, but Maman told me that it was all like living in a palace of glass: shiny, but breakable.

But of course, I know what it was that really broke the spell for her. It was not an economic crash, or the coming of the second Great War, or even just the slow turn of fortune's wheel.

It was me.

And now, to make matters worse, I realize that I have deluded myself into thinking I am in the center of beauty and light, just as she was. New York is not Paris—it will never be Paris, for all of the fuss people make over it—and this group is no Papa here, or Fitzy, or Stein. There's no Josephine, or Pablo, or Pound.

In twenty years, all of these people will be exactly what they are now, except they will look a lot more pathetic to boot.

I enjoy Teddy, but I shall have to tell her that I can't keep such company. Blue is right, I am tempting trouble.

I can't let myself be dazzled by this fool's gold. I have to keep moving forward.

When the waiter comes around to pour the bottle of champagne that has been ordered in my glass, I cover it with my gloved hand.

"No, thank you."

He raises an eyebrow at me. He will have been paid not to inquire about my age, or Teddy's, or that of any of the other young girls who flock around Harlan and his friends. He nods and goes on.

Harlan breaks off from his conversation to stare at me from across the table.

"Darla, what's the matter? That's premium stuff."

I have never once had a drink, not so much as a sip, of alcohol since I came to this country. If he had paid the slightest bit of attention to me, this would not be any kind of surprise.

I grit my teeth. "Delphine."

He snorts. His cheeks are ruddy already. I guess he would know all about the quality of the champagne. "Ah, yes, that's right. Forgive me. Theodora's new French pet."

Teddy leans forward and scowls. Her face is red, even her ears are red. I have never seen her look so furious.

Her voice is hateful. "Do *not* call me that."

He chuckles. "Ah, doll. Calm down. It's your Christian name, after all."

The Greyhound laughs with him, because of course he does. "A nice Christian name, for a nice country girl."

Teddy plants her hands on the table. Her face does not change, but her voice drops two octaves. "I don't remember asking for your opinion, Jacob. Considering that you're inbred trailer trash from the backwoods of Kentucky, and you sold your ass to pay your way up here. Frankly, I can't imagine why anyone would want it, even for free, but as you have no other useful talents, I can't blame you for making do."

I hear a wheezy little giggle, and Fiona shoves her fist into her mouth and looks at her lap as if she's found a fortune down there. Harlan guffaws; he is a buffoon who loves nothing more than to sit back and watch the conflict that he has created. Everyone else looks awkward, as if they are not sure how to react, and they had better do nothing until they are told.

The Greyhound looks at her as if he'd throttle her. "You don't know anything. Stupid girl."

She shrugs and stands up, pushing her chair back with such force that it makes a screeching sound. "I know enough."

"Oh, stop it. Stay," Harlan says irritably. "I want you to stay. I know the singer, I want to introduce you. You always say you want to meet more people."

She tosses her head—even in anger she's elegant—and strides off as if she has a million better places to be. I scurry after her without a word to the rest of them. We wind our way through the lines of tables and out the front door. I nearly smack into a waiter in my haste to keep up with her. The crisp evening air makes her shiver, and I tuck her arm underneath mine.

"I can't stand any of them," she says bitterly.

"Do you want me to take you home?" I say cautiously. I don't want her to storm away from me too.

She rolls her eyes. "No, of course not. I don't want to go anywhere he'll find me."

I see an opportunity forming before me. "Would you like to come with me?"

Her eyebrows shoot up. "To Harlem?"

"It's perfectly safe," I assure her, trying to keep the pique out of my voice. "I told you I live above this adorable restaurant. It's Parisian, almost."

"Is it?" she asks doubtfully.

She must see the annoyance on my face, and she waves a hand. "Oh, you know I don't have a problem with colored people. Daddy didn't like them much, but Mama said we were all trash anyway, just different shades."

"Louise says that bigotry is a sin against God, who created all human beings with the same amount of love."

She giggles, and it's nice to see her face soften again. "That's the nun, right? That doesn't sound like what my preacher used to say."

I shrug. I cannot understand religion in this country, which appears to be both passionate and fundamentally irreverent.

"So will you come?"

She hesitates. "Won't your friends mind me calling so late?"

I don't want to sound overeager, but I want to show her my novel. I want to show her the sketches Delia is teaching me to draw that I've put up on the walls, of all the things I miss the most from home. I want to show her Papa's picture and see if she will exclaim that she sees a resemblance, an undeniable link between us.

"No, I told you. I live above the café, they won't even know I have company."

She leans her head against mine. "Oh, all right."

I flush. "I'll hail us a cab."

Her eyelashes flutter. "Mhm."

I feel the same mix of fear and excitement I used to feel when I swiped little candies from the store when nobody was looking, or smuggled bottles of liquor home from the black markets during the war. I feel as if she is a stolen thing but soon will be rightfully mine.

. . .

She doesn't look very impressed.

She looked pale the entire cab ride and tossed the driver some extra money when she told him the address and he balked at her. White girls, particularly a white girl dressed like Teddy wrapped up in her sables, with pearls around her neck, do not venture out of the white neighborhoods in the evening.

Though I have seen cars full of white boys driving through our neighborhood in broad daylight, hollering at the girls on the sidewalk to come for a ride. When I asked Delia if that meant trouble, she laughed in my face and said, "Not for them."

When we got here, the car sped away the second we had shut the door behind us, and Teddy clung so tightly to my arm I thought she would pull it off.

Blue was watching us from the window. I raised my hand, and he nodded, glanced over at Teddy, and then let the curtains fall shut.

One of them always stays up for me. Maman never did that.

Once I got her up the stairs, I expected her to relax, but she sat on the bed and drew her coat tight, though the heater has made things toasty for us.

I go down to the restaurant kitchen and fix her a cup of hot cider, but she just grips it between her hands and doesn't drink it.

"Do you want to see my novel?" I offer, and I congratulate myself on how disinterested I sound.

She bites her lip. "Haven't you only written a few pages?"

I flush.

"And you haven't even named the characters," she goes on. "You've just called them Boy and Girl."

I feel the familiar ripple of shame. "Well, yes, but I . . ."

"Perhaps when it's finished, then?"

I turn a bit towards the mirror, and I see the quaver of my lower lip though she does not.

"Of course. You're right, it'll be much better that way."

She puts the cup aside. "Let me see your mother."

I am taken aback by the request. "What?"

"I'm curious," she says. "She sounds so glamorous. Don't you have a photograph?"

My first instinct is to lie. I teeter for a moment, and she inclines her head. Slowly, I kneel down between her long legs and pull the antique jewelry box from its hiding spot underneath the bed.

She watches me intently as I take the delicate key and turn it in the lock. It is an antique that has been passed down in my family since the time of Napoleon—porcelain, with gold leaf on the sides and a lid edged with mother-of-pearl. It is a phenomenally heavy monstrosity worth its weight in gold, but Maman would never sell it. She had pawned off most of her jewelry by the end but never the box she kept it in.

I don't think it was dignity that made her keep it. The war robbed the dignity from us both; the Germans stripped Paris of its pride like a vulture will pick at a carcass until there is nothing left but bones. Hunger cares nothing for human vanity; it will grind it into dust without a second thought.

The only explanation I can think of for her obstinance is the only reason that ever made sense for her. I think it was love.

I pull out the photograph of Maman, and as soon as my fingers graze it, I am drenched in a cold sweat. I remember how frantically I snatched it from her bedroom wall as I fled my home for the last time.

I went to it straightaway, without thinking. It was always my favorite picture of her.

I hand it to Teddy with trembling fingers.

She takes it and gasps. I hear the familiar lilt of surprise in her tone as she says, *"That* is your mother?"

I turn my eyes away from her bright face to look at the picture.

It is of Maman as a young woman of twenty-six, her vivid blue eyes visible only to me in the black-and-white photograph. Her face is turned up towards the light, framed by ringlets of her hair. There is a smile on her face that proclaims a certain joy.

She is radiant, and Teddy sees no resemblance between us whatsoever.

I smile weakly, though it costs me a great deal to do it.

"She's so pretty!" Teddy goes on, oblivious to the implication of her excitement. "My goodness. She could have been an actress, a real movie star."

I let out a low hum that she takes for agreement. This is not how this visit was meant to go. Teddy has drawn things into whatever direction suits her, as she always does, and I have bobbed along like driftwood caught in her tide. I quash my anger. I used to be furious all the time and I'm . . . tired.

To my great surprise, she turns the frame over and undoes the latch on the back. She slides the photo out and holds it close to her face.

"She was a poet," I whisper. I want to tell her more, but I don't want to at the same time and so we both fall silent. It swells and fills the room with so much hot air that I honestly think we are both going to float away.

She turns it over, as I knew she would, and reads the writing on the back. I can't see it with my eyes, but the words are engraved onto my skin, in the same sprawling cursive.

Finally, she breaks the silence by reading Maman's words out loud. It is delicious torture for me to hear the words, pleasure like a sharp knife. I stop hearing Teddy's voice. I hear my mother, as clearly as if she were sitting beside me and whispering in my ear on

our balcony, with the city stretching below us and the stars in the
night sky dimmed by its light.

We were all
Briefly golden
Like a flickering candle
In a patient dark

Chapter Four

~~~~~~~~~~~~~~

Gravity

Harlem, New York
February 1, 1946

There is no such thing as a lie. Only a metaphor.

I have always thought of it this way. This is what makes me so gifted at deceit. At the heart of it all, I am telling the truth, and often an excruciatingly painful one. It is not my fault that the world is too stupid to decode my runes. It is not my fault that I have to put things in a certain narrow box to make people understand me, and to make it so that I can survive in this godforsaken world.

I never felt guilty about lying. Not for a second.

I do now.

Delia's disappointment is crushing. Her expression is anguished, and I see the tears sparkling in her eyes.

I am seated in the living room with Blue and Delia standing in front of me, clearly about to pass judgment. I knew as soon as they called me in here that I was in trouble.

The only thing I don't know is for what. Which of my many crimes have they discovered? I sit on my hands to stop them from shaking.

I am utterly terrified, but I do my best not to show it. Once when I was a little girl, a burglar broke into our home in the middle of the night.

Maman leapt out of the darkness as he approached my bedroom door and sliced him across the face with a switchblade. He nearly bled to death on the floor in front of her, her pretty pink slipper on his back, her knife at his throat waiting to finish the job if he attempted to move. She called for me and told me, very calmly, to run down the block and alert the police. After they came to fetch him, she went onto the balcony and smoked a cigarette.

Later, I asked her if she had been afraid, and she shrugged her slim shoulders and said, as if she were talking about the price of a loaf of bread, "You are my daughter, Delphine."

I tell myself that I have her courage, but I feel the sinking realization that I do not.

Blue shakes his head. His voice is eerily calm, but that does not comfort me. "Didn't I tell you to come to me with any trouble?"

"Yes," I squeak.

He nods. "So you didn't understand me?"

I wish he would yell at me. This is so much worse. "I did."

"Then," he goes on. He pauses to adjust his lapel. He's been in the house all day, but he is still wearing a suit and tie. "You decided to disregard me."

It's not a question.

"I don't know what you mean."

Delia shakes her head at me. "I found it. In your trash can."

Her voice is full of horror. "I thought you were too smart to go messing around in this bad business. And to bring it into *our home*."

I really have no idea what she's talking about, but still I do not feel innocent, and I cannot force innocence onto my face.

"Miss Delia . . ."

She holds up a hand to silence me. "I knew it. I knew it when you started keeping strange hours, and hanging around with that good-for-nothing girl."

"But Miss Delia—"

She is incensed. "Hush," she whispers, and the vitriol, from someone who has always been so kind to me, stuns me into submission. I gawk at her and feel my own tears rising.

We are staring at each other like two fools about to cry.

Blue steps in between us.

He peers into my face with such intensity that I want to squirm, but I force myself to sit rigid. I don't squeeze my eyes shut like I want to. On one of his visits to Paris, years ago, he and Maman took me to the circus, and we watched the lion tamer. That man stood in the middle of the ring while the lion circled him, and he was absolutely still.

"If you lie to me," he says coolly, "I will ship you straight back to Paris. Tonight. Understand?"

I let out a breathy little wheeze of affirmation.

His face is hard. "Are you on that stuff?"

"I don't understand," I plead piteously, and at last I give way to the sense that I am telling the truth. The tears fall down my face. "S'il vous plaît, I don't understand."

He repeats it for me in French, but still I can only shake my head. I understand the English, I understand almost everything people say to me now, but I have no idea what he is talking about. I may be a charlatan who has conned my way into their home, but today at least, I have no sins to add to my tally.

He looks at me for a long moment and then he turns to face his wife.

"She's telling the truth," he says simply. "It's not hers."

Delia starts to argue, but he wraps his arm around her and draws her close. "Trust me, I can tell."

The anger goes out of her, and she gasps with relief. "I'm sorry, Delphine. I'm sorry. Oh, thank goodness. I should have known."

She goes into the other room and comes back quickly. She holds the wastebasket before me, and I can see, as clear as day, the syringe lying at the bottom. The foil. The remnants of pale brown powder.

Teddy.

We stayed up late talking, and then she spent the night. I slept on a blanket on the floor so that she could have the bed. She was gone before I woke.

I don't know much about this foil, but I know it spells doom.

Maman, though usually such a passionate rule breaker, absolutely refused to indulge in anything besides alcohol, and she would have boxed my ears if I had ever dared. She was a slave to her passion for Papa, and later to the bottle, but not this. Never this.

My throat is dry. "Oh."

I meet Blue's eyes, and I feel a wash of dread at what he is going to say.

"You're not to see that girl," Blue says quietly. "Ever again. Or you're out of this house, Delphine. I'll send you right back to your mother, and tell her to lock you up in your room for the next five years."

He does not ask me if I understand this time. He knows that I do.

. . .

It is hopeless pleading my case to Blue. He never changes his mind about anything. He was a musician for years; there's not much he hasn't seen. Every time he sees me, he gives me a rueful smile, as if to say that he is sorry for my pain, but there is nothing to be done about it.

After a few days it is Delia that I turn to.

I catch her while she is rolling dough for biscuits, but she shakes her head and sighs as soon as I walk through the kitchen door.

"Please," I say. "She will be wondering where I am."

She wipes her hands on her apron. "Let her wonder."

I am wringing my hands like a soprano in an opera, but I don't care. It is all I can do not to throw myself at her feet.

"You don't understand. I can fix her."

She stops what she is doing and turns to look at me. Her eyes are full of pity, and I hate pity.

"My dear, sweet child. You cannot."

"I'm not a child," I say firmly. "And I have done this before. I can get it right this time."

Delia reaches for me, but I step back. If she touches me, I will cry.

"Delphine," she says gently. "This isn't your fault. It's not your burden. This girl, this Theodora, she'll have to turn to her own family for help. You can make a new friend. Why don't you try

church? There's some Catholic churches in the Italian neighborhoods."

I cannot decide what sounds worse.

I don't know how to make her understand. Ordinarily I feel like
I can talk to her, but now my tongue is all in knots, and I don't
know what to say.

"I can't just abandon her."

"You aren't abandoning her. She's abandoning you, and everyone else who cares about her with the decision that she's made.
You should be using that typewriter we bought you, not worrying
about this."

I rack my brains for something that will appeal to Delia. "But
wouldn't Jesus want me to help her? He helped the lepers, didn't
He? He didn't just leave them to suffer."

She doesn't miss a beat. "The last time I checked, you are a
teenage girl. Not Jesus."

"But—"

"Has she asked you for help?"

"No, but—"

"Then nothing doing. You can want all your life to help
someone, and if they don't want to be helped, it's never going to
happen. When Jesus comes back, He can handle it Himself."

I stare at her in vengeful silence.

She smiles softly at my scowling face. "I know you care about
her. But this is the way of life sometimes, honey. You think I haven't
had to let some people go? I feel sorry for this young woman, I do,
and I'll be praying for her. But the one I've got to worry about is
you. Your mama left you in our care, and as long as you're here
we've got to decide what's best for you."

Nobody has ever done what's best for me. I don't need them starting now.

Delia touches my hand, her fingers brushing over mine with such tenderness that I have to use all of my willpower not to fling myself into her arms.

"And it's more than just our responsibility, Delphine. It's been a real pleasure to have you here. I can't . . . I can't have any babies of my own, and that's been an old wound I've had to learn to live with, because it's as the good Lord sees fit. But having you here . . . you feel a bit like my own."

I twitch away from her. There is no point in thinking what things would have been like if she had been my mother. I cannot choose. Nobody can choose, and it's the worst thing in the entire world.

"I don't want to leave," I say, and it is true. I have never been so well cared for. "And so I will do what you ask. But please, at least let me tell her why. At least let me say goodbye to her."

Delia hesitates.

I swallow hard and remind myself not to whimper. "Please. She has been kind to me. Let me give her that much."

She looks conflicted. "I'll have to ask Joseph."

I nod. "And may I tell her that if she stops this, I can be her friend again? Once she is better?"

Her expression is full of sadness. I don't think that all of it is for me. "Better doesn't always look the way that you think, Delphine."

"I know that," I say stubbornly. "But things will be different this time. They have to be."

She shakes her head and goes back to making her biscuits. "I wouldn't count on it."

. . .

There is nothing left to distract me from reading Louise's letter. As I open it, my hands tremor slightly and I chide myself for being such a ninny and remind myself that she is an ocean away and that her words are powerless. I picture them falling into the sea one by one, so that by the time her letter reaches me it is nothing but a blank page.

> *Dear Delphine,*
>
> *You are a willful fool, just like your mother, but you lack her talent for charming the world into turning a blind eye. You seek trouble in every corner. You are a storm chaser, and if you continue this way you will get too close and not be able to escape in time.*
>
> *You are in America to find the man you believe to be your father, are you not?*
>
> *You cannot mind two masters. I serve God, and so should you. But as you will not, you should at least learn to serve your own best interest.*
>
> *Your mother left your soul in my care, and I urge you to consider it above all earthly whims. There is no substitute for a calling fulfilled, which you will learn if you are spared to grow old.*
>
> *Your loving godmother,*
> *Louise*

I crumple it up and toss it away from me as if it will explode if I hold on to it. I am shaking with indignation.

Of course she would feel the need to remind me that she held me while I was naked and screaming, and a priest sprinkled tainted water onto my forehead and blessed me.

She always makes me feel like a little child again, when I am clearly most of the way to being a grown woman, if not one already. I am not her ward.

I am Delphine Auber Hemingway. I am going to be a great writer someday. I am a lady.

I will not reply. Louise has been my constant, though sometimes she feels like a North Star and other times like a shackle around my ankle that I cannot break.

I realize that I am panting, and I try to calm my breathing, but it's really no use, and before I know it, I have retrieved the crumpled ball and ripped it into a dozen pieces.

I kneel on the floor, put my head against the bedsheets, and fall into a fitful sleep.

It is Delia who wakes me up hours later, as the sun is going down.

"Wake up, child," she says, her hands gentle on my shoulders.

I raise my head to look at her, still groggy. She is dressed for going out, in a pretty red dress and white gloves, with her curly hair bouncing just above her shoulders.

She takes in my face in one quick glance. "What's wrong?"

"Nothing," I lie. But my voice is weak.

She sighs and doesn't bother contradicting me. "Blue and I are going to a party. Will you be able to manage? I've left a plate for you."

It's all I can do not to let out a manic-sounding giggle. Can I manage? Maman was gone for days sometimes.

"I'll be fine."

"I spoke to Blue," she continues. "And he's agreed that you may say goodbye to your friend, and tell her the cause. Perhaps it will motivate her to change."

I spring up at once. "And then I can see her again? Once she's better?"

She holds up a hand. "None of that was said. You can do this one thing, and then you had better focus on yourself and that book you want to write so badly."

This is so close to what Louise was telling me that I want to get angry, but now that two people have said it, I have no choice but to accept that it must be true, and I can only huff in frustration. Besides, my rage is all gone, and I feel soft as a jellyfish.

"But I can see her?"

"Tonight, if you wish. But you had best be back here before too late."

"Oh, thank you," I gabble. "Thank you, Delia."

She kisses my cheek. "Take care, my dear girl."

I don't know why she looks so sad.

The worst is behind me. I can't tell her, of course, so she still thinks of me as a young girl and not a woman who has held a knife and twisted it in the back of someone I loved.

Nothing can be worse than that. And so I have nothing to fear and everything to hope for. I am determined that things will improve from here on out.

. . .

I pen a rushed reply to Louise before I leave, while I am still puffed up with my victory. My hand whizzes across the page, my handwriting is sloppy—I will make sure to show her that I could not even take the time to write nicely.

> *My dear Louise,*
>
> *I am touched by your concern, but it is not necessary. I know my destiny better than anyone; indeed, I am the only one who has ever believed in it by your own admission. I will not be distracted from it by anyone. I understand that Maman placed me in your care that day, but she also placed me in the care of God. And if He cannot be bothered to do His duty, I think it is safe to say that you are free of yours.*
>
> *Delphine*

I leave it on my desk. I'll send it out tomorrow.

I go to the kitchen and try Teddy's number three times, but nobody answers. I am too impatient to wait any longer. It's only Wednesday, and I think there is a decent chance that she's home, or that she's out to dinner but will be back before it gets too late. I think Harlan has some kind of gentlemen's club on Wednesdays as well, where he and his good-for-nothing, sniveling rich friends get together to smoke cigars and look at slides of all the places their ancestors pillaged for fun.

I bundle up in my emerald green coat with the silver buttons, which is really Maman's old coat that Delia has taken up for me, and I catch the streetcar to head downtown.

It is bitterly cold, and I wish I had worn a scarf. My cheeks are ruddy and my lips are chapped by the time I've walked the remaining blocks to Harlan's apartment building.

The doorman stops me. "Visiting?" he asks, because obviously I don't live here.

Maman carried herself like she came from money, because she did, but it was all spent by the time I came along, and no one has ever mistaken me for high class. She always insisted that we weren't poor in the real sense of the word, just in a gentile way: *Poor people don't have antiques, Delphine.*

Still, clearly I look like riffraff to this man, because his nose is all scrunched up even though he is smiling.

"I'm visiting Miss Theodora Dolan," I say clearly.

"Nobody by that name lives here," he says gruffly.

"Of course she does," I say irritably. I have no interest in arguing with someone so obviously clueless. "She lives with Harlan."

He looks very serious. "No, she doesn't live here anymore. You're going to need to leave."

He looks the sort to put his hands on a lady—or at least on me—and toss her right into the gutter, but still I stand my ground.

"I want to see Harlan, then."

The man looks at me as if I am boring him. "Who are you, exactly?"

I could kill him. Really, I could. He is every man who has ever held the door for a beautiful woman and then let it slam in my face; he is every teacher I have ever had who rolled their eyes at me and fawned over another girl. He is this vulgar city, where no one is special because everyone is.

I feel a tap on my shoulder, and as I turn the scowl vanishes from my face.

It's Harlan, with Teddy draped across his arm. Something in her eyes is off, but she greets me with a pleasant smile.

"*There* you are," she says brightly. "I thought you'd been swallowed by the pit."

"I tried to call," I say meekly. She is dressed like a young girl for once, in a dark blue blouse and a tan skirt, with her hair uncurled and falling pin straight to her shoulders. She wears light makeup, and I can see that her once-smooth skin is now covered in fine bumps. There are violet shadows under her eyes.

I point at the doorman. "He said you didn't live here anymore."

She glares past me at him. "He's not very bright."

Harlan has that smarmy look on his face. "It's all right," he says to the doorman. He crooks his finger at me. "She's with me too."

Then he continues on through the ornate lobby, leaving me to trail after him. Teddy slides away from him the second that we enter the lift, putting her hand on my shoulder.

"Are you ill?" she asks. I hear the pique behind the concern.

"No," I say quietly. Harlan is looking at me as if I am a fly he'd like to swat. I don't want to speak in front of him.

She studies my face, raises her eyebrows, and nods ever so slightly.

That is one of the things I like most about Teddy. She's quite brilliant at reading people; it is a trick I must learn. It's a wonderful quality when she means to be kind, but when her mood turns and she decides to poke with a sharp stick, one can never pretend that she hit the right spot by accident.

"Harlan, sweetheart, why don't you go on? Delphine and I will chat up on the roof. I won't be long."

He looks like he wants to protest, but she pats his thigh and he mumbles a word I don't know and turns away.

When we get to their floor, he steps out and we keep going. As soon as the lift doors close and we rattle farther upwards, she turns to me and shakes her head.

"So if you're not sick, then what?"

My lips move but no sound escapes.

I try again. My ears are burning with guilt. "I'm sorry."

"I didn't ask you to be sorry, I asked you why," she says tartly. "I can't do anything with your 'sorry.' That is the most useless word in the English language."

I try to smile at her, but my cracked lips make it painful. "In any language, I think." My English is good enough now to realize that there are a dozen ways to apologize and none of them do much good.

The lift stops, and Teddy takes my hand and pulls me out. We climb a dimly lit set of stairs, and then she pushes open a heavy metal door and we emerge onto the roof.

I am chilled to my bones in an instant, my knees knocking together, but Teddy merely pulls her ermine coat shut and walks over towards the edge.

The view is breathtaking. The buildings below us jut towards the sky as if they'd own it entirely, and the multicolored lights dance before me. The city in all its splendor. It's not Paris, but it's growing on me. This place, these people . . . it could never be home, but it's something.

If I were not so miserable, I would take a moment to appreciate it.

I go to Teddy and take her cold hand in my own. "The needle" is all I say. It is all I can bring myself to say. Teddy has always been golden to me. I want to obliviate reality if reality will tarnish her. I want to push the truth off the edge of this rooftop and watch it shatter.

She goes white but nods. At least part of her was expecting this. "I should have been more careful."

I say nothing and she gives me a sardonic smile.

"Surely this isn't such a scandal to you? You're not from a small town by the backwater. You must know that this would hardly count as news. Everyone does it."

I don't want to lecture her. "Not everyone."

"Everyone I know." She dismisses me with a shrug. "Harlan knows. His own doctor supplies me."

Though I am cold, my fingers are tingling as if I am holding sparks between them. I am here to tell her goodbye. I am here to tell her that I can't see her anymore until she abandons this vice.

But instead, I find myself saying, "Come away with me."

She laughs, but it's humorless. "What? Will you whisk me away to Paris?"

I could almost say yes. But I know that I can't, and I don't want to lie to her. I have never felt so disinclined to lie to anyone before in my life.

"Stop this, and I'll take you somewhere better than here," I promise her.

She shakes her head. "I have to stay. Harlan's got me an audition."

I grit my teeth. I can't stop myself any longer.

"He is never going to make you an actress. Can't you see that? He's stringing you along so that you'll keep taking your clothes off for him."

74

Her face is whiter than salt, her eyes bloodshot. She moves away from me, wordless, and I follow her. I am relentless once I get started. The threads of my self-control are starting to fray, and I feel the rush of fear and temptation that have caused me so much harm.

"Teddy, please. I beg you. Stop selling yourself to a man who doesn't deserve you. I've got to move on soon anyway, I've got to go to my father. You can come with me. We'll look after each other. We don't need men."

She rounds on me. "I'm not a whore," she snaps.

"I didn't say—"

"I don't need you to mother me," she spits. "My mother is in Indiana with our postman, and I'll give her a call if I want a lecture."

I try not to wince. "I'm not trying to lecture you. I just want to help."

"Help?" she crows. She rears back and clutches at her belly; her laugh is full-throated and spiteful. "As if you have anything to offer! I don't need help from the likes of you, when I was the one who picked you up off the side of the road like some stray dog."

I take a deep breath.

"You do," I say simply.

"It's recreational!" she screeches, so loudly that I cringe away from her. She flies at me, arms flapping. "At least I haven't given up on every dream I have and become a shut-in like your mother."

I grip her wrists, but I don't squeeze. I just look at her with quiet malice, an unspoken mixture of a warning and a plea. But to challenge her is a mistake, because she is as stubborn as I am, and sharper tongued.

"You know, I haven't told you this because we're friends," she says, as if it is a mere afterthought. "But I do think you're wasting your time chasing after this writer, whoever he is. Your mother probably made the story up to spare her own blushes. Your real father is probably any one of a dozen barflies. She probably doesn't even know his name. She probably hiked her skirt up in an alleyway and had the business done with."

I fling her away from me with all my strength, and she catches on her heel and goes down. She yelps in pain, and a year ago I would have been on her, like a wolf scenting weakness.

But I cannot turn to rage. I can't do anything but stagger away from her.

"Not you," I gasp weakly, and I know that I am crying because I can feel the tears freeze onto my cheeks, and it feels like a burning.

Teddy pushes herself halfway up, cupping the side of her cheek. "Get out!" she hollers at me, as if I were a dog for her ordering and this rooftop were her very own living room. "Get out . . . you . . . you . . ."

I wait for her to call me something horrible. Something that will infuriate me so I can forget, just for a split second, how much this all hurts.

But she doesn't finish her sentence. She just looks at me with the coldest eyes and then turns her face away.

She looks out over the sparkling expanse below us. "Just go, Delphine," she says wearily. "I have finished with you. Don't come back."

I am trembling. I stumble through the door and stagger down the stairs. I all but collapse when I enter the lift but I manage to stay upright. I start to walk towards the train, but I really don't think my legs will carry me that far, and I go back to the front desk and ask if they will call me a taxi.

They look horrified at my tearstained face, and they hurry up and oblige to get rid of me as quickly as possible.

I sob quietly the whole way home into the sleeve of Maman's old coat.

Chapter Five

~~~~~~~~~~

Wild for to Hold

Harlem, New York
April 1946

The book smells like Sunday mornings. I hold it to my face and caress it like a lover.

I am home.

I open the pages and kiss the words.

Papa's words, handwritten.

An early draft of a work never published, given to Maman as a gift. Mine now. Kept safely in the jewelry box beneath my bed, known only to me.

I can actually see the two of them together, their heads turned towards each other as if they would kiss, strolling past the riverbank in the evening. I can hear them discussing poetry, philosophy, and politics. I can see him reach for her, and I can see her go to him as if she is being pulled by a golden thread that she will never manage to sever, even after he is gone.

I am not wrong. I am not mistaken. I am not the daughter of a whore and a nobody. It's not possible.

But when I try to write, I cannot help but wonder if I have inherited any talent whatsoever.

I wish I could confess to someone that I haven't the faintest clue what I am doing, but half of being a writer appears to be keeping this fact to oneself.

How am I to create an entire world from nothing? If I were a genius, like my father, wouldn't I know it by now?

. . .

I tell myself that I do not regard Teddy as a great loss.

Amazingly, it is my past that comforts me most. I remember the searing agony of what has come before, and I can smile grimly and get on with life now.

I work in the restaurant, and I chat with the customers in much better English than before. They leave good tips and start to treat me like a regular fixture in their lives. I help Delia around the house, and she is teaching me to sew—I am abysmal at it, but it's nice to spend time with her. Blue is working on a new business venture and I haven't seen much of him, but when I do he smiles warmly at me as if he is proud. This too makes the loss go down smoother.

I have made good use of my new typewriter, and I am making fewer mistakes now than before. I have decided to name my protagonist Beatrice, which I think is some progress. I have set the story in Antibes, and I plan to have only female characters, no men at all, which will probably mean that nobody likes it. But for once I've decided to suit myself.

Sometimes I go to the New York Public Library. I sit in the

Rose Reading Room underneath the bright chandeliers with a stack of delicious-smelling books in front of me and forget the world. I pore over the words of Louisa May Alcott, Jane Austen, George Sand—whose real name was Amantine Lucile Aurore Dupin de Francueil—and Betty Smith, whose book *A Tree Grows in Brooklyn* came out just a few years ago. She gives me more hope than any of them because she is still alive. She is walking this earth right now, doing exactly what I dream of. I like her book so much that after I return it, I buy a copy and put it in Maman's jewelry box. I know this is the kind of book I will read over and over again, until the pages are frayed with love and I am mouthing the next lines before they happen.

This is what I want to learn to do. I want to make complete strangers see inside my imaginings. I want them to visualize the rosy cheeks of babies, smell the filth of desperation, and hear the triumphant laughter of people who will not be broken. I want to turn the ink on the page into the dearest friends of complete strangers. I want to be a magician whose only trick is my voice.

I realize in that piece of myself whose existence I deny that even if things go as badly as they might with Papa, I will never stop writing. I won't give this up.

I have thought about seeing if I can get another job, perhaps something secretarial now that I can type. I will need more money and I will need it soon.

Papa is in Cuba.

I had heard rumors before but now a newspaper article has confirmed it for me.

I don't know exactly where, but I do know that Blue keeps an address book in the top drawer of the mahogany desk in his office. And he has kept track of everyone from the old days; he is the keeper of their memories. He is one of the few still alive from those days in Paris some twenty years ago now, still unscathed by the fire that burned so brightly but disappeared so fast.

I will need passage and enough money to book a hotel for quite some time. I don't speak a word of Spanish, and I doubt anyone will be willing to give me a job. I want to be ready by the end of this summer, and I am absolutely certain that I will find a way to manage it. I've been here too long; it will have been nearly a year by the time I'm ready to leave. I don't know how I will manage to look Blue and Delia in the face and tell them I'm leaving. Will I play the coward again and slip away in the middle of the night?

When I get to Cuba, I don't plan to introduce myself to Papa right away. I will put myself close to him but stay hidden. I will be his flickering shadow. I am sure that he will notice me on his own.

I do not consider an alternative, because there is no alternative to consider. The only other place for me, if not in his orbit, is at the bottom of the river Seine, and I have already given up that option.

I still have not sent a reply to Louise.

What can one say to a woman who is always right but who is too humble to glory in it? And anyway, I don't want to write to her, I want to see her. She had a way of calming me just with her presence. I feel uneasy all the time, and I cannot sleep for the buzzing in my ears.

Delia has tried to talk to me about my moods, but I am fatally obstinate, and I overheard Blue telling her to leave me be.

But mostly, everything is improving. If I look at it clearly, I am actually in a much better state than I was when I lived a life of mundane desperation in Paris.

Maman was always so adamant that she loved me, right up until the moment she didn't.

. . .

Harlem, New York
May 1946

Dear Louise,

If you had ever asked my mother, she would tell you that she never regretted being a passionate fool. Even though it brought her very low, and me with her. But I don't think she would want me to walk in her footsteps and sink into her melancholy.

You know, sometimes I think that I will go mad. I feel a voice calling to me some nights, and it is very far from the voice of God. I think that my determination to fulfill my calling is the only thing holding me up.

I would never wish my destiny away, never. Not for anything, not for all it has cost me. Not for all it cost her.

But sometimes I think it might have been nice to be a very beautiful girl who was not clever enough to be dissatisfied with the ways of the world, and to have lots of friends and be happy. I think it would have been nice to have a family who considered me first and not to have to fight so very hard for what should be mine.

But of course, this is vanity.

Isn't it?
Your loving goddaughter,
Delphine

.   .   .

June 1946

Dear Delphine,

It is not vanity. So often you mistake vanity for humility, and humility for vanity.

My darling girl, if you could bring yourself to come back to me, I know it would be such a help to us both. Your soul would thank you. And your mother would thank me.

Come back. Finish your schooling. Go to university, as your mother wished, and study literature. You can write all of the books you like. When the time is right, you can marry a good man, and he can give you children of your own to lavish love on.

I know you have so much love in you. Do not waste it, as your mother did. Plant it somewhere that it can bloom.

You do not need him. And my dear, I am very sorry to tell you that most of the women who have needed him have found themselves gravely disappointed.

God has chosen you for greatness, of this I am sure, but I am not at all sure He has chosen you for this.

All my love,
Louise

.   .   .

Asha Lemmie

Harlem, New York
July 1946

I have become very quiet. I like to tell myself that this means I am becoming introspective and wise, but all I hear in my head most of the time is the sound of boiling water.

I can think of half a dozen ways to get the money that I need. Louise would be horrified by all of them. Perhaps even my mother, with her flexible conscience, would disapprove of how dark my thoughts have become. She was always kind, whatever else she was. She never took advantage of anyone if she could help it.

I keep trying to avoid the most frequent thought, but it's like a ball on a track: it always comes back.

Teddy is gone. It's summer now, and I still don't have enough money to continue my quest. I have to do something, and soon.

Blue and Delia have a safe.

He keeps it in his office, and I have seen him take out whole stacks of money, more than you would suspect they have with their relatively simple lifestyle. But the restaurant is always very busy, and they are not shy about buying me gifts. I think they are quite well-off.

I don't know the code, but it is possible I could guess it. Or perhaps he'll leave it open one day.

I could find a way to pass it off as a burglary. It's possible.

But when I think of it, my stomach begins to cramp, and I have to sit down.

I love them. I do. They are wonderful. If they had raised me from the start, I would be better for it.

But . . .

I know, and I don't know how but I do, that I am running out of time. Papa will not accept me if I am old when I meet him; he will not see his child in my face if all the childhood is long gone.

And nothing I do will be impressive if I wait until I'm old to do it.

The bitter seed in me says that it is one more sacrifice, and what is theft compared to blood? Nothing, really. If I heap a lesser sin on top of a greater one, it hardly counts.

But then I remember that Delia has taught me to braid my hair before bed, and to let it out in the morning so that it is fuller and thicker. I remember my typewriter, and that I have never gone hungry or felt unwanted since I set foot in this strange country. There is a crooked piece of me that has started to straighten, like a bone will heal when it is properly set.

I am torn in two, going back and forth between the darkness and the sad, flickering spark of light.

I try to write for weeks but the words refuse to come. The empty white page is my purgatory.

I have to get out of the house.

It is an exceptionally quiet night. Usually there is always some sound in this city, it is never dead silent, but tonight it is. As I lie in bed, my mind begins to run away from me. I try to rein it in, but my thoughts are too fast for me and they land, as they always do, in a place that I don't want them to go.

I see the dead woman's sightless eyes.

I can't do this. I have to go. I have to get to Papa. I have to go *now*.

I wait until the little hand on the clock has moved past two to get up. I pull a dark blue cardigan over my nightshirt, put on my shoes, and go down the stairs as carefully as I can.

I cross the street to the main house and unlock the front door with the key in my pocket. They have trusted me with this, as they have trusted me with so much.

I creep through the foyer and down the hallway a little ways to Blue's office. It's a large room with hardwood floors covered in thick rugs. There's a decanter full of what looks like sherry on a silver tray on the right side of a plush armchair, and a record player. The safe is behind a large oil painting of the canals in Venice dominating the wall closest to the door.

There's a large desk of darkest wood and a high-backed leather chair behind it.

But what I am instantly drawn to is the far wall, which is covered in bookshelves. I cross to it and run my fingers over all the well-worn tomes. These books are not for show. These books are loved. They are filed in alphabetical order by the last name of the author, and my hand goes without thought to Papa's section. They're all here. Every single one.

I go to the letter *F*, and I find the entire body of work of Maman's beloved Fitzy. She ripped herself to pieces when he died. I found her shrieking on the floor when she got the letter from his daughter. I had never seen her so upset.

When she calmed down, she asked for her books, and she read her favorite poem over and over again. It made no sense to me, but I have a strong suspicion that she wasn't really speaking to me at all.

The Wildest Sun

Noli me tangere
For Caesar's I am
And wild for to hold
Though I seem tame

When I finally gave her a little white wine and put her to bed, she slept for a day.

She got worse after that.

A car speeds by and recalls me to the present. I shake my head. The entire point of leaving Paris was to bury my past, but it seems to have woven its way into the back of my eyes. I don't know how to stop seeing it.

I move to the desk and rifle through the papers, hoping that luck will be on my side and Blue will have left the address book here. Of course, he hasn't.

I look in the obvious places for the key: underneath the potted plant, in the ashtray, underneath the seat cushion.

"Can I help you find something?"

I nearly jump out of my skin. Blue is leaning against the doorway, fully dressed, watching me with the alert calm of an owl.

My lips pucker; I gasp and sputter, but I am speechless. I am almost never speechless, but something in his face makes me so.

He takes a step towards me, his hands in his pockets. "I said, can I help you find something, Miss Delphine?"

I am cringing like a snail being doused in salt. "I . . ."

"Yes? You?"

I back up towards the bookshelf, holding my empty palms before me to show that they are empty.

"Please don't throw me out," I blurt.

"I don't make a habit of keeping thieves in my house."

"I'm not stealing!"

I am not such a fool as to mention that I have seriously considered it.

I back all the way up to the curtains and bunch them in my fists as he continues to come towards me.

"Then what?"

I look to the right and then to the left like a trapped animal, trying to think of how to escape. I can think of nothing. I am debating whether I am clever enough to lie to him successfully; it is a miracle that he has not realized the letters he sends through me to my mother have never passed beyond my hands.

"I advise you not to lie," he says, prying into my thoughts. "I'm going to give you one chance to tell me what's going on."

I shift from one foot to the other, and then I realize that I am only making myself look more guilty and I force myself to be still.

I see no way out of this but the truth.

"I wanted the address book," I tell him, my eyes roving in the general direction of his face but not looking at him. "Not to steal. Just to copy an address, just one. That's all."

"And you couldn't have asked?"

I look at the floor.

"Hm? You plan on going somewhere so urgently that you couldn't ask me?"

I can't seem to make myself say anything else. I want to merge through this wall and out onto the street, where only the night air can judge me.

I see his shoes move away, and I glance up. He goes to the desk, pulls the key from his pocket, and unlocks the top middle drawer. He pulls out the address book and tosses it to me, so quickly that I have to scramble to catch it.

I look at him incredulously.

He nods. "Which one is it?"

"S-sir?"

"Who is it that you think is your daddy?"

The air vanishes from the room. My knees begin to knock together.

Blue takes a seat in his chair, looking at me like a hanging judge. He gestures for me to sit too, and I sink into the armchair beside the bookshelf before I collapse and make a fool of myself.

"That's it, isn't it? Why you asked your mama to come and stay with us. I've been wondering about that. Surely it would have been easier for you to stay in France."

I absolutely will not cry. I am like some sad creature who has been pulled out of its shell, writhing in the merciless light without any dignity. But I will not cry.

"Yes," I whisper.

I can be packed in an hour. Two at the most.

Blue leans back. "I figured. Last time I saw her, she mentioned that you were getting insistent about meeting him."

I bow my head. "Did my mother ever tell you who he was?"

"Not exactly. She never said who, but I suspected it had to be one of those men she was running around with eighteen years ago. I don't mean to say she was fast, 'cause she wasn't, but she liked male company, that's for sure." For the first time his face softens, and he allows himself a small grin. "She went to stay with her cousin in the country, and ten months later she popped back up with you in her arms. I figured if she'd wanted me to know exactly who your daddy was, she would have told me. She was direct enough when she felt like it."

My anguished gaze goes to Papa's section of the bookshelf.

Blue observes carefully, and he puts it together without me having to say a word. I don't think I could say it out loud. I still can't for some reason, as if I am afraid that it is some special magic that will dissipate once it hits the air. I have to keep it inside me until the perfect moment.

He shakes his head. "Huh. That's unfortunate. He never was my favorite."

"What's wrong with him?" I demand. My skin is hot, like someone has lit a match and struck every single one of my nerves.

Blue looks surprised at my sudden fierceness. "Nothing in particular is wrong with him. He's just a braggart, in my opinion. A braggart and a bit of a fool."

"He's a genius," I assert. "*The Torrents of Spring*? *A Farewell to Arms*? *For Whom the Bell Tolls*? How can you not think he's brilliant?"

I think of my favorite quote from *The Sun Also Rises*: "You can't get away from yourself by moving from one place to another." How much I have always loved that line and how desperately I am still clinging to the hope that it's wrong.

He shrugs. "Maybe so, doesn't stop him from being a damn fool." He chuckles at my expression. "Look, it doesn't matter what I think of him. You're going to have to form your own opinions. I just warn you not to idolize him too much."

I don't say anything. I don't like that he knows my special secret, and that he is so unimpressed by it. And I don't want to hear anything bad about Papa. Maman complained, but that was her right as a woman he had discarded—her only right.

"I want to find him," I say simply. I am very aware of the book in my hands, which is suddenly almost too heavy to hold. "I'm sorry, I should have just asked for what I wanted. I just want to find him."

He looks at me with something akin to pity, and it makes me want to scream.

"You're just seventeen. It's gonna be some years yet before you're ready to be chasing that man all over the world."

"I thought he'd be here," I say weakly. "This is New York. Everyone is supposed to be here."

"Well, you can't go to Cuba," he says flatly. "Your mama would never allow it. And even if she would, I wouldn't. You're under my care, unless you want to go back home."

I do want to go back home, but I can't. Not ever.

"I want to stay here," I say. "My mother is . . ." I wave a hand. "She's not well."

Blue raises his eyebrows. "I know all about it. She's not the first slave to a bottle and she won't be the last. But she seems to be improving, from her letters."

"She improves because I am gone," I say bitterly. "We don't deal well together. She doesn't even like me."

He looks uneasy. I have knocked Maman loose from her pedestal, and it gives me pleasure to see him hesitate. "I'm sure that's not true."

"How are you sure?" I snap at him. I slide into anger like a familiar pair of pants. "She was always at her best when you were there, always showing off. You knew her as she wanted you to know her. And yes, I know how beautiful she is, but she was also useless. I did everything. I had to take care of her as if she were my child. I never had anything that was not her castoff, I never met anyone who did not judge me against her. I was not at luxury to enjoy all of her charms when I was making sure she didn't waste away." I feel my color rising. "Everyone gossiped. Everyone laughed at us, at *me*. So even if she does like me, even if she loves me, what good does that do me? Quel bien?"

He is calm in the face of my passion, and as the silence stretches on it begins to feel like more of a tantrum than anything. He has the same gift Louise does for making me feel like an imbecile without doing much.

"So," he says coolly. "You wish to stay here with Delia and myself?"

I nod. Where else can I go, if I can't find a way to get to Papa?

"Then you had best promise me I won't catch you sneaking around in my house again," he says sharply, and I wince.

"I promise."

Blue sighs. "You know, Delphine, I believe you when you say things weren't as they should have been. You're as jaded as a woman twice your age, and I know that your mama has her troubles. But she's trying to get better."

I am reminded that I have to keep up the lie. I hate writing those damn letters; I feel like I am tempting fate every time. I speak through lips that feel thick and clumsy. "Of course she is."

"Maybe it will take you some time, but I think it would be a good idea to get to work on forgiving her."

I offer up a polite smile. Is he mad? Am I not the only person in the house sliding towards—what would Maman call it—a patient dark? Forgiveness?

Maman and I are far beyond such things. There is nothing between us but salted earth.

I love her and I hate her as I have always done. But there is no hope of forgiveness. We are frozen in time.

"I will do my best."

My best is worthless, so this at least is true.

He looks unsure. Maybe he can see the ticking behind my eyes. "Good night, Delphine."

I muster a look that I hope is penitent. "Good night."

When the door shuts behind him I let out a breathy giggle. I'm not remotely amused, but it slides out of me like a death rattle, against my will.

I copy down the address I need, my hands shaking the entire time. I hold it to my face, but I don't feel any connection to it.

I catch a glimpse of my reflection in the mirror behind the desk, and my complexion is wan, my eyes empty-looking. My mouth is pinched as if I've eaten something foul. I look very far from triumphant tonight.

I glance at the painting that hides the safe, then back at myself, and I see that my eyes are strained but dry. I may be sickened by what I am willing to do, but that will not stop me.

Nothing will stop me.

Chapter Six

~~~~~~~~~~~~

Tournesol
(Sunflower)

Harlem, New York
September 1946

I put on a veneer of demure obedience, and I pretend—so well that I trick myself some days—that I have accepted staying here for the next several years. Blue takes us all to a friend's vacant lake house upstate for two weeks, and it is nice to be free of the smothering heat of the city. I even start to dream again, like a normal girl who is not haunted by destiny or ghosts. I catch myself humming Ella Fitzgerald and Billie Holiday. I smile at boys on the street when I take my daily walks, and some of them smile back.

When I sat down to write at the shores of the lake, the words flowed out of me, in a way that had never happened before. It felt like the simple act of a penitent, with all the pure beauty of a nightingale's song.

We have been back in the city for all of three days when the call comes.

I hear the phone ring, and the sound of Delia putting her knife down and going to answer it.

"Delphine!" she hollers from the kitchen. I am in the living room playing checkers with Blue. He looks at me curiously and I shrug. No one has called me in months.

I get up. "Don't cheat while I'm gone."

He chuckles. "Girl, I don't need to cheat. You're terrible at this game."

In the kitchen, Delia is pretending to chop her tomatoes, but something about the rigid way she holds her body tells me that she's going to be listening to every word.

I pick up the receiver. "Hello?"

I don't recognize the voice that comes through. "Hello? Erm, hi. This is Fiona."

I really have no idea what she's talking about. "Who?"

"Fiona, from . . ." The line goes fuzzy. "Supper club."

My eyebrows shoot up. The pretty dark-haired one from months and months ago.

"What do you want?"

I don't have the patience to dress up my question like a lying American. And I don't want to think about before.

I hear her swallow. "I bet you think it's odd I'm calling you."

I think she has five seconds before I hang up the phone.

"It's Theodora."

My stomach lifts, somersaults, and then drops back down. "What?" I gasp.

"She's in a bad way," Fiona says, very low, as if she doesn't want to be overheard. "I thought you'd want to know. The rest of us . . . everyone else has washed their hands of her. Harlan threw her out. She's not doing well at all."

My mouth is full of cotton balls. "Did she ask you to call me?"

"No, no," she says hurriedly. "I just didn't know what to do."

"We aren't . . . I haven't seen her. I haven't spoken to her."

"I figured. But I thought I'd tell you anyway." She goes quiet for a minute, and I hear footsteps come and then go. "The last I heard, she's staying at a motel on the Lower East Side called the Cranston. I have to go now."

"Thank you," I whisper, and I think I hear her breath catch before the line clicks. "Thank you."

Delia is looking at me, owl eyed, waiting for me to tell her without her having to ask. I bunch my hands into fists around the fabric of my yellow skirt.

"I've got to go."

She starts to protest, but I cut her off. "I'm sorry, Delia. I don't take any pleasure in defying you. You've been so good to me, and please believe me when I tell you that I'm so grateful to you. But I've got to help Teddy."

Blue has materialized behind me and is listening.

I turn to face him. His face is hard as a slab of marble, but his voice is calm as always.

"Seems to me you've made up your mind."

My voice trembles a bit, but I look him in the eye. "Yes, sir."

"Then you gonna be changing it?"

I am aware of the ticking clock and the hum of the refrigerator. The delicious smells of Delia's cooking, the distant shriek of laughter as the neighborhood girls play jump rope. All of these things are familiar to me now.

"No, sir."

He gives me the same look he gave me when he caught me rifling through his office. Disappointment mixed with curiosity.

The silence stretches on. It's unbearable, heavy with terrible possibilities. At long last, he shrugs.

"Some things in this life a person just has to do. That's how you feel, go on, then."

I don't feel as relieved as I should. "Can . . . can I come back here?"

Blue's expression doesn't change. I know he is tallying up my transgressions, weighing them against his love for my mother and his affection for me. "I'm gonna have to think on that. You'd best be back by dark if you want me to consider it."

I nod. I know that's all I'm going to get out of him now. He never allows himself to be rushed into decisions. If I had been raised by him, he would have curbed my natural rashness; he would have tamed my wild temper as sure as if he'd taken a whip to me. He would have made me a self-assured, thoughtful woman.

And I wouldn't be dashing past him, fighting the voice of reason that tells me to stay. But now I am grabbing my satchel from the rack on the wall, the one I keep enough money in to make a quick escape if need be, and running down the street.

This is rash, contrary to my best-laid plans. It would have been much better for me if the phone had never rung.

And even though I have no idea what is going to happen to me, and my stomach is turned upside down with dread, I know that I am smiling.

I am hurtling towards the sun once more.

.   .   .

To call this a motel is generous indeed, and perhaps also a bit insulting to the rest of the category. There is a layer of visible grime on the glass in front of the reception desk, and I wish that I had worn gloves like a proper lady to protect my hands, though I doubt you'd ever find a proper lady here. The man behind the counter looks at me like one would appraise a cut of meat, and from the little grunt he gives, I take it he is not impressed.

"I'm looking for Miss Teddy Dolan," I say. "I am her friend."

He looks down at the clipboard in front of him, but he does not do it very carefully. "Not sure if she's here."

I reach into my pocket and slide three dollar bills across the counter at him. "Please check."

He takes the money without so much as a thank you and then points to the dank staircase at the other end of the lobby. "She's in room 310. Don't think she entertains female guests, though."

I hardly hear him. I'm already going up the stairs, taking them two at a time, not holding the railing because I don't want to die of tetanus, and I go faster than I thought possible. By the time I reach the third floor, I am panting, my heart hammering in my ears, the blood hot in my veins.

I go down to the end of the hall and knock on the door. There's no answer, so I start to pound, with one fist and then two.

The man in the neighboring room pops his head out and glares at me, and I give him a look that makes it clear I don't care at all what he thinks. He goes back into his room and shuts the door, murmuring "bitch" under his breath. I am unfazed—it seems to me that men in every language use the same handful of words to describe us, depending on whether we're doing what they want. As far as I am concerned, they need new material.

"Teddy!" I shout. "Teddy, open up."

There's a rustling behind the door, and I know she's there. I can almost see her peeping through the keyhole. I can feel her, as surely as I can feel a spring breeze.

"Teddy, it's me," I say again, my voice softer this time. "Please."

The door opens, just a crack, and I see one of Teddy's deep brown eyes, widened in surprise.

She opens the door all the way and snatches me inside before slamming it behind me.

"What are you doing here?" she demands.

I don't answer. I can't. I am shocked at the sight of her.

Her skin is sallow and looks greasy. Her hair is free of its platinum blonde dye and is a tangled crop of brown. It looks as if she has taken a pair of scissors to it. She has lost weight, and her wrists look dangerously bony and frail. If she fell down, I think she would break in two.

"My God, Teddy. What's happened to you?"

She flushes, and I realize too late that offending her is a bad start. "Nobody asked you to come," she says resentfully. "Really, I don't know why you're here."

I pinch the inside of my palm to stop myself from reaching for her. "Fiona called."

Teddy lets out a sardonic bark of laughter and turns away. "That slut! I bet she did."

"She's just concerned."

Teddy goes over to the bedside table and picks up a box of cigarettes. There's something about the way she moves now that is unsteady. All of her grace is gone.

"So very concerned!" she shrieks. "Sleeping in my bed, fucking my fella. I'm sure she's just gutted over it!"

I absorb this new information in silence.

"You can't stay here," I say flatly. "I won't allow it."

She looks at me with her nose scrunched up. "You don't have to do this. It's not as if I was a good friend to you."

"I still want to help you," I say carefully.

"I don't need your help," she insists. She fumbles for a cigarette, dropping the box and then picking it back up. "I don't want it. Run back to Harlem."

I smile at her spite, and she balks. She does not realize that I have done this before. I know what it is to love someone who loves poison. I know what it is to wait out all of their resistance and to wear them down and get them to do what I want. Addicts are clever, but they are also very stupid, and not good at long games.

In a little while, she will be desperate for another fix, and then she will do whatever I say if it means she thinks she'll get me out of her way. I don't know how to wean with this particular substance, and I don't dare to ask anyone.

I have to be cautious. Teddy isn't Maman. She isn't interested in putting on a show for me, pretending that she wants to change. I am determined to atone for at least something I've done, and I will help Teddy if it's the last thing I do.

I have to find a way to make Teddy care. To make the prospect of the horizon worth the hellscape she will have to crawl through.

Maybe offending her is exactly the right thing to do.

"Please let me help you. You don't look well at all. Your beautiful skin . . . ruined. Perhaps for good."

She looks at me, her red-rimmed eyes wounded. "What?"

I use my snake charmer voice, the one I learned from her. "You will have the skin of an old lady," I predict. "Like leather. No one will want to hire such a face to work as an actress, you must know this. And it's a real shame. They'll never know how talented you are. And you were so pretty!"

She is horrified, her lips actually blue with fear. "That's not true."

"Look at yourself," I challenge her. "Teddy, look in the mirror. You've ruined yourself."

She is shaking. "I haven't."

I stride across the room and grip her shoulders. "Look around. You're living in squalor. Is this what you left Ohio for?" I know the mere mention of her home state will send her into a fury, but I have to risk it. "Is this why you ran away from your father?"

She lets out a little gasp. "I didn't mean for any of it to happen," she chokes out. "It all went wrong. Harlan . . . he got cross with me, and I slapped him." She shuts her eyes. "I suppose I thought after all the times he did it to me he deserved it."

I think of his smug face, and I want to do more than slap it. "He threw you out?"

"Not that time," she mumbles. "Not for good, anyway. But we'd been having problems. He says I'm ungrateful. That plenty of girls would be happy to have what he gave me."

"He's a liar," I say hotly. "And a pompous fool."

Her eyes flash, and I see the old Teddy again. "He's an arrogant jackass, but he's not a liar. He tossed me out and moved that slut Fiona in two days later. She's wearing my mink coat, and going to my auditions, and I am nothing."

"Let me take you out of here," I implore. "Please. We can go to a better hotel."

She shakes her head. "I can't pay for that. I can barely afford this. I pawned a necklace."

"I'll pay for it." I'll use the money I brought from Paris. Papa's face blurs before me as the words leave my mouth. Maman's face too, somewhere deeper.

She hesitates. Teddy is always alert to any sign that anyone is feeling sorry for her. "No."

"Yes," I insist. "And we'll have some lunch. When is the last time you've eaten properly?"

Her thin wrists give me my answer as she raises her hand to her mouth. "I don't have much of an appetite."

Not for food, anyway, but I intend to fix that. I won't fail this time. I can't fail twice.

I stroke her flushed, tearstained cheek. "Teddy, I want to help you. And it's not because I pity you. It's not that at all. It's because you have a calling, and I have a calling. I understand you. And we promised to help each other, didn't we? We promised."

She sobs and leans her forehead against mine, and I take her hot face in my hands and kiss one cheek, and then the other.

She giggles weakly. "Very French," she whispers. "I could almost think I was in Paris."

If this were Paris, Maman would be here. She would have a

smile, and a pithy remark, and just maybe someone in her address book who could offer us help.

But this is New York, and we are alone.

I twist our hands together, interlocking each one of our fingers so that we are joined, one to another. I can do it this time. I can save her.

"Trust in me."

. . .

By the looks of her I don't have much time before the real trouble starts. I bundle her and her one suitcase into a taxi, and tell the driver to take us to a hotel I've passed by two dozen times on the Upper East Side. I wish I could take her back to Blue's with me, but I'm afraid if they saw us coming they would change the locks.

She groans into my shoulder, and I stroke her hair.

"Let me out," she whines. "I've changed my mind, Delphine, let me out. I don't want to go in the car."

"It's all right," I soothe her. "We're going somewhere worthy of you. I'll get us their finest bottle of champagne."

She perks up a bit at the thought of this, giving me a small half smile. "You don't drink, though, do you?"

"I don't," I confess. "But for you I will."

She groans again, and I tell the driver to pick up the pace. He gives me a dirty look, but I don't care. I am already coming up with the list of things I'll need. I dig into my satchel and pull out my notebook and a pen.

Hot water
Towels

Chamomile tea
Vodka
Blankets
Oven mitts
Fresh mint
Ice
Crackers

They should have most of it at the hotel, and if not, I can send a boy for the rest. From the way Teddy is growing restless, I am guessing it's been at least a few hours since she's taken anything.

"Do you feel okay?" I ask her quietly.

She shrugs and smiles, but she's white, and the skin around her collarbone trembles. "Been better. Been worse. I'll feel better after we eat."

I nod, but already I am settling into the grim determination I will need to see us through this. I will have to grow immune to her tears; I will have to look at the pulsing veins in her delicate throat and feel nothing.

When we finally arrive, after what feels like eons, she is teetering on her feet and I sling my arm underneath her and half drag her into the lobby.

"I need a room," I say, without any pretense. "Preferably one that's somewhat private."

I may be surrounded by expensive artwork, and the gentleman before me may be wearing an exquisitely tailored suit, but I swear he gives me the same look as the man before.

"Madam? A room?"

As if I'd want anything else at a hotel.

"Yes, a room. Please."

He shoots a sidelong glance at Teddy, who is mumbling to herself quietly. "For both of you?"

I am so frustrated that I nearly dissolve into a tirade in my native tongue, but I check.

"Oui. Yes, a room for two." I think hard on how long we will need. "Four nights," I say at last. I'm cringing at the thought of spending the money I stole so carefully, but I can hardly take her back to the brownstone. That should get us through the worst of it. I wish I had brought more clothes. I hope Blue lets me back in to get the rest of my things.

The employee looks doubtful even as he writes it down and holds out his hand for the payment. I count it out carefully and hand it to him. He hands me a room key.

"And will you be needing help with anything else?"

I hand him the list. "Anything that can't be found here, please send a boy to go and get it. I will pay."

He looks at me as if I am dancing about in a motley cap. "We don't do that, madam."

"Please," I ask quietly. Teddy's head has lolled onto my shoulder. She's taller than me, and it is awkward trying to hold her up. "Sir, please. Our father will be here from Washington next week, and I know he'd be so grateful if you could help us."

That lie does it. He tweaks his mustache. "Indeed?"

I look down, as if I can't say more. This is always the best way to go about it. Let people wonder, and they'll come up with whatever story suits them the best. He reads my list.

"This should be easy enough. I'll have the kitchen send up what we have, and I'll sort out the rest."

I smile and flutter my eyelashes, as if I am overwhelmed by his kindness, and then I heave Teddy over to the lifts.

"I'm hungry," she says irritably as the doors close. "What's to eat here?"

I touch her forehead and find it hot. "I'll find out."

She's not going to want to eat anything soon. I am both comforted and disgusted by the fact that I know almost everything that is going to happen. I wonder how I have managed to move half a world away and still find myself in the same place.

I have the unpleasant thought that I could go to Ethiopia, I could go to China, and it would still change absolutely nothing, because the problem is what lives inside me. Maybe Papa was right after all. Before, it was easy to blame the choices that trapped me in what can only be called dysfunction on Maman. But Maman is gone now, and here I am. It's me. It's my mind. And I cannot run from that.

We get to the room, which is thankfully clean and comfortably appointed. I can breathe in clean air, and the oversized bed looks plush and inviting. Teddy lets out a contented hum. This is the kind of setting she longed for when she came to New York; this is the gilded dream.

"Better," she concedes, and we both giggle.

"Now, Teddy," I say gently, turning her to me and looking into her glassy eyes. "Why don't you have a shower?"

She flushes. "Do I stink?"

Like a barn. I can almost taste the cigarettes and sweat. "Of course not. But it will restore you. Why don't you wash up while I fetch us something to eat?"

She hesitates, and I take the liberty of starting to unzip her dress. She's in no state to make decisions, and besides, I can't have her hesitating. I have to take hold of this ship and steer it.

She lets me undress her, and I try to be as quick and gentle as possible, and to avoid staring, but by the end of it I am red as a brick. I kneel down and remove each heeled shoe, and I slide off her socks trimmed with lace. I can see why men desire her, and I can see ever more clearly why they do not desire me.

"How perfect you are," I mumble.

She beams with pleasure; she is endearingly vain, and my admiration must feel like a balm.

She does a little half spin for me, steps out of the heap of clothes, and I guide her over to the bathroom. I run my fingers through her hair, which is greasy but still thick.

"Take your time," I urge. "It will relax you."

I usher her inside and I wait until I hear the water running for a few minutes before going to work.

I pick up the pile of clothes and go through every inch. Starting with the dress, I check the outside pockets, and then I check to make sure there are no pockets sewn onto the inside. I check underneath the collar, and I check inside her brassiere and underwear. I check her socks, and I check her shoes. I find the bag inside her left shoe, filled with that hateful beige powder, and I immediately run to the far window, open it, and toss it out into the street. It feels like it should be dark by now, but these are the late days of summer and it is still defiantly bright outside.

I remember the day that de Gaulle came to liberate Paris. I remember hanging my body off the balcony, almost balancing on my belly like a swallow, with the tears streaming down my face and the joyous song of freedom in my mouth.

Maman took us down to see the troops marching in, and I will remember every solitary second of it until the day I die. I never expect to have such a perfect day again. She wrapped her yellow scarf around my waist and danced me around the street like we were Fred and Ginger.

When the Nazis came, Maman shut herself away. She told me that Paris without joy was like a garden without flowers, and that if she could not stop the city from dying, she would at least be damned if she watched.

I have never seen her as happy as I saw her the day we were freed.

I like to remember her that way.

I go through Teddy's suitcase with my pulse fluttering, and I find the kit she uses to fix, but no more drugs. I put everything back just the way I found it, and then I fly to the door when I hear a knock.

A handsome young colored boy in a uniform hands me a bag, and I thrust a big tip into his palm and kiss him on both cheeks before he can stop me. He has a hazy grin on his face as I shut the door.

I am halfway through setting up when Teddy emerges from the bathroom, naked as the day she was born, with a towel wrapped around her hair.

She looks a little better. It won't last. "What was that?"

I look at her painted toes. "It was nothing, just an errand I had done. Put a robe on."

She tuts impatiently and fumbles around in the bathroom for

one. When she comes back out, she lets her hair down and sits on the big bed.

"I'm so tired," she yawns. "I feel like I haven't slept properly since I left Ohio. There's too many lights in this city."

I sit beside her and wrap an arm around her waist. "Teddy, there's no easy way to say this. You've got to stop. I can help you."

She tries to shrug away from me, but I hold her fast. "Time enough for that," she says with a nervous laugh.

"No," I say firmly. "Now. Today. If you fall into tomorrow's you'll never get out."

"Nobody appointed you my keeper," she says nastily.

"Do you see anyone else?" I ask calmly. "And I don't need anyone to appoint me. I've decided."

I think I understand now why I ran into this girl on the street that night. Teddy is the closest I will ever get to atonement. Why else would I be willing to spend my own desperately needed money to help her? What else could it mean that when I am with her, in quiet moments, God seems to sit in the room with us?

She glances around as if an escape route might open up if she just looks hard enough. "I'm hungry," she whines. She's trying to distract me. "Can't you go get something for us to eat?"

"You can have crackers," I rule. "Anything else is pointless."

She blinks, as if it's just dawned on her that I had planned this all along. "What are you doing, Delphine?"

"Something I'm good at," I say wryly.

She is white as the sheets beneath her fingers. "I can't do it," she gasps. "I don't want to do it. I'm going to get sick."

I don't bother lying to her. "You will," I say simply. "It will pass. I'll be here."

"No!" she shrieks.

"Yes."

She bolts up and goes for her things, where she dropped them in the middle of the floor.

"There's no point in that. I threw it away."

She's trembling now. "Oh, God. Oh, God, spare me."

She goes for the door to the hallway, and now I move, catching her before her long white fingers can graze the handle.

"None of that," I say briskly.

She wriggles, but I'm stronger than her, emaciated as she is, and I put one arm around her waist, the other around her chest, and drag her into the bathroom. She lets out an ungodly howl, and I slap my hand over her mouth before someone comes. I push her inside and slam the door shut, propping my body against it to keep it closed.

"Shush, Teddy," I urge. "Save your strength."

She hollers at me to let her go, she swears at me for a fool, and she slams her body against the door.

The thuds dissolve into banging fists, and then slapping palms, and then a low whine as she sinks to the floor and cries.

"Listen to me," I say clearly, loud enough so she can hear me over her own misery. "Listen to the sound of my voice. I want you to drink some water. And stay near the toilet. Put some towels down on the floor. Do you want a blanket?"

The string of expletives she lets loose would make a sailor blush. She's not trying to open the door anymore—she's run out of strength. I allow myself to sit down, my back leaned against the wooden panel between us.

I can hear her sniffling and blowing her nose. Then, a few

minutes of quiet—cruel, really—and then the sound of her crawling over to the toilet and heaving.

I close my eyes.

This is the sound of my childhood, as familiar to me as a lullaby. All that's needed is Ella Fitzgerald's voice to croon above it all, to make it feel less like a nightmare and more like a dream.

. . .

Day two.

I count out loud to her. I tell her it's been another hour. She sleeps in fifteen-minute increments, but I don't sleep at all. I give her water and crackers when she'll take them, and I dab ice on her neck to cool her down as she burns with feverish heat.

I want to put her in the bed, but she is sweating so much I'm afraid she'll ruin the sheets, so I build her a cocoon in the bathtub.

She's past rage now.

. . .

Day three.

I am able to move her to the bed, where she leans back against me and whispers through cracked lips. I order some soup for us, but she scarcely touches hers.

She speaks of dying. She says that she dreams of it and that she can smell decay on her fingers.

She says that her mother ran away to Indiana, which I knew, but then she also mentions that her sister ran off too—to Iowa. Apparently her father used to beat the three of them for the slightest offense. "Stone-cold sober too," she adds. "He never touched a drop. Somehow that made it worse."

Her legs are still shaking. She shifts around, looking for a comfort she won't find.

"I hate people, you know."

I nod. "I know."

"I'm sorry for what I said to you. Before."

I don't trouble myself to think of which specific instance she is referring to. "Don't give it another thought. It doesn't matter."

"You're not ordinary," she whispers.

"Ah, Teddy." This is all I could ask for. "I'm leaving soon. Come with me."

She mumbles something incoherent. In a moment she has fallen asleep, and I lie perfectly still and listen to her fragile heartbeat.

She will be awake in ten minutes, and I think of what I can tell her to make her cling to me, to hold fast to the future that I could give her.

When I was very small and brimming with bright hope, I used to tell Maman that I would build her a glass castle in Antibes and fill it with all of her friends. I swore to her that I'd paint her poems on the wall in gold. I told her that I'd find Papa and make him come back to us. I told her I'd give her a fountain full of champagne and a sun that never set.

She would smile at me with a deep sadness in her eyes and say nothing but that I was her angel, and she was sorry.

. . .

Day four.

Teddy has an appetite today, but I make sure she eats slowly, and I limit her to soup and bread. I bathe her and change her into a fresh dress, and then I brush out her hair and braid it so that it will curl when I let it loose, just like Delia taught me. The brush shakes in my hand as I think guiltily of how worried they must be, and I push it down.

Teddy complains about her natural color and says that she will dye it again, but I say that I like it better this way.

Then she says she wants to call Harlan.

"What?" I ask, more sharply than I mean to. "You can't mean it."

"I do, I want to talk to him."

I will rip that man's face off with my bare hands if I ever see him again. "I really don't think that's necessary."

"Well, he owes me," she says flatly. "If he wants me to keep mum about what I know, he can pay me at least. Then he and that slut he's shacked up with can go straight to hell."

My grip on her braid eases. "Right. So you'll call him?"

She peers at me in the mirror. "No, I want to see him."

I jerk, and I nearly yank her out of her chair. "You can't!"

She winces and pulls away. "Of course I can."

If I let her out of my sight now, he'll drag her right back, or worse.

"But don't you want to come to Havana with me?"

She laughs. "Havana? What?"

"My father's in Cuba, I know it for a fact now. I have his address." I swallow. "I'm not wrong this time."

"How lovely for you," she says warmly, and I know that she means it. "And who is it again?"

I hesitate. "I'll tell you soon," I promise. "As soon as you're better."

She winks at me. "I'll hold you to that."

"Shall we go for a walk?" I suggest lightly. "A short one, just for some fresh air?"

She stands on shaky legs and gives me her old, indomitable smile.

"We'd better. It's really not fair to the god-awful people of this city to keep myself indoors like this. I've got to show myself to the public, after all."

. . .

Day five.

Yesterday's walk lasted eight minutes. She got queasy as soon as she saw all the people, but she put on a brave face and we walked around the block and tried to enjoy the nice weather.

I've called a doctor, and we're waiting for him to come. I call Delia too, and tell her quickly that I'm okay, and that I'll see her as soon as I can. It's the first time I've called her, and I feel so guilty that I hang up before she can get a word in.

We have to leave the hotel in a little while, and I'm climbing the walls thinking of where to take Teddy. If I know anything now, it's that she stays with me.

If I stopped for a moment, I would ask myself why I am doing all of this, and I would remember that I miss Delia's cooking and Blue's calm wisdom. I would wonder if I had another letter from Louise, sitting unopened on my desk. I'd think that I have not written a fake letter from Maman in a while, and that this whole house of cards is going to come crashing down on my head.

So I don't stop. I pack up all of our things, and I plan to go back to Blue and Delia's tonight to get the rest of my belongings. They'll let me do that, I think. They're good people.

I can get us tickets to Florida, we can stay in a hotel for a night, and from there we'll go to Cuba when I have enough money.

The doctor finally comes, and Teddy looks at me sweetly and asks me to wait in the hall so she can speak to the man alone. He's in his fifties, gray haired and with whiskers sprouting from his oversized ears. He demands his payment before he'll even see her.

I don't want to go, but I step outside and I keep my ear pressed against the thick door the entire time. I have a wild thought that he's not a doctor at all, but a dealer, and this is all her elaborate plan to slip back into the filth I just pulled her out of.

I take deep breaths and remind myself that the hotel found him for me. He looks respectable.

After half an hour, she opens the door and the man leaves, mumbling to himself the way that old people do, complaining just for the pleasure of it.

I rush inside and find Teddy sitting on the bed, legs crossed, face blank as a marble slab.

"What is it?" I demand.

She shrugs. "It's just the sweats. I've seen other girls go through them before, and they'll pass."

"Nothing else?" I am doubtful and can't mask it.

"Nothing I don't deserve," she says with forced cheer. "Just the desserts of my folly. It will all pass. Now, tell me more about Havana."

I am immediately planning again, and I take her hand and pull her towards the window, where we can stand in the sunlight streaming through the cream-colored blinds.

"Well, you have a passport, don't you?"

She giggles. "God, no. Nobody ever expected me to go any-where. I was supposed to live and die on the patch of shit I was born on. It's a miracle I'm even here."

"I'll take care of everything, but you do . . . you do want to go, don't you?"

The look on her face is avid. "I could go for an adventure. But I can't speak Spanish."

I go quiet. I can never make her understand. I have never had one single thing that was only mine. I have never had a sun in my heavens that was not a thousand miles away, oblivious to my name, to my very existence. I have been seen only to be dismissed.

I've never had anything like her.

· · ·

We agree to meet again in twenty-four hours. She swears to me that she is restored, that she is better than that, she is reborn. I try to dissuade her from confronting Harlan, but she is resolute. She says it's something she needs to do for herself, to reclaim her dignity. She says that he'll give us the money we need if she threatens to spill secrets, that she knows of backroom deals and money laundering. That she'll call his holy-roller mother and sing like a plump canary.

She is shining with confidence. I search her face for my mother's well-meaning lies, but I don't find them. She's dressed like her old self, her face made up, her nails painted. She really does look brand-new.

"It's the only way," she assures me. "How else will we get enough money? Will you have enough on your own just from working at the restaurant?"

I can't argue with her because I don't have a better idea. I just look at her with a sinking feeling in my belly and a smile stretched across my face.

"Oh, don't worry that I'll use again," she huffs, as if it is an unreasonable assumption.

"And he won't hurt you?" I dare to name my greatest fear.

She raises her eyebrows. "He can damn well try, but I think he'll find I hit back these days." She pats my cheek. "I don't think he will, don't look like that. He wants me out of his life. He won't miss the money, and he won't miss me."

I cover her hand with mine. I don't want to let her go. I would bind us together with invisible string if I could. Truth be told, I don't really trust letting her out of my sight. I'm afraid she'll be drawn back towards those who can give her more than I can.

"Just one day."

"Just one," she promises. "And then we'll go find your papa. And I'll learn to dance with fruit on my head."

"And we'll meet right here? At ten o'clock in the morning?" I confirm. "And you're staying the night with . . . ?"

"With a girl I came up from Ohio with. Yes, yes. Right in this very spot. I'll wear red, you won't be able to miss me."

We kiss on both cheeks, and she beams at me.

"See you tomorrow."

And with that she bounds off, free as I have never been except when I am tilting towards trouble.

In a moment she is swallowed by the crowd, and I have to turn away and walk my own path to a place I love, where I am no longer welcome. This feeling is familiar, and bitter to swallow down.

I dawdle, but eventually I arrive at the brownstone. My throat is so dry it hurts.

Even though I still have keys I don't use them. I knock on the door, and after a beat, Delia opens it.

"Oh, God," she exclaims, and she pulls me into her arms and into the house. She smells like flour. "Oh, God, child. You've come home."

I have to screw myself up very tightly not to cry. "Hi, Delia."

She hollers for Blue, and he comes running down the stairs, his tie crooked. It's the first time I've ever seen him with a hair out of place.

He hugs me tight, and I dissolve into his arms. I cling to him for a moment and then I let go.

I force the words out. I hate lying to them; it tastes foul. "I've come . . . for my things. I can't stay. I . . . I've decided to go back to Paris. To Maman. Tomorrow morning."

Delia gasps, but Blue takes it all in without flinching.

"And your friend?"

Now I am grinning.

"She's well. She's excellent. She's going home to her family."

Delia looks as if she hasn't heard me at all. She trembles and then goes still. "You're leaving?"

The pain on her face is unbearable.

"I thought you wanted me to go," I say weakly.

We look at each other with unshed tears, and she shakes her head and doesn't bother to contradict me.

"Well, if you've made up your mind, that's it, then," Blue says gruffly. "And you're sure?"

No.

"Yes," I whisper. "Yes, sir."

He puts a firm hand on the top of my head. "I'm glad you're going back to your mama. I expect to hear word from you both the second you arrive."

I can't speak. I am choking on the lies like they're putrid meat.

"I'm going to miss you both," I say brokenly. "Truly, I . . . I'll never forget either of you."

Delia knots her apron in her hands. "You ever come back here, you consider this your home."

I bow my head in shame. "I don't deserve it."

"You don't have to deserve it," Blue rules. "That's the whole point of having a home. Everything else in the world a fella's gotta earn, but this one thing you just get."

If I had an ounce of sense I'd drop to my knees and thank God for the both of them. I would pack away my fascination with Teddy, I would crush my ambitions, and I would bloom in this concrete where I have been planted.

But I don't have common sense.

Only a secret name, and a known destiny.

"I'll go and pack. And then I'll help with dinner."

. . .

I am such a hateful coward. I don't even wait until they're awake the next morning to bundle up all of my things and go. I toss Louise's unopened letter into my satchel with the thought that maybe I'll feel up to reading it once I arrive in Havana. Maybe the words won't be able to touch me as deeply there.

I leave the keys and a note on my desk, and I steal away without a sound.

I'm getting too good at this. This isn't who I wanted to be when I came to New York.

But I don't have time to feel bad about my lack of common sense right now. I toss it into the box in the back of my mind that is full to bursting, and will likely kill me the day I decide to open it up.

Absurdly, I am wearing my best, with my finest hat crammed onto my sad hair, and low heels that I don't stumble in. The last time I arrived in a new place, I looked like I'd been dragged out of the nearest gutter. But this time, I have Teddy.

I have been permanently altered by what happened on that once-beloved balcony back in Paris. I have only one method of surviving, and that is to charge straight ahead, always.

I take the train to the right part of town, and then I have a breakfast I can barely taste at a cramped café right off the corner of where I'm meeting her.

I am waiting for Teddy at the designated spot twenty minutes early, trying to look like I'm seriously occupied and not waiting for anyone at all. I pull out my notebook and scribble down my name two dozen times. My typewriter is snug and heavy in its traveling case, just waiting for me to have a real idea.

I check my watch. Ten past ten. She's probably just running late. Teddy doesn't even carry a watch—she has this notion that people will wait on her anyway, and here I am proving her right. I will have to ask her one day where she gets her confidence from.

I start to sweat in the temperate weather. Fifteen past now.

I catch a flash of red coming towards me, and I crane my neck to look, my heart leaping, but it's not her. A middle-aged woman in an ugly scarlet sweater brushes by me, and I let out a low curse.

This isn't going to go wrong. I'm not going to let it go all wrong again.

I take off as fast as I can without running towards Harlan's apartment. I feel sick picturing her in bed with him, tangled up in his sheets and his lies. Or worse, maybe she's gone to meet her dealer, and I will never find her again.

I make eight blocks in record time, and then I am through the lobby and nearly to the lifts before someone stops me.

"Excuse me, you can't go up there. Who are you here to see?"

"I'm going up to see Harlan," I say briskly, and I jerk away from him before he can grab hold of me. "You can tell him or not tell him for all I care."

The man frowns. "You'll have to wait here."

What luck, someone is coming out of a lift, and I am able to glide into it quick as mercury. For the first time, alone in the small confines of the elevator, I start to wonder if a normal person would do what I am doing for Teddy. And then I wonder if a normal person is a good bar in the first place.

The thought has left me before I stride into the hallway, to the door at the end of the hall, and bang on it like I'm trying to rouse the dead.

Fiona answers it, her eyes wide in her pale face, her big smile dropping when she sees that it's me.

"Delphine?"

"Where's Teddy?" I demand.

"She's not here, and you really shouldn't be here." She glances behind her and lowers her voice. "You had better go."

I start to push past her, and she yelps.

She holds out her scrawny arms to stop me. "It's true! She was here, yesterday, and she and Harlan had a terrible argument about something. He made me leave, and she was gone when I got back."

I search her face for a lie, but all I find is strain. "Where has she gone?"

She shakes her head, her dark hair sticking to her face. "I don't know, exactly. Harlan says she wasn't well, and he sent her to a doctor."

The lift doors open behind me to reveal the man from before, along with another brawny fellow, and they stride out and shout at me. I wince, but Fiona steps out and shuts the door behind her.

"She's our guest. Leave her alone, please. It's all right."

They both look doubtful.

I give her a swift glance and try not to show my shock. "Why, yes. As you can see here, we're all friends." I beam at them. "You can go now."

The first man looks at me as if he'd throttle me before he turns and stalks off, his companion following. I take a deep breath.

"Why did you do that?"

Fiona sighs. "I know you must think I'm awful."

I shrug. I know I'm supposed to hate her in solidarity, but all my ire is reserved for Harlan.

"I really don't know where Teddy is, exactly. But I have a guess. Based on what I overheard, I think she may have gone to see Dr. Porter."

At once my stomach does a somersault. "A dealer?" I gasp.

"No, no," she says in a rush. "This is a different type of fellow. He deals with ladies' troubles."

I look at her uncomprehendingly. "What?"

She looks embarrassed. "You know. He helps girls who are in the family way."

I really wish people in this country would say what they mean. She makes a gesture towards her stomach, and I finally understand. The blood drains from my extremities.

"Find out where he is!" I snap.

She nods and goes inside in a hurry, leaving me to wait for her return in the hallway. Somehow I know that she'll come back, even though she doesn't have to.

She comes back and hands me a scrap of paper with a hastily scrawled phone number on it.

"Tell him Fiona Higgins sent you," she says hurriedly. "He only takes referrals. Safer that way. He'll tell you where you can meet him, he's always moving."

I can't think of the sufficient words to thank her. Already, I feel the urgency pulling at me, forcing me to leave, but I have to say something.

Finally, I stumble on the simple truth. "You deserve better, you know."

She looks taken aback, but then she sighs and cracks a tiny smile.

"Probably."

And with that she goes inside and shuts the door. I hear a small click as it locks, and I know that I can't come back here again.

.   .   .

My hands are sweating as I fumble for coins in my purse to use the pay phone. I take off my good gloves because I don't want to ruin them. I know about these things only in the vaguest sense.

Maman was hardly shy about educating me about the doings between a man and a woman—and the consequences. But she always told me that if I got myself into trouble to come directly to her and not to any silly friends. She knew the right people. There was no shame between us. It is one of the things that I miss more than I thought possible.

I dial the number, holding my breath the entire time. I am both terrified that no one will pick up and that someone will. Finally, after what feels like weeks, a woman answers the phone. Her voice is clipped.

"Dr. Porter's office, Anne speaking."

"Hello?" I realize that I sound like a child and I force myself to deepen my voice. "This is Delphine. I'm a friend of Fiona Higgins."

I wait for her to say something, but she doesn't. I'm not sure what to say but I know that I can't let her hang up the phone.

"Please, I'm calling because I need help." I swallow. "I was told that you could help me."

The sound goes muffled for a moment. I hear her say something to someone. There's a pause and then she says, "It's going to be one hundred dollars. He can see you tomorrow at noon. Come alone."

I try not to speak too fast. I can't let her hear how nervous I am. "I'm looking for someone. Teddy Dolan. She came to see the doctor. I'm her friend. She never came back and I'm just trying to find her."

The woman goes quiet and I'm afraid she's going to hang up. I sound like I'm being a busybody and nobody likes those, especially when they're doing something against the law.

"Please, can you just tell me where she's gone? Or even if she's okay? I can pay you."

There is some more muffled chatter on the other end of the line. Then I hear a man's voice.

"What do you want?" he asks sharply.

I assume that this is the doctor.

"Please, I'm not trying to make trouble. But I know that Harlan Ross, or maybe Fiona Higgins, sent a Miss Teddy Dolan to see you. She's tall, with light brown hair and brown eyes. She's pretty, you'd remember. She's eighteen, but she tells everyone that she's twenty-one. I just want to know if she's all right. She was supposed to meet me, and she never did."

Please echoes inside my mind, and I am filled with bitterness that I am once again a supplicant. *Please tell me.*

He mumbles something under his breath. "Hospital," he says shortly, and then the line cuts out.

. . .

A hospital. Common sense tells me that it's probably a close one. I only have to check three of them before I find her.

I can't understand how Teddy could be in a place like this. I triumphed just yesterday. It's not possible that things could have gone wrong so quickly.

I tell the nurse at the front desk that I'm Teddy's sister, and she checks her records. I can't even hope that Teddy isn't here, because then how will I find her?

The nurse looks at me. "Write your name down, and you can go up and visit in a little while."

She notes that I'm carrying everything I own, and that I'm sweating. I'm afraid she thinks I look like a vagrant.

"Did you just get in this morning? She was only admitted a few hours ago."

I swallow. "Yes, yes, just off the train from Chicago." I don't know very many American cities; this is really the only one I can think of on short notice. "Can't I see her now?"

"Your sister's lost a lot of blood," she says in a low voice. She puts emphasis on the word "sister" as if she knows I am lying. My accent is fairly obvious. My skin is frigid, even though I can't stop sweating. "But she'll be okay. The police have already been in to see her."

"The police?" I croak.

She looks at me as if I'm slow. "Of course. We have to call the police when we suspect this kind of thing."

I nod and say nothing. I can't think of a single thing to say to make this better, so I press my lips together and hope like a little girl that all of this will stop.

"You want to see her," she asks.

"Please." It's barely a whisper.

"She's on the fourth floor, left wing. Room 418. You can see her for one hour."

She calls for a dawdling orderly, who leads me upstairs and down a long hallway. I had to take Maman to the hospital once or twice. I remember her face, white as the sheets tucked up to her chin. I remember the way that the nurses treated her—like a fool who had brought all her trouble on herself—and I doubt that Teddy will fare better.

He opens the door to her room, which is all the way at the end of the hallway and is the size of a coat closet.

"She's in here."

I fly to her side. She was dozing, but she opens her eyes wide when she sees me. She is pale but smiling, and her eyes are still clear. Her suitcase is in the corner. I drop everything I'm carrying and take her hand. I see a glint of metal, and I realize that her right wrist is handcuffed to the railing running along the side of the bed.

She takes in my horrified gasp, my face full of questions, and she closes her eyes again.

"Don't look like that," she croaks. "It's only temporary."

"What did you *do*?"

She blinks up at the ceiling.

"What I had to. Don't lecture me, Delphine. I'm tired."

"We're going to Cuba, remember?" I say. "You promised. Now . . . did this doctor do this to you?"

She groans. "No, no. I did this to myself. All by myself. I didn't have the money to pay him, so he sent me off with some vague instructions and I did it myself. When I couldn't stop the bleeding, I went back to him, but he turned me away. He told me to come here after making me swear never to mention his name."

I am so distressed that I can hardly speak. "Oh, Teddy, why didn't you tell me?"

She shrugs and the metal clinks. I am chilled to my toes by the sound.

"Some things I've just got to keep to myself."

"I could have helped you!" I wail. I remind myself to lower my voice. I don't want anyone interrupting us. "I have money."

"That's your money," she insists. "For finding your papa. It's got nothing to do with me."

"It's my money, and you've got to do with me. Don't tell me

what I can use it for," I rage at her. "Look what you've done! What will they do to you?"

"They don't have any proof, only suspicions," she says stubbornly. "I'm unmarried and young. But I was alone, so there's no one to bear witness against me." She gives a mirthless laugh. "I was completely alone."

I pull the chair in the corner next to her bed so I can sit beside her. I have to be calm. I am not known for my brilliant decision making, but it seems I will have to be the reasonable one between us. "Why didn't Harlan give you the money? That's why you went to see him, isn't it?"

Her complexion, already white, goes whiter still. She is tight-lipped in her fury. "I'll kill him, Delphine. So help me God, I'll kill that worthless son of a bitch."

I stroke her arm. "We'll leave here and never think about him again. I will make us filthy rich when I finish my novel, which really must be any day now, and we won't think about him, or any of the other people who didn't believe in us."

She shakes her head. "You're funny."

"I'm not making a joke."

She cracks a faint smile. "No, I mean you've got a funny way about you. You'll be all right."

I have to ask. I have to ask, though I am sick to my stomach. "How did . . . how did you do it?"

She skims her eyes away from mine. "Crochet needles. I washed them first. I had tried pennyroyal tea before, but it didn't work."

I could slap her. "Teddy!"

"Oh, don't you judge me," she says crossly. Her temper puts a bit of color back in her cheeks. "I've gotten enough of that. The nurse who first looked at me when I checked myself in all but called me a whore who should be left to die."

"I'm not judging you for what you did. These things can happen. Maman always warned me, and of course she would have known."

She sits up a little straighter, as if I am her jury and she is going to plead her case. "Harlan never liked rubbers. Every time I insisted it was a fight. I got tired of fighting. He promised he'd take care of me."

I'd sooner trust a snake than a man trying to get my underwear off, but I think I'm learning some of that tact Louise is always on about, because I clamp my lips shut on the words.

"It doesn't matter now."

"I wasn't going to do it." Defiance lights up her deep brown eyes. "I wasn't going to slink back home, knocked up, pathetic, a stupid girl with failed dreams. And do what? Beg for a man who'd take a secondhand woman? Hope one of the boys from the neighboring farms still held a candle for me, so he could marry me and stifle some of my shame? I wasn't going to walk in the same miserable footsteps as my grandmama and my mama. I choose my life, it doesn't choose me. Even if it's disastrous. It's *my* disaster, goddamn it."

I am quiet in the face of this outburst.

"You think I'm selfish," she accuses me.

I raise my eyebrows. "I am the last person in the world who is going to call you selfish for daring to want things and fight for them. I am not going to criticize you for refusing to slink back to the dirt you were born on."

"But your mother gave up everything for you."

I feel a hysterical laugh bubbling up in my throat. "My mother is not a good example. There is no nobility in doing something you're not meant to do. That's hardly an argument."

She rattles the handcuff on her wrist. "Well, this is what I get, apparently. Swell. I liked to pretend that I was in control, with Harlan. That I was using him, or at least that we were using each other. But I see now that he's had a dozen pretty idiots before me, and he'll have a dozen after. I'm a cliché."

She leans back against the pillows and lets out a low, thin moan. "Jesus, I'd rather be dead than go back to Ohio a cliché."

I place my hand on her hot forehead. "Don't distress yourself like this. Things can only improve from here." I know this. Of course I do, I, who lost my mother and my home. I, who have had Blue and Delia and let them go in pursuit of a papa who could atone for my mother's failings and shed enough glory onto me to help me atone for my own. I know that the way to survive is to go forward and hope that you are going up towards the light.

She shivers and pulls the covers up to her chin. "I'm tired."

"Sleep. I'll stay here with you. And when you've rested up a bit I'll sneak you out and we'll be off to Cuba."

She grins. "They might not even check on me. They've got me back here all alone like I'll contaminate anyone I touch."

I feel a powerful urge to do something. It's not in my nature to stand still. "Can I get you anything, Teddy?"

"Theodora," she whispers. "A boring name for a boring girl."

"You're not boring!"

"I don't mind. Nothing bad happens to girls who don't want too much. So I'll be plain old Theodora again, and I'll leave all the dreaming to you, and catch the breeze from your wings. I'll be just fine."

The door opens and a nurse comes in. She's unsmiling.

"Visiting time is over. You'll need to leave now. You can see Miss Dolan tomorrow."

"Can't I stay?"

"No," she says, without a glimmer of sympathy. "The police will be back to question her later. You can come back in the morning, past nine. And don't bring all of those things with you, this isn't a boardinghouse."

I shoot an anguished glance at Teddy. "I'll be back."

She smiles as if she has never doubted it, as if I am incapable of telling a lie. "Of course you will. Ma belle, Delphine."

.   .   .

I book a room at the nearest hotel, just one block over. The bed is large and comfortable, I can sleep crossways like I prefer, but I don't sleep a wink. I toss the covers back and watch the goose bumps appear on my arms.

I don't know how I am going to fix this.

For a moment in the darkness, when it is so quiet that I can hear all of my unwanted thoughts, I consider going back to the brownstone in Harlem. Delia would make me a cup of tea and put clover honey in it. Tomorrow morning I'd help her make biscuits. Blue would beat me at chess and laugh, and I would know I was safe. I'd have my typewriter to write on, and a new dress for Christmas.

Blue is real. Delia is real. Even Maman, when I had her, was flesh and blood.

I am chasing smoke and shadows.

No, no. I can't do this. I can't allow the doubt to creep in. I can't look back. I will end up with nothing.

I try to turn my mind towards my novel. I can control that.

I'll set it in Havana. I will be there soon—I ignore the fact that I will not be able to afford to live for long with the money I have—and I will be alive to every detail, every foreign scent and vibrant color. It's perfect. It's meant to be.

Except I still have next to no idea what it will be about.

Do geniuses know that they are geniuses, or is part of their brilliance that it all seems mundane to them?

I'm sure the fact that I have to think about any of this means that I'm a dolt.

I turn my face into the stuffy heat of the pillow and wait for the light to creep over me and tell me that it's time to go.

I am up and dressed by six thirty, and then I have to wait. I put on a short-sleeved yellow dress with white buckled heels, and I brush my limp hair until it shines. Teddy is the only one who would appreciate it if I wore lipstick and I don't think that's her primary concern right now.

I pin a yellow hat with tiny white feathers onto my head and cock my head in the mirror to make sure that it doesn't fall off. I refold all of my clothes and check the antique jewelry box to make sure that it's not damaged. I've wrapped it in layers of brown paper and so far it seems to have worked. On the way over here from France, I kept it in my lap constantly, hidden in a burlap sack.

My fingers find the key on the gold chain around my neck. Just a peek wouldn't hurt. Just to make sure that nothing has shifted, or turned to dust and floated away.

Maman's picture is there. I graze my fingers over her eternally frozen smile.

Papa's book is here too, signed and dated. It's addressed to his *tournesol,* his sunflower. Apparently he has nicknames for everyone. I wonder what he'd call me.

I read awhile but when I look up, it's still only eight o'clock. I can't wait anymore. Teddy is probably awake now, and the sooner I get to speak to her, the sooner we can plot our way out of this. She was wrong to wade into trouble alone, when God knows I am a natural-born companion for such a thing. I think she understands now. From the look in her eyes when we parted, I think she finally trusts me. I find that I don't want to betray that trust. It makes me proud. I want to honor it.

Checkout isn't until noon, so I leave my things in the room and head down to the lobby.

I walk the short distance with my head held high. My mother walked the streets like she owned them, even when we were down very low on our luck and she knew that the neighborhood gossips had been shoveling dirt on her name, calling her a drunk and a slut, a scandal and a madwoman. I can manage some confidence. Or if not, I can fake some.

I arrive at the hospital and walk up to the front desk in the lobby. The nurse, a young woman with strawberry blonde hair and a scattering of freckles across her nose, looks at me with a smile.

"Good morning," she says pleasantly.

"Good morning. I'm here to see Miss Theodora Dolan, please."

She checks the binder in front of her, flips a few pages. "I'm sorry, I don't see anyone by that name."

My stomach clenches. They can't have taken her away already. "She's here. I saw her yesterday. I'm her sister. Delphine."

"I can ask someone."

"She's here, I'm sure. Room 418. Please do."

She gets up and walks down the hallway to her left. She's not gone long. When she comes back she's still smiling, like it's stitched on.

"Theodora Dolan, correct?"

My heart leaps. I got here in time. "Yes, yes. Can I see her now?"

She taps her clipboard with her pen. "I'm sorry, but Miss Dolan passed away early this morning. Around three thirty. If you want the body released to you, I can have someone bring you the paperwork."

I just stare at her. I must have misheard. I must not have understood the words.

"No. I'd like to see her now."

Her smile drops a little. "I'm actually just a candy striper. I volunteer. I really shouldn't be telling you this. One of the doctors is coming to see you. Please just have a seat."

I don't understand.

"What?"

She goes pale. "I don't know how to do this part. I'm just covering for one of the nurses."

I start to walk past her. She touches my arm and I slide away; I don't even feel her. I see her lips move, the cracked lipstick with the flakes stuck to her front teeth. But I can't hear her, and I just keep walking.

She follows me down the hallway, but when I get on the lift she stops. Her smile is gone now, and she just watches me go, her eyes large in her face. "I'm sorry," she says again before the doors close in her face.

I realize that my hands are shaking. That girl isn't a doctor, she isn't even a nurse. She doesn't know what she's talking about.

And I probably didn't understand anyway.

I walk down the hallway. The space around me seems to warp, and I feel the hair on every inch of me standing straight up.

I have been here before. The old wallpaper with roses. The cathedral bells chiming in the distance. The broken bottle of Chardonnay, sticky beneath my bare feet. The blood. The empty blue eyes.

Home, gone.

No. Stop. Stop.

The door to the room at the end of the hallway is open. I can see someone's back. A flash of light brown hair. Teddy.

I'm running. My legs move without me and I'm in the doorway, knocking aside the woman standing there.

The girl laid atop the bed is not Teddy.

Teddy has brown eyes like melted chocolate, but lighter in the center and bright when she laughs. She is bursting with passion, defiance, energy, a desire to love and be loved. I saved her.

The thing in the bed is lifeless, still, a chimera wearing Teddy's face.

This is impossible.

"You shouldn't be here," someone says urgently. "I'm sorry, but you'll have to wait downstairs."

I move forward. This is not Teddy's hand in mine. It is cold and stiff. So why am I crying? Why is there a soft, pathetic whine creeping from me?

"Teddy's fine. This isn't her. Where is she?"

The woman I knocked into turns to her companion. "Get the doctor," she says rapidly. The other woman, a nurse, dashes from the room and now there are hands on my shoulders, pulling me back.

"I'm sorry," she says softly. "She's gone. She went septic; that can happen with this kind of thing. It's a nasty business. There was nothing we could do. It all happened very quickly."

I take the hand in my own and kiss the white fingers, turned to marble stone before me. I close my eyes to blot out the sight, but nothing can stop the tears from falling.

"No. We're going to Havana."

Her pull grows more urgent. "I'm sorry. You can't be in here. We have to move her, we need the room. Is there anyone we can call for you?"

No, no, no.

The answer to her question, and the only word I can pick out from the white hot agony behind my eyes.

No, no, no.

.   .   .

I didn't mean to kill anyone.

That's what I told Louise when she found me. That's what I tell the shadows that hunt me, scenting blood and weakness. That's what I say to myself every morning, noon, and night.

Most of the time I can tell myself it was an accident. The kind of accident that could happen to any unloved girl with a temper like mine.

I didn't mean to kill her.

But I did mean to set the fire.

If they ever catch me, I will tell them everything. I will tell them how I went to the mansion on Long Island, the very same one I celebrated the dawning of the new year in. How I hid in the woods behind it and waited until dark. I will tell them how I broke a low window with a rock and climbed through. I unlocked the back door to bring in all of the gasoline I bought.

I will tell every detail: how I filled the flowerpot from the kitchen with gasoline and went from room to room spreading it in every corner. I refilled it more than once. The bitter seed inside me burst open, and it was a relief to sink into the malice and freedom that have always waited for me. I lit the matches and let them go, and all of my despised helplessness went with it. It was the most pleasure I have ever felt, feeling the flames at my back as I left the way I came.

If they ever ask me, I will tell them the truth: that I did it, and I would do it again.

I found the instructions written on a piece of paper in Teddy's purse, scrawled in her messy script. This was the last thing that she ever wrote. She was thinking of me, even as death was pulling her away. *To Delphine: Look in the third guest bedroom of the mansion on Long Island, behind the painting of Harlan's grandfather. The ugly one. Eight-five-seven.*

I took all of the money from the hidden safe. Ten thousand dollars. It's enough, more than enough for me to go wherever I must.

She is cold in the ground. Worms will eat her beautiful eyes, and the man who helped to kill her will eat caviar and not think of her at all.

She will never see Cuba, she will never grow up. She will never learn, as I have, that it is better to be a miserable, ordinary woman than a special dead girl.

So I don't consider death. I will face torment every time I close my eyes, I will see Teddy's face alongside my mother's now, and I will accept the pain as the price of being alive.

Because when you are dead, others will write your story for you.

I will burn down the world before that happens to me.

I am Delphine Auber Hemingway. I am the daughter of a poet and a genius. I am destined for greatness, and I am damned to do terrible things to achieve it.

I claim it here, now, as I sit in my cabin and feel the waves making me sick as I am carried far away from the shores of America.

I cannot speak it, I can barely even think of it, but I can write it. I can write down the truth and watch the words flow onto the page.

I can't hide anymore.

I take the pen in my hand and let the words come, slanting crooked on the piece of paper in my notebook. I force myself to look; I don't flinch or avert my gaze. I stare at them, undaunted, and I let out an endless breath as they blaze forth and become real.

My name is Delphine Violette.

I was born on the eleventh of January, nineteen twenty-nine.

I am the only daughter of Sylvie Margot Auber and Ernest Miller Hemingway.

I am seventeen years old.

I killed my mother.

PART II

Chapter Seven

Nocturne

Havana, Cuba
December 1946

In my interview with Madame Celia, I stick to the truth whenever possible, but I obviously can't tell her why I'm really here.

She reminds me of a bird, with a huge mass of thick curls piled high on her head and a diminutive frame that seems crushed beneath the weight of her hair and gaudy jewelry. She dresses like a woman several years younger.

Her office is hot and stuffy. I feel like I've been given a demerit the second she looks at me, though the nuns at my school would never have worn so much makeup.

I lick my lips. My Spanish is fledgling, but she picks up on that and switches to heavily accented English. I suppose she deals with tourists.

"Rita, is it?" she asks, looking down at the application I've filled out.

"Rita. Yes."

She cackles as if she knows my name is most certainly not Rita.

"How old are you, Rita?"

"I'm twenty years old, madame."

She gives me an unblinking stare. "I don't think so. Eighteen maybe. If that. Just a little girl."

I flush but hold my tongue. This boardinghouse is in a central location, with good rooms and good rates, and it caters to women only. I need a roof over my head. I'd feel better if that roof didn't have men beneath it. I let her stare at me and look down at my hands folded in my lap.

"I will pay on time," I say quietly. "In advance, if you want. I'm really . . ."

I can't say that I'm trustworthy.

"I won't cause any trouble."

She shakes her head. "And you're here with no family? All alone?"

She has no idea. She has no idea that I can take care of myself because I've always had to do so.

"I have business here." I try to sound prim, but it fails. The tired ache in my bones has spilled into my voice. "I just need a place to start."

"And you don't speak Spanish?"

"I will learn."

"And is that business some love affair by any chance? Because I'm a good Catholic woman. I won't condone any carrying on outside of marriage."

"It's not," I say flatly. "My mother says that love is wasted on men. She told me to get a puppy and be done with it."

She flashes a quick smile and then jots something down in the open notebook in front of her.

"Well, we don't allow dogs here. On two legs or four. So you're Rita. Twenty. French. Wants a room on a higher floor. And has business to take care of. That's you, is it?"

I swallow and force myself to look at her. It's a peculiar feeling to lie to someone who knows it as well as you do.

"Please let me stay, madame."

She leans back in her chair. "Oh, fine. You can stay here as long as you need. You are hardly the worst of them."

. . .

My room is on the top floor overlooking the harbor. The walls are palest blue, like Teddy's dead lips. I have a bed, a small wooden table with two hideous floral cushioned chairs, and a desk facing the window. The clothes Blue and Delia bought me are in the closet; an unfinished letter to Louise is tucked beneath my pillow. Maman's jewelry box is underneath the bed, and the key is around my neck. The money I've put into a safe that I have bolted to the closet floor. I can't risk losing it to thieves. Half the women here have a shifty look about them. I'm sure I'm one of them.

I have my typewriter. It was difficult to carry all this way, but I could hardly leave it behind.

I have written eighty-two pages now of the novel that I started in New York, much of it on the journey here. The stack of paper is neatly bound in the top drawer of my desk. I never let myself read it over again once it's written. When it's finished, I plan to, but not for now. I sit down every evening, with the scent of the sea air still clinging to me, and I pour everything out before I have a chance to doubt it. I sign my name as Delphine Auber Hemingway now. I think Maman, for all her flaws, made me into a writer too.

I do not allow the thought that I am a broken, loveless thing to enter my mind until I am finished. I have all the long hours of the night to make up the time.

I don't dream of them. Their ghosts are always at my shoulder during the day, so close I can feel their breath on the back of my neck.

But at night I'm all alone.

I think that they are off somewhere, enjoying the happiness that was denied them in life. Maman is a great poet and lucky in love. She has no daughter, no need for a silver medal in place of a golden dream. Teddy is glamorous, famous, beloved. She lives for herself and is free of a world that would damn her for it.

There are no gentleman callers allowed inside the building, not even inside the common areas, and so no temptation to use a man as a lackluster distraction.

Though there is a man in my life, or at least a boy.

Javier costs me five dollars a week, which is a bargain, or so he tells me. He's my translator and guide. He can't be more than eighteen, though he tries to fool people with a sad little mustache above his top lip. Madame Celia, the owner of the boardinghouse, told me where to find him.

The first time I saw him he was playing guitar in the square near the Hotel Nacional. He really is a horrible singer. In a city full of gorgeous, vivacious sound, he stands absolutely no chance.

I flipped a coin into his nearly empty guitar case, and he looked at me like we'd just made love.

This morning he is waiting for me outside the front door when I come downstairs after breakfast.

He has a tan, warm complexion and deep, engaging brown eyes that appear to be slightly different shades from one another in the light. His hair is curly, slicked down on the sides with product and fluffed at the top. He has bad teeth that he hides behind a close-lipped smile. He's my height but much better built, with strong arms and a long torso. He's not handsome, but he is not ugly either, so at least we have something in common in that we are both mostly unmemorable.

Today he is wearing a tight yellow shirt and white pants. He smiles.

"Bonjour, mademoiselle."

I nod and fall into step beside him. I never know where he's taking me beforehand. He always takes me to a new part of the city—and what a beautiful city it is. It makes New York look like a festering dump.

But it's not Paris.

We take these daily walks, and he points out landmarks to me and tells me what streets to avoid after dark. He knows all the best places to eat, and he always gets into boisterous conversations with the cooks, who laugh and pile our plates even higher. I have developed a fierce love of plantains, and I would never have guessed that a simple plate of rice and beans could be so satisfying.

He's teaching me Spanish, and I pick up what I can in bits and pieces. It's easier than English, and less ugly.

"So are you going to tell me your name today?" he asks as if he doesn't much care either way. He waves at a man he knows who drives by us in a brightly colored car.

"I told you my name."

He grins. "Rita Hayworth. Right."

I consider the obvious lies almost like telling the truth. I shrug.

"I'll tell you when you tell me how you learned French."

"I told you I learned in school."

We pass underneath the awning of a bright pink building and I revel in the brief shade. Javier has told me that Old Havana is centered around five main plazas and that I will learn to tell them apart soon enough. The Plaza de Armas is the city's birthplace and reminiscent of medieval Europe. Tourists flock there to see El Templete, a monument erected in 1827. "But the real magic is the ancient ceiba tree across from it," he whispered in my ear. "Make a wish, circle it three times, and your wish will come true."

I don't believe this for a second, but I pay closer attention when he says that he will take me to the many book vendors that have set up shop across the street from the grand palaces, and then to a quiet street that is paved with wood so that I can read them.

The Plaza de la Catedral is widely considered to be the most beautiful place in the city, with towering cathedrals galore. The Plaza de San Francisco de Asís is home to a former convent, but more interestingly it is home to the Hotel Ambos Mundos, where Papa stayed for a time when he first arrived in the city.

I feel a tingle in my fingertips when he tells me this. Already, I am learning things and I didn't even have to ask.

The Plaza Vieja is the most colorful of all and there is no shortage of things to eat. "You can't miss it," he assures me. "It's gorgeous. And even if you're blind, you'd be able to smell it."

Finally, there is the Plaza del Cristo, which is much smaller and doesn't attract as many tourists. Javier says it's his favorite.

Next week, I plan to see what kind of history books the Biblioteca Nacional has for me to borrow.

Already, I am thinking ahead to where I will live in the years to come. I favor the Moorish-style rooftops and stark white balconies against colorful backdrops. When things are a bit more settled I will look for one with ivy climbing the walls, painted blue as a peacock.

I mop my brow with a handkerchief Delia made for me.

I have always dreamed of the warmth, but I did not dream that I would sweat so very much. I swear I never used to sweat so much before, but life before New York also grows hazier by the day.

I glance at Javier. "I know what you told me about your French, I just don't believe that's the entire story."

He looks amused. "You're not very polite. Aren't you European girls supposed to be delicate? Proper?"

"I have no idea what I'm supposed to be like. And you shouldn't generalize. I don't expect you to smoke cigars and dance all the time."

"But I *do* dance all the time," he says, quite unabashed. "Is that supposed to offend me? You would make a terrible bigot, Rita Hayworth, if you can't think of anything worse."

"I would make a terrible bigot because I dislike just about everyone equally."

He laughs and I'm left feeling like I've said too much. I point to a fancy-looking building in the distance and ask what it's called. He likes to talk. The more he says and the less I do, the better.

I wonder if he's a criminal and that's why my landlady was willing to give me his name. If she is assuming that I'm a fugitive, I can't blame her for thinking that no one reputable would want anything to do with me.

After a while we stop and sit on a bench and watch the cars go by. Though the palm trees will take some getting used to, there is something about this city that reminds me of Paris. I like the cobblestone streets, the looming cathedrals, and the general feeling that important things have happened here. I did not come here to be happy, but under different circumstances I think I could be.

Never in my wildest dreams did I think I would end up on an island. I don't even own a bathing suit. Blue and Delia offered to get me one when we went up to the lake house, but I was content just to dip my toes into the water.

He sees the vacant look in my eyes. "Do you miss New York?"

"No."

"What about Nice?"

I have to remind myself that I told him I was from Nice. I've never been, but I've seen travel brochures. I had a classmate, Henriette, who went every summer and brought back little tokens for everyone in our year but me. There were only fifteen of us. It was rather obvious.

"I do miss it." But I am thinking of the view from my little balcony. I can smell Maman's lilac perfume as she comes to my side and tells me that she's feeling better today, and would I like to go to the picture show with her?

"A Frenchwoman in Cuba," he muses. "That could be a song I could write."

I roll my eyes, but I smile a little despite myself. Javier is the only company I have who lives and breathes. If I am not with him, I am in my tiny room trying to wrestle the jumble of words inside my head and the burning in my chest into something resembling a book.

"I don't think music is for you," I say, and it's only after the words have left my mouth that I realize it sounds rather mean.

"Music is for everyone," he corrects me. "It's like air."

"*Good* music isn't. Just like how anyone can slap a sentence together, but not everyone can really write. Not everyone can move a stranger to tears over people that aren't even real. The problem with the arts is everyone underestimates them. There's a difference between doing something because it amuses you and being recognized as great."

His lips twitch upward. "So are you ever going to tell me what your novel is about? This *House of Pristine Sorrows?*"

I wouldn't even if I knew. Or maybe I would, maybe that would make it real? So much of my life exists only in my mind. The part that exists in brick and stone has been crumbling around me. I turn my head away. "You can read it when it's finished."

He holds his hands up. "You're not very charming."

"I didn't come here to be charming. And I've got something I need to ask you."

"I'll consider it, Miss Hayworth. As a favor between friends."

At once I'm on my feet. "We're not friends. I'm paying you."

I can't have friends. That has been made quite clear to me. They are a distraction I can't afford.

He puts his hand over his heart. "You wound me. Just because you've hired me for a job doesn't mean we can't be friends."

I start walking, without a clue where I am headed. He slides ahead of me with all the grace of a dancer. He's light on his feet. I think he could lose me in a crowd without an ounce of trouble.

Maybe one day he will.

"So what is it that you want me to do? As your hired help and Spanish teacher, and not as your friend?"

I take a big breath. I feel as if I'm stepping one foot onto the right path at long last.

"Find out everything you can for me about Mr. Hemingway. Discreetly. Find out where he goes, what he likes."

I've been wanting to ask him this from the start, but I've been afraid that he would think I was some sort of madwoman. Perhaps he would even report me to the police.

He looks at me with curiosity all over his face. "The American writer?"

I force myself to look him in the eye. "Yes. I think that he lives in a farmhouse a little ways outside the city. I want you to find a way that someone might get close to him."

He juts out his chin. "For what purpose? You don't pay me enough to be an accomplice to murder."

I seize onto his arm as he touches on my fear. "I would never hurt him!"

"Ah, I see. So it's la pasión, then. A schoolgirl crush. He's rather old, you know, but I'm not judging."

"It's not that either!"

He chuckles at the horror in my voice. "So what then?"

"I'll pay you four times your usual weekly rate. And no questions."

He throws an arm around me and looks into my eyes like he's trying to pick out the truth of my intentions. He's always so casual with me, you'd never guess we had not known each other for very long. He is always teasing me and touching me, not in a lewd way, more like an older cousin who has assigned himself the task of keeping me on my toes. I don't mind it. It's new but I think I could get used to it.

I take a closer look at him to confirm that he is perfectly average looking, because you'd never know from his confidence. Maman always said men were like that.

He lets me go. "You're an odd girl, Miss Rita Hayworth from Nice. Half a world away from home, all alone, no family or man to protect you, and refusing the chance of a friend. Doesn't make much sense to me."

"I don't need friends and I don't need to make sense to you. Just find a way for me to get close to Hemingway. Can you do that?"

"I can do that," he confirms. "But what will you do when I tell you what I learn?"

"What I was born for," I say simply. "And that is none of your business either."

. . .

That night, I write twenty words on my typewriter. Just twenty. That is what my life, and all the death it has brought, is worth. If I could crack my skull open and pour out the words, I swear I would do it. I have such ideas in my head, but when I sit down to write them they all flutter away. I think it is punishment for my sins. Like Sisyphus.

After a few hours of frustration, I give up and rest my head against the windowpane. I miss Louise. I wish I could see her and hear her voice, but I know that I don't deserve either. She would be ashamed of me. I haven't written to her since I arrived in Cuba and I know that she'll worry.

I make my way back to the desk and pull out a sheet of paper.

Dear Louise,

I'm sorry. I'm not dead.

I'm in Havana, Cuba now. He's here. I'm sure this time. I'm going to find a way to see him. When I finish my novel and when I'm very, very famous, I'll tell him who I am.

It has to be in that order, and not before. He won't understand otherwise. He won't see me as I need to be seen.

I have been thinking of what you once told me. That pride is not the answer to shame, but its root. I have tried to give up my pride. Truly. But I can't.

So that is why I am still ashamed? Because the two are stuck together?

I know what I did to my mother is unforgivable. And then there was Teddy, my dear friend Teddy, who I failed. Another pretty dead face in my dreams.

I think my shame is keeping me from writing. I think I am past my fear. I think it is the shame that is choking me and keeping me frozen in place.

So help me banish my shame. No riddles or religion. Something useful. Something even I can't botch. Help me, or I'll die voiceless, and it will all have been for nothing.

Her death, and mine.

Your loving goddaughter,

Delphine

Louise responds best to desperation. She could have been a wealthy woman all her days but instead chose to spend her days helping the destitute.

I pick up another sheet of paper from the stack. This letter is harder. This one is for Blue and Delia, who took me in as if I were a good, honest person, which God knows I am not. Delia loved me. I should have tried harder not to let her but I was weak, like a plant thirsting for a drop of rain.

It was never easy with Maman, but it was worse during the war years. Toward the end. Everything was.

We nearly killed each other every day. I risked my freedom sneaking out to the black markets past curfew to buy her liquor, or steal it when there was no money to spend. I couldn't live with her when she was sick. She was miserable, and I thought she would die sometimes when she shook so badly.

I didn't realize death was so final. I know that is a stupid thing to think, but I still cannot believe that I will never see her again. She will never choose anything over me again. She will never have the chance to see the great writer, the great woman that I know I can become. And there is nothing I can do. This is not a story that I can edit.

I'm powerless. When it comes to her, I am always powerless.

But with Delia, everything was peaceful. Easy. And I lied to her. Over and over. I gave her no better than what the world has always given me.

I can't do it anymore. When I try to write more comforting lies, my hand seizes up and the pen clatters to the floor. I wonder if this is what it feels like to have one of those souls that Louise is always going on about.

Dear Blue and Delia,

My mother is dead. She's been dead since I came
to you.

I'm not in Paris. I'm not in France at all. I won't
insult you with sorry.

Please don't try to find me.

Thank you for everything.

All my love,

Delphine

I can't think of anything else to say. I don't even know if I will send either of these letters, or if I'm just writing them now because I am a coward who needs to sleep.

It's working at least. As I look out at the distant moon, my lids start to grow heavy.

I whisper to myself about Papa, the same stories that Maman used to tell me on the nights she was feeling well enough to tuck me into bed instead of the other way around. I can almost feel her fingers running through my hair, almost hear the perpetual giggle in her voice as she whispers to me about the parties, the hotels, the restaurants, the bars, the shows. The way they were all drunk on the best wine and their own youth and talent, the belief that the bad times had passed over them and would never come again.

But more than that, the magic of quiet moments. He used to rub her feet in front of a roaring fire. He used to run his fingers through her thick hair and promise he'd bring down stars for her to wear as earrings. She was his sunflower, the brightest, most beautiful of all the girls in Paris. Should fate tear them apart, even then, he would never forget her.

I used to walk in his footsteps. I never told my mother, or even Louise, but I would go to the rue du Cardinal Lemoine and stand outside his first flat, the one he shared with his dutiful, long-discarded first wife. Then I would go to 39 rue Descartes, the flat he rented just to write in. Sometimes for my birthday, on the good years if I begged, Maman would take me to La Closerie des Lilas for dinner.

How many Sundays did I spend going to the places he'd been, trying to hold on to him, hoping he could sense me wherever he was? Hoping that just maybe he'd sense my longing and come back for me? For all of Maman's charm, she was unbearable to live with most of the time. Believing in Papa kept me alive, kept me stubbornly marching on. I never let myself feel abandoned by my father, I never thought of it that way at all. If anything, a secret, hateful part of me blamed my mother for not being able to hold him.

She blamed me for things too.

When I was eleven, I poured all of her wine bottles down the drain. When she discovered what I had done, she chased me through the apartment, shouting at me with tears in her eyes. Glasses were broken, picture frames knocked off the wall, books thrown from the shelf. I was faster but she pursued me with all the fury of a wounded animal. She finally caught me and we toppled onto the floor, her hands pinning down my wrists. I can still see her face looming half an inch over mine, obscuring everything else, the vein in her forehead pulsing. I can picture the hateful look in her eyes so clearly. Even in Havana it chills me to the marrow of my bones.

Look what you've done, she hissed at me. *After everything you've cost me. Look what you've done.*

On the boat journey here, I slept with kitchen scissors clutched in my hand, the stolen money burning a hole through my suitcase, stashed underneath the tiny bunk.

I heard Maman's voice in my head over and over, calling to me from the tainted corners of my mind.

Delphine.

See?

See what happens?

You've done it again.

Look what you've done.

To drive the voice away, I forced myself to think of Papa's ghost becoming real, solid, a thing of flesh and blood, not a name in a book or a story. I thought of his eyes meeting mine and having real expression, not frozen like in a photograph. This love has been a one-way mirror all my life, and now it is a door that I can step through.

That's what I focused on every time I closed my eyes. Not Maman's corpse. Not Teddy's.

Not Blue and Delia's fear and disappointment.

I thought of the fire I set and all the ghosts burned away.

Then I could picture Papa's eyes on me, blissfully oblivious to who I was before. A new chapter.

My lips move as I tell myself the story until I finally sleep.

Papa comes to Paris.

Papa loves Sylvie.

Papa leaves Sylvie.

Delphine is born.

Papa meets Delphine.

Delphine is born again.

Chapter Eight

~~~~~~~~~~~~~~~~~

Cantabile

Havana, Cuba
January 11, 1947

Papa loves cats. Loves them so much that he has eleven of them. Maman would never even let me have one. He has peacocks too, in Florida. And he has a new wife—a fourth wife, named Mary.

I'd rather know the names of the cats.

His precious sons are all with him too, from what Javier tells me. I think we'll get along fine, so long as they accept that I'm not any less than they are. But I'll have to do what Louise says, and show them grace, because what else is there to offer to people you absolutely can't get rid of?

I've learned that Papa shaves with a straight razor. I've learned that he likes whiskey, and mojitos, and which downtown bars he prefers to get them from. I'm told that he's brawled in a bar more than once and that he goes off like a shot when anything touches his pride—which means he will not shy away from my rough edges. Maybe he'll even see himself in me.

But best of all the things I've learned is that he has a boat that he loves and spends hours on. Sometimes with his family, but often, often enough, gloriously alone.

And that, I think, is my way to him.

Eighteen today. Practically grown. I may still be flat chested, but at least I'm getting smarter.

I inspect myself carefully in the mirror in the peach pink light of the early morning. I think I am less gawky. A tan suits me and brings out a little depth in my brown eyes. It could be worse. No point in thinking of the ways it could be better.

I wear one of the dresses that Delia refurbished for me, one of Maman's old things that's been tailored to the modern style, with the hem hovering just above my knees. I think I've grown again. The dress is an eye-watering shade of red. I hope the boldness will seep into my skin. I do my hair up in pin curls and put some blush on my cheeks.

When I meet Javier in the morning, the same as nearly every morning, he is clearly surprised by the trouble I have taken to look nice. We walk to the Hotel Nacional, one of the first buildings he showed me when I met him. He tells me it was built in 1930 in the Spanish style, and I eye it and think how hideous it is, but it is apparently quite important for tourism since a lot of fancy people like to stay there. Javier always takes the time to explain things carefully to me, and I appreciate how patient he is when I ask questions.

I am starting to feel comfortable now. I can approach a vendor and know when he is offering me a rate that is too high; I can understand a bawdy joke or pick out the meaning of a song when I pass a musician on the street. On the way to the hotel, a kindly-looking old man with skin so dark that it is nearly blue, shiny like

the patent leather on good new shoes, lets me slap his conga drum after I gave him a tip. The woman beside him smiles a toothless smile at me as she strums her guitar.

Javier takes no offense when I ask him if there is an idiotic racial hierarchy here as well as in the United States, and he says that there is, but a lot of Cubans will deny it if you ask them directly.

He says that even though his mother is mostly Spanish, he is a mulato, and he says it with a swell of pride in his voice.

"I don't want to be a conquistador," he says flatly. "Though you'll find plenty of people happily claiming their Spanish great-grandmother and denying everything else. Though the drums they dance to come from Africa, and the tobacco they smoke was culti-vated by the Taíno people long before anyone from Europe set foot on these shores. Even the word 'mambo' comes from the language of the slaves. It means 'conversations with the gods.'"

I smile at his enthusiasm. "You know a lot."

He shrugs. "I know my history. It's the last thing the powerful want, you know, is for the rest of us to know the history they won't teach. For this my mother calls me a radical. I tell her she was a radical when she married my father, but she says that all she did was fall in love."

We sit down on a bench outside and he hands me something hot and delicious-smelling wrapped in paper.

"It's pan tostado. Nothing fancy."

It's the first time he's ever brought me anything. "Thank you."

"You look different than usual."

I offer him a sideways smile. "Good different?"

"Pretty different."

I can't decide whether to be offended or flattered. The playful warmth in his eyes makes me not want to be angry with him. As much as I have tried to crush the part of me that wants to have someone who can make me both laugh and think, I am starting to like him. And it's not like with Teddy. I just feel easy with him.

"Today is my birthday, you know."

He raises an eyebrow.

"Is that so? And you're twenty-one now?"

I just look at him.

"Something like that."

"Well, I'm taking you out."

I nibble on my breakfast. Oh, butter. How I missed fresh butter during the occupation. I could probably bathe in it daily and not grow sick of it. "Out where?"

Outside of eating, my tours, and Spanish lessons, Javier and I don't socialize. This seems dangerous. I can't decide what worries me more: the thought that he won't like me or the thought that he will.

"Dancing, of course," he says.

"That won't be necessary," I say quickly. The color rises to my cheeks. "I'm not a dancer."

He looks genuinely bewildered. "That doesn't mean you can't dance. You don't have to commit your life to a thing to enjoy it for one night."

"I don't enjoy anything that I'm not good at."

He shakes his head. "That's sad."

"Not really," I protest. "It's not wrong to want to be great at things."

"But no one is great at everything, Rita Hayworth. And there's so many, many things in this short life. You'll wall yourself off from most of it with that attitude."

I'm starting to regret opening up to him. "Stop calling me that. You know it's not my real name."

He shrugs. "I do. I also know that you have a temper, that you want to know everything there is to know about the famous American, Hemingway, and that today is your birthday. I know that you want to write things, but only if other people tell you that they're great, and that you're maybe eighteen at the most. I know that you've come to a foreign country all alone, so you probably don't have any family or at least not any family worth having. I know that you've come into some money from somewhere. I know all of this, but you won't tell me your name."

Maman used to change the subject masterfully; she could give you a look through her lashes and get you chatting about the price of a loaf of bread like it was the most interesting thing in the world. I can't do that.

"Did you find out where his boat is docked? *Pilar*, isn't it?"

"Is that your price? More information for your name?"

I have to remind myself not to let him rile me up. "I'm the one paying you. Just tell me, please."

"I did."

"Good. Take me there. I want to buy a boat."

I've done the math and I can afford this expense, since the rest of my lifestyle is not extravagant.

He turns his entire body towards mine. I can see crumbs on his shirt from his own breakfast. "A boat?"

"A sailboat, yes. Or a small yacht. Whatever I can afford."

His look is incredulous. "Do you know the first thing about sailing?"

I look him in the eyes and smile serenely. "Of course. I grew up in Nice. I sailed all the time."

"Alone?"

"I was usually alone, yes." This part is true. I wonder what God's penalty is for half lies? Louise would not be amused by the question.

Javier doesn't even pretend to believe me. "Well, then you'd know you don't buy boats from a dock, you buy them from a shipyard. And you can't always just get one the second you want it. These things can take time. You may have to put your name on a list."

"I want one immediately. I'm sure you'll find me something. And I want to name it too."

He laughs in my face. "Rita Hayworth, you want a great many things. I don't work miracles."

I put my hand out to touch his chest. Nothing bawdy, just a graze. "But you'll try, won't you?"

His gaze follows my hand and then flicks back up to my face. "I'll try. But no promises."

He wags a finger. "I'll try, *if* you let me take you dancing. You should try enjoying something in life before you die."

I take a moment to moderate my tone. "I have a long time before then, I hope. After I've done what I need to."

"Well, we all hope. But nothing is promised."

For once I don't rush in to reply. I let the silence cover us, and I think of Maman's vivacity, and Teddy's determination to never be forgotten. They did not get enough tomorrows. And whether I deserve it or not, I'm the only one of us who is still here.

I look around the park. It's no Jardin du Luxembourg, but it's the middle of winter and there is still green here. Even in January, there is still green, and blooming, and new life. It never stops.

I know I could learn to love that about this tiny country.

"Fine. Take me dancing."

"I believe the custom is to say please, Rita Hayworth."

I start to get up. "It was your idea in the first place!"

He laughs at me, without a hint of malice. I think now that he laughs just because he likes laughing. I don't need to fear it, or guard against it. It has nothing to do with me at all.

"I know it was, señorita, but now I'm going through all the trouble of getting you a boat."

. . .

That night as I dress, I tell myself I'm not going to look too nice for him. I don't want him to think I'm trying to impress him.

But he called me pretty. And I find that I don't want him to change his mind. I'm not interested in him, but I will take whatever admiration I can get.

So I wear the shortest dress I have, one of the few things I've store-bought in years—but I can't wear Maman's hand-me-downs tonight, I just can't. It is sleeveless and in royal blue with buttons down the front. I put on heels even though I will trip over the cobblestones in them. The waist on the dress cinches tight, and I feel a little breathless already.

I pile my curls on top of my head and empty half a bottle of hair spray to keep them there. I even spend a full minute practicing a coquettish grin in the mirror before realizing how dumb I look.

Javier can deal with my natural expression since he's the one who came up with this idea. And it's really a stupid idea. But I find that I'm giddy. I'm sure to make a fool of myself, but I'm still grinning. Not just because of tonight, but because of what comes after.

Next week I'm going to meet Papa. It has to be perfect. I'll use the boat and I'll find him when he's alone, and somehow I'll make him love me. I've never been one for details but surely it can't be that hard? This time, something will turn out right.

I could have gone there the first day and knocked on the door. But I can't show up like a stray dog. I'll never erase that image if that's where we start.

I've thought about it for years, and I've realized that he doesn't have to know who I am from the first day. We'll have years for all of that. I don't need him to love me in a rush of petals and light. This is not a fairy tale and I am not the kind of girl who gets to be in one.

No, the important part is to make sure that there's a blank page between us. The important thing is that there's hope.

Javier picks me up at eight o'clock. He pulls up in a gigantic convertible, the ghastliest shade of yellow I have ever seen, like neon mustard. It may be hideous, but it looks brand-new. He honks loudly though I'm standing right in front of him on the steps to my boardinghouse.

"I'm not getting in a stolen car," I shout at him. "I've got enough problems."

He gets out of the driver's seat, comes around, and opens the passenger-side door. He's dressed in a mulberry-colored short-sleeved shirt that looks a size too small and gray slacks. "Well, good evening to you as well. The car's not stolen. It's my own, I got it last birthday. Now, get in."

I hesitate. "If you have a car, why have we been walking every-where all this time?"

"Walking is good for you, Rita Hayworth. It's healthy for the body and soul. But Havana is beautiful at night. So get in and let me show you."

I do as he asks, settling into the plush leather seats and letting him close the door for me like I don't have hands. It's silly but nice to feel like I'm someone who needs cherishing. He pulls off, too fast.

We whiz by a block of flashing neon signs and palm trees gently illuminated by streetlamps. When we pass the ocean, I take a deep inhale. I am growing to love the clean, salty smell of the sea. Javier makes a steep turn, and now I spot many other partygoers bustling about, all dressed to the nines, the men with their hair slicked back and women with their jewelry brightly shining, showcasing lip-sticked smiles. The women here have a sophistication that I must learn; I rarely see any of them with a hair out of place. Already, I can hear music floating in the air, the sharp percussion of drums and the rich blare of trumpets. Even I, devoid of any rhythm, start to tap my foot.

My mother would like it here.

I turn to Javier. "Where are you taking me?"

"Are you always so pleasant when a man takes you out?"

"Men don't take me out."

"Not ever?" He chuckles. "Well, on second thought, you have the disposition of a stable cat, so I'm not so surprised."

I flush. "This isn't a date anyway."

"It's not a date," he agrees, and I feel my heart sink a little de-spite the fact that I don't even want him in that way. "It's a birthday present. I could never take a girl as ill-mannered as you on a date. And the purpose of a date is to get to know someone. You won't even tell me your name."

"Why do you care so much what my name is? I don't know your full name either."

He runs a stop sign. "My name is Javier Alejandro Castillo Moya."

I huff. "I didn't ask."

"No, but I told you."

I take my time thinking of what to reply. I recognize that he's trying to be kind to me. I know that Teddy would want me to embrace this night, this chance at lighthearted joy, but I don't know how I am meant to.

"In my experience trusting people ends poorly. Even with the smallest things. But I do appreciate you taking me out tonight. So thank you."

He nods. "I see. I'm guessing you've never been salsa dancing before?"

"Maybe once or twice."

As soon as we pull up to the club, with its flashing sign and a line of exquisitely dressed patrons outside, I wish I hadn't lied. Everyone here looks like they know how to do salsa and every other dance in existence for that matter.

"This looks fancy."

A valet comes up and opens my door. Javier hands him the keys and a few bills.

"It is fancy," he says with a bemused look. "Some of the mob bosses come down here from Miami. The mayor comes here too.

But I've never known a woman to complain about being taken to a nice place for her birthday. Did you want me to take you to a hole in the wall?"

"Yes," I say frankly. "Somewhere no one important will see me looking stupid."

He offers his arm and I take it.

"Did you find me a boat?" I ask, trying to keep urgency out of my voice.

"I've made some inquiries. I can get you a fifteen-foot yacht. Lightly used. You can name her whatever you like."

Javier waves to a man with a handlebar mustache who calls out to him.

"The boat is a she?"

"Boats are always women. They were named after goddesses in ancient times. You know, I really shouldn't do this; you'll sink and drown since you clearly don't know anything about sailing."

He leads me towards the line but instead of going to the back, he nods at the bouncer, who pulls back the velvet rope and lets us in immediately. As we step into the darkened ballroom, I look up at him in a new light.

He told me his full name without any hesitation. He stands in the square and plays his guitar, and sings off-key, and smiles his crowded-toothed smile like he has no care for what the world thinks of him. He's far more honest than I have ever been or could ever be. I don't even think it's confidence, it's not that he thinks he is special—he just wants to have fun.

I cannot comprehend being that free.

A waiter comes up to us and leads us to a table in the very front of the packed room, with a clear view of the musicians on the stage. I am dressed plainly compared to every other woman I see. I see bare arms and several inches of leg. I see red lipstick, and gold hoop earrings, and decadent fur coats, tall gloves and taller heels. Louise would keel over to see me in a place like this.

The waiter looks at me curiously and I flush. Javier orders us drinks and leans back in his padded chair.

"I haven't been back here in a while."

"You're barely eighteen, how long can you have been coming here?"

He laughs a full-bellied laugh. "I used to come here with my mother."

I pause. This is the first time he's mentioned her to me without being prompted. I want to ask, but I don't want him to ask me anything in return.

"They let a child in?"

"They let her child in," he corrects me.

I force myself to hold back. "You seem very well liked."

"Does that surprise you?"

"Not really."

Our drinks come, two mojitos, and I push mine towards him. "I'll just drink the water."

He studies my face in a way that makes me squirm. "Not eighteen?"

"I could be fifty and I wouldn't touch it. I hope you're not offended."

He takes my drink and sips from it, before sipping from his own. "Who was it, then?"

I balk. "What?"

"The drunk in your family. It's not a normal thing for a young girl to turn down a single drink, unless she has watched a single drink turn into many."

I want to rage at him, but I'm too tired, and besides, I have taken the trouble to curl my hair and I don't want to be angry today. "It was my mother. And don't call her a drunk. She preferred to be called an enthusiast."

Sometimes, if she drank just enough, she was happy enough to grab me and dance the Charleston around the living room. She was an excellent dancer. When she finally collapsed she'd toss a coin at me and tell me to buy something sweet.

"Sweet like you," she'd say, and then she'd laugh like a girl and tuck her stockinged feet underneath her.

I smile at the memory and Javier smiles back.

He is so easily and perpetually amused. It is his singular emotion; indeed, he seems to have no other aspiration in life but to skip about smiling. It must be nice to be a boy.

"I can order you one without alcohol in it."

This reply is more thoughtful than I expected. "Oh?"

"Yes, of course. You should try the mojito. Your Hemingway has developed quite the taste for them."

I am instantly alert. "Has he? I'll have one, then. Without any liquor. Thank you."

"I'll get you one after we dance."

I flush hot and I can feel the burning in my fingertips. "No, no. I told you I can't dance."

But he is already up and sliding my chair back. I grip the table like it can save me, but he is insistent, and since I am here on his charity I can hardly refuse him. While I don't think he'd report me to the police as a suspicious person, I don't want to chance it.

"It's your birthday, and you should have a dance. You should be carefree for a little while. I'll show you the steps."

"People will stare. I'm already foreign. I don't need to stand out anymore."

"Rita Hayworth, everyone is here enjoying themselves. No one is looking at you. You are far less important than you think."

He leads me onto the crowded floor. I can smell sweat mingling with cigar smoke, the mint on his breath as he pulls me close. The music is deafening; it swells around me and seems to push us closer together. His fingers are digging into my lower back.

The band starts a new song, and he leans his head towards me and speaks loudly in my ear.

"One, two, three, four. Hands in close position. Forward and back. On the beat, on the beat—don't dance to the words."

He holds me tightly, and when he releases me for a spin I manage it without breaking an ankle. I am hot from embarrassment but smiling. The music crescendos, and he twinkles through the steps like he was born in dancing shoes. I've always noticed his grace. He walks on the balls of his feet; there is a spring in his step every second of the day. My mother would have been a far more appropriate partner for him than I am.

We dance all night, stopping only for me to down my liquor-free mojito in three desperate gulps. They really are delicious; I love the mint. I am drenched in sweat, and I know that my curls have fallen and my stringy hair is clinging to my forehead. He picks me up bridal style and whirls me around to the beat when my feet finally give out on me. He is dauntless. The music makes him come alive; nothing can stop him. On this island, with the music running through my veins, I feel the weight of all that has happened slide away, if just for now. I am so light that I swear I could take flight like one of the gulls that ride the wind, hovering between water and sky.

When the last song comes to an end, I collapse into his arms and he howls with laughter at the state I'm in.

"You're a horrible dancer. I really thought you were being modest."

I giggle when a few hours ago I would have wanted to defend myself. "What now?"

"Now they bring the car around and I take you back to your lodgings."

I make a split-second decision as I hobble into the night air, leaning heavily on his arm. My feet will be as fat as hams in the morning.

"I don't want to go back yet."

He is quiet for a moment. "Is there somewhere else you'd like to go? Are you hungry?"

Actually I am, though I had not thought of it before he mentioned. "I have a craving for some tostones."

He shoos the valet away gently and opens the passenger-side door for me. "What would you know about that, flaca? Un potaje?"

"I read about it in a guidebook," I confess. "But I want to try it. My mother was a terrible cook and we didn't have much money for restaurants. It was like heaven for me when I stayed in New York, trying new—"

I clamp my mouth shut. If he knows about New York, he could

know that I am on the run. At least they *might* be looking for me. Harlan, or the police, or both.

He sees the terror on my face, I know he does, but he doesn't say anything. He takes off, driving just as fast as before, and I look at the illuminated city before me. As we drive down one street, I can see the dark water shining, and I ask him if he enjoys swimming to try to distract him.

"Very much. I've been swimming since I could walk. You?"

"I never did much of it."

His tone is teasing. "Really? In Nice?"

My throat is dry. Despite the air blowing in my face, I am still hot. "Javier . . ."

"You don't have to bother with that," he cuts me off. "You clearly won't tell me the truth. That's your prerogative, Rita Hayworth. But you don't have to lie either."

I feel absurdly guilty. As if I owe him anything.

"I'm sorry."

He shrugs and turns on the radio. We sit in silence for a while, and then he takes us up a hilly road that grows more and more winding. The trees close in around us, until a branch whips the side of the car and I duck down to avoid a smack in the face.

"Where are you taking me?"

"You've been in the car for twenty minutes and you're only now asking me?"

Suddenly the path clears, and I see a large house with black wrought iron gates in front of it. It's white brick, with bushes of red flowers surrounding it, vibrant even in the dark. As we grow closer, I see lights on the path and two armed men standing in front of the gates.

At once I'm afraid that he has known who I am all along and that he is turning me in. I fumble for the handle to the passenger door, but I don't dare jump out and run. I don't even know where we are and my Spanish is still rudimentary.

"Where are we? Whose house is this?"

"It's my house, silly. Who else's? You think I'll take you to a stranger's house at this hour?"

I check my watch and see that it is nearly three in the morning. The front doors to the boardinghouse will be locked. Madame does not wait for naughty girls; she told me frankly when I arrived that if I found my way into a young man's bed, I'd better make sure I pleased him enough that he'd let me stay there until morning. "Why are we here? What do you have in mind?"

He laughs his brash laugh. "Not that kind of thing. I'd sooner place my privates into a crocodile's mouth. I'd get a warmer welcome."

I am speechless. We trade barbs all the time, but this one strikes true. I am not attracted to him, but it doesn't matter. I don't want to hear him say what I am certain everyone else thinks. I turn my head away before he can see the quick tears spring to my eyes.

I hear him say something to the men. I understand enough Spanish now to know that they address him very respectfully. I hear keys jangling and the gate opens. Javier pulls onto the wide pathway, and someone immediately rushes out of the house and opens the door for him.

He shoos the man away before he can open my door and offers me his hand.

I look at his face, half hidden in shadow.

The realization that has been slowly gathering around me

finally solidifies. He is not a street urchin at all. He plays the guitar in the square because he wants to, not because he needs to. The money that I give him is meaningless. I thought I had some power over him, but he has been humoring me all along. And now I don't know where I stand. My judgment has failed me. Again.

He looks at the stunned expression on my face and sighs. "Come inside, Rita Hayworth."

"You're rich."

He docs not deny it. "Yes, indeed."

My temples begin to pound. I let him lead me inside, and I close my eyes on the hand-carved bespoke furniture and the large oil paintings on the walls.

I let him sit me down onto a plush love seat and push a glass of water into my hand.

I'm such a fool. Louise was right, I am an arrogant fool, and I should have stayed in Paris and let her waste her time trying to mold me into something better.

I feel the weight of Javier sitting beside me. "Don't look so distraught, Rita Hayworth. Why does it matter to you whether I'm rich or not?"

"Why are you doing this with me? If you don't need the money?"

I open my stinging eyes to find that his expression is serious for once.

"Your landlady is my stepgrandmother. She asked me to keep an eye on you. She said you looked like you were in some trouble."

This kindness is too much for me to take in. "Madame Celia?"

"Yes. She was the second wife of my grandfather. He owned several factories and made a small fortune. So no, I don't seek employment because of necessity. I just don't like to be idle."

"So you're not an orphan?"

He raises his eyebrows. "Not at all. My parents have been happily married for twenty years and live in Miami for half the year."

I could sink into these couch cushions and never come out of them. "So this . . . you being my guide is what exactly? Charity?"

"I'm doing it because I want to, and I have the time of day. I also happen to enjoy your company when you are not intentionally trying to be disagreeable."

My stomach rumbles loudly. "I don't understand why you didn't tell me any of this."

His tone hardens a little. "Because you have been so forthcoming with me?"

I bow my head. "Javier . . ."

He stops me. "Look, I understand. You're young, and a girl, and far from home. I understand why you wouldn't trust everyone. But you have to trust someone. You're here for a reason. If everything had gone right in your life, you'd never be crazy enough to be here alone. But we all need someone in this life, Rita Hayworth."

"Is this you volunteering?" I can't bring myself to trust him.

"This is me trying. I can't force you and I won't try."

I look into his honest brown eyes and take the leap. I have nothing anyway unless I can find a way to Papa. And I want to believe that every connection I forge in this life will not be false, or failed, or doomed.

"I'm not from Nice."

He sighs deeply, like a man relieved of a great burden. "You're from Paris. I spent five summers there. I know. You're very obvious. You could never be from anywhere else."

I have no more humiliation left to feel, so I just nod and go on.

The words come tumbling out and before long I've told him nearly everything. I am so relieved to tell someone that I feel lighter by the time I catch my breath.

I tell him only one lie: that my mother drank herself to death. I don't want him to look at me the way Louise did when she found me cradling my mother's bloody body. I don't want anyone to look at me like that ever again.

My voice cracks when I tell him about Teddy, but he is patient and listens to me quietly. I even tell him about setting the mansion aflame and stealing the money from the safe. He does not flinch.

"Do you make a habit of setting things on fire?"

"No. It was just the once. I . . ." I lower my gaze. "I have a temper."

"I can see that. So this is why you're so afraid. Because you're a criminal."

I chafe a little. "I committed a crime. I'm not a criminal."

He hears my tone and lets it go. "Why do you need the boat?"

I still can't say it out loud. But Javier is no fool. If I lay out the puzzle pieces he will put them together.

"Papa has a boat. He spends a lot of time on it. I thought . . . I thought I could find a way to get close to him."

His eyes gleam, and I see the exact moment that it clicks, I can almost hear it. He strokes the peach fuzz on his top lip.

I brace myself for the scorn I faced from my classmates, or Louise's skepticism, or Blue's pity.

I get none of that. Instead he draws my face into his rough hands and looks at me quite seriously.

"I'm sure Mr. Hemingway will be very glad to meet you."

This simple touch brings me to tears. He has pulled just the right thread, and now the tight knot of fear inside me is unraveling. I have never wanted to tell anyone my first name before. It has never felt special. But at this moment it does.

"My name is Delphine."

"Delphine," he repeats, like I have told him something beautiful. He tilts his head back ever so slightly and lets me go. "A pleasure to meet you."

I wipe my face, but the tears don't stop. "So you'll help me? Even though I have nothing that you need in return? Knowing what I've done . . . will you truly help me?"

"I will help you. Family is the most important thing in the world, and besides, I love a good story. And as strange as you are, I'm sure yours will be very entertaining."

Chapter Nine

~~~~~~~~~~~~~~~

Pilar

Havana, Cuba
February 1947

Today.

This is what it means to hang one's entire life on a moment. This is what it is to have only one purpose, one reason for drawing every precious breath. This is what it is to be oblivious to everything else and see only one blazing star in the sky.

Today I am alive for the first time, truly alive, in vivid color and not a sad pantomime.

I can hardly believe it, but here I am. I am standing on the deck of a boat, my very own boat that I bought from Javier. She is called *Tournesol*. We have even had the name emblazoned on the side in bright letters, impossible to miss.

I am also not seasick, which is miraculous—I was sick as a dog on the way to America and coming here—though we have been on the water for two hours at least.

Javier has it on very good authority that Papa will be here, today, in this very spot. He comes here to fish. Apparently he likes to mount the biggest ones on his wall, which is a male fascination I will never understand, but I am sure he has very good reasons.

"The wind is with us," Javier shouts, though he is standing right beside me. He is clearly familiar with the ways of a boat, actively enjoying himself, bright with a child's enthusiasm as he uses seafaring expressions that mean nothing to me.

I tug on my long white shorts. My sky blue linen shirt covers a bathing suit top that I bought when I was feeling ambitious. The wind has whipped my hair into a bird's nest but I don't care; I am bright with more confidence than I have ever felt.

"Nothing will go against me today. I have waited my entire life for this."

"So what are you going to do exactly? Jump out of the boat, chomp down onto the hook, and let him catch you?"

I give Javier a dirty look. He has become a friend, something that I didn't think I would ever have a use for again. Still, I don't want anyone else here right now. If I didn't need him to sail this thing for me, I would have left him behind.

"I haven't worked that out exactly."

He cannot contain his amusement; his forehead wrinkles as he struggles not to laugh. "You've been dreaming of this your entire life, but you haven't worked out the details at all?"

I close my lips on a retort. God help me, I think I am developing this patience that Louise is always on about. "It's difficult."

He shrugs. "Not really. You're making it difficult. You could just walk up to his front door and knock, you know where he lives. You could have done that the day you arrived."

"I can't do that!"

He cracks a beer open and has a seat. "Of course you could. You won't, but you could."

I shake my head. "No, no. He has no reason to believe me. He won't want some street rat turning up reminding him of some long-forgotten love affair, claiming to be his child. And I'm a girl at that. I can't just turn up. Nobody in their right mind would welcome that."

"What does being a girl have to do with anything?"

I give him a hard stare. "Don't play coy. Being a girl has everything to do with everything. I have to do more, be more, to be worth the same. It's always been that way, it will always be that way."

"I think you're being melodramatic, my dear."

"Well, you would," I say pertly. "And that's another thing. That word. 'Melodramatic.' What's the difference—in books, in film, in life itself—between drama and melodrama?"

He hoists up his sleeves, pushes them up past his suntanned elbows. He looks tired already, but I know he'll make the effort to listen to me. It's one of the things I like best about him.

"I'm sure you will tell me."

I certainly will. I've been reading since I was three, and reading book reviews in the newspaper too. When I was in school, being lectured by the dull nuns, literature and history were the only classes I ever really paid attention in. And with the shadow of Papa's life hanging over me, I have had more cause to think about books than most.

I point to him. "One refers to things about you, for you, by you. Better if you're European, lovely if you're old, and perfect if you're dead. An old European man writes something where star-crossed lovers sing all the time, wring their hands, and everyone dies in the end, and we all crown it high art. A tale for the ages. A beautiful tragedy. Opera. Right?"

He looks interested despite himself. "Yes. That's true."

"Meanwhile, if a woman wrote that same thing, someone would refer to her as melodramatic and licentious. Silly. Perhaps someone would condescendingly refer to it as 'quaintly charming' or 'sweetly imaginative' instead of just coming out and saying that it didn't suit their personal taste. I have come to accept that everything is considered more ridiculous when women like it. Why do you think women put men's names on their books? For their health?"

He pauses. He looks at the flush on my cheeks. "I see you've thought a lot about this."

I shrug and crush my hands together, interlocking the fingers. My hair slaps against my cheeks in the wind. That has always been one of the worst parts of having such a temper. I am condemned already as emotional, possibly mad, unstable by nature. The jury passed a sentence on me long before I was even born.

I clear my throat and look away from him. "Well, I'm going to be a writer. I have to think about these things. The words we choose betray us. So I hope to choose mine with more care."

"In real life or just in your stories?"

I glance at him. He is not smiling for once. I think he's serious. I take in for a moment that he has actually considered what I had to say.

"Both," I concede. "I really ought to do both. Thank you for listening to me."

He motions for me to come sit beside him, and I do. He absent-mindedly hands me a glass beer bottle from the cooler on his right, and I take it, hold it in my hands, let the condensation sweat onto my fingers. He knows I don't drink, but I think his mind has gone somewhere else.

He inhales deeply.

"I love the sea, you know. That's the island in me. My grandfather used to take me fishing almost every day. He wasn't from Havana, just a mulato from a little village. He taught me how to put the bait onto the hook and wait, eyes wide open, for hours on end. 'Sing in your head, Javier! Out loud and the fish will swim away. You're off-key anyway!' We would go snorkeling sometimes if it got too hot. He taught me how to sail, how to keep track of direction by the North Star and which way the sun sets." He closes his eyes. "He was a good man, my grandfather. Born nothing but a poor country boy. But he worked hard. And now I never have to."

I don't interrupt his reverie. I can tell by his voice that he is not as happy now as he was then.

After a while, I say, "So you're aware that you sing off-key, then?"

He cuts me a look and I grin.

Then, more seriously, I say, "You're lucky. It's a special thing to have someone think the world of you and take the time to show it."

He nods. "I know. Tell me about Sylvie."

I flinch away from him. I make my way back to stand in front of the wheel, shield my eyes with my hand. I think I see a boat coming towards us, but I can't see what it's called.

"She was my mother. She loved me sometimes, and now she's dead."

"Did you love her?"

I fumble for the pair of binoculars Javier brought on board to shield my face. Despite all of Javier's nautical lectures, I am still uneasy on my feet out here. "I don't know."

"But you named the boat after her? The name your Monsieur Hemingway gave to her? Why?"

I can't find the damn things. But I see it clearly now. Maybe not with my eyes. Somehow I know. I turn to look at Javier, whose tan face is glistening with sweat, his deep brown eyes bright. I tell him the truth as I know it.

"She deserves to be remembered."

When I turn back, the other boat is drawing closer. And I don't move. I let his boat come towards me, guided by the water, the most natural thing on earth. I let it be.

After all of my chasing, everything that I have done, finally now I stand still as a statue. The blood pauses in my veins in reverence of this moment. I don't even blink.

Only my mind keeps churning on. I remember everything in a flash so powerful that I don't know how I stay standing. The war years I try so hard not to think about, the taste of fear in my mouth and the persistent hunger in my belly. More than once I pilfered a can of sardines from a store shelf. The ration lines, the crying babies and the smell of shit. The raids, people disappearing from their homes, people turning on each other for a loaf of bread. The dry days, when Maman was first irritable and then sick as an old dog, howling with fever shakes. Stealing bottles of wine from the black market stalls, holding a shard of broken glass I found in an alley to the throat of a pursuer when he tried to take them back.

The end. The brief joy, the transient sun. Maman's auburn hair against her butter yellow dress, hoisting her handmade sign into the air. Both of us shouting, hugging, crying, because it was over, and we were free.

The brief calm. The truth. The shouting. The knife. Her blood seeping into my clothes, my hair, dripping off the side of the balcony I loved. Louise's scream of horror when two days later she found Maman's stiff body in my arms.

And everything that came after.

But none of it matters now.

Papa's here at last.

. . .

At first he doesn't see me staring, and so I have the benefit of taking him in for the first time unobserved.

He is tall. I knew he would be tall. He looks strong with good, thick hands like a man who could wrestle a bear and win. He is wearing an oversized blue button-down shirt and I can see wiry chest hairs poking out from the top two buttons he has left undone. He has gentle eyes, the exact same shade of brown as my own. He's got a thick, dark mustache above smiling lips and a full head of hair. He is forty-seven years old and still handsome. His movements are confident and assured in a way that I instantly admire without envy. I beam at him and I cling to this moment. I open my pores and let the wonder of it all sink into me, so deep that I can never forget it.

He is perfect. He's my father.

But . . .

He is not what I pictured.

I realize, with a start, that the photograph I have of him as a handsome soldier in the Great War was taken more than twenty years ago. The skin on his forehead is browned and wrinkled from the sun; there are crow's feet around his eyes that go all the way up into the sides of his receding hairline. The hair on his arms is thicker than the hair on his head. His cheeks are puffy and ruddy and he has a slightly rounded belly visible even underneath his shirt.

There is the most minuscule part of me that is absurdly disappointed. He looks like anyone's kindly old uncle. Not the kind of man who could keep a woman like my mother under his spell.

I am beaming and close to tears at the same time. He looks up from fiddling with his line and spots me.

This is the crucial juncture. He will wake up tomorrow the same man, but my life is dependent on this meeting and I am utterly breathless, waiting for the executioner to decide if I will live or die. I have reached the end of what is in my power. Only he can decide if there will be more to this journey that I've been on my entire life.

His gaze takes me in quickly, intelligently. Does he see a resemblance? Or just an ordinary young woman gawping at him like one of the fish he's trying to catch?

His judgment is quick. When he smiles at me, I see even rows of slightly yellowed teeth. Discreetly, I thump my wrist against the steering wheel to confirm that this is all real. He has laid eyes on me and found me inoffensive. He has looked at me and seen the kind of person with whom he could make a start.

He has given me nothing but a warm look and is already a

thousand times more meaningful than every promise my mother ever made me.

When I wave to him, without realizing what I am doing, he waves back amicably before busying himself setting up his fishing rod.

Javier comes up behind me. I can hear my own excitement in his voice. God bless him, he has become invested in my story.

"Is he what you thought?"

I tear my eyes away from Papa. I can't look too eager. I have to play this scene with all of the wisdom I have hand-wrung out of my disastrous choices.

"Better. Will you give me a rod?"

He scoffs. "You don't know what to do with it. I told you to pay closer attention when I showed you."

"I'll get the hang of it. Give it to me and go below; he's more likely to talk to me if he thinks I'm alone."

I have no idea if this is true or not. I simply said it because I have to decide something. I can't stand here aimlessly, or Papa will think I'm a halfwit.

Javier raises an eyebrow. "Delphine, are you certain?"

I am looking at Papa out of the corner of my eye. There's a buzzing like a swarm of angry bees in my chest. "What?"

Javier places an urgent hand on my shoulder. "Are you certain you want to be alone?"

My tone softens on its own at this touch. "I'll call for you if I need you. Don't worry. I won't try to move the boat without you, I'll probably sink it."

He hands me the fishing rod and guides me over to the side of the boat nearest Papa. He sits me down next to the bucket of worms and bends down to whisper in my ear. I notice for the first time that he has a small patch of dark, curly hair on his left ear.

"Wiggle it a bit if you want to make it look like you've got something on the hook. Old people love to comment on that."

"Thank you," I whisper, and he nods and springs away. I think he has absorbed my anxiety and turned it into his usual boundless energy. He must teach me that trick.

One day when I am able, I should make some grand gesture to thank him. Something obnoxious that I will hate and he will adore. I have come to have faith in him, just as he said that I should. And I have faith that he will not abandon me. He is too loyal and honest to slink away now. I can't help but marvel at my luck in finding him.

I put a worm onto the hook and try very hard not to focus on how disgusting it feels as it wriggles between my fingers. What an odd hobby. I can't imagine why people do this for amusement.

The sun beats down on the back of my neck. I definitely should have worn a hat. My legs will be stiff and my back sore for sitting for so long.

But I am grinning like the joker on the pack of cards.

I look at Papa through my lashes.

I drink in the sight of him, sometimes daring to raise my head and stare at him directly. He is so absorbed in what he's doing that he doesn't notice. Occasionally he pulls out a silver flask and takes a quick gulp from it, wipes his forehead with the back of his hand. I think I hear him humming.

One hour goes by. Two. Three.

I am afraid to do anything else but sit here and look at him, but I can't let the fear stop me.

I look at him, clear my throat. And then I say, far too loudly in English, "How's it going?"

He glances up. He doesn't look startled. Did he see me watching him after all?

"Oh, all right."

And there it is, the sound of his voice. It's deeper than I imagined, rougher sounding.

There's a mocking blankness where my thoughts should be. The words come out before I can stop them.

"My name is Delphine."

"Hemingway," he says, like he has no first name. Like he is just anyone and not one of the most famous writers on earth. "You're a Parisian."

It's not a question. My heart is pounding in my bone-dry throat. "Yes."

I am hoping that he will ask me more questions, but he doesn't.

"I don't see many young ladies out here."

"I'm eighteen," I blurt. Does that mean anything to him? Did Maman tell him something about me after all? Did he know she was carrying me when he left France with his second wife? Maman said she never told him, but in this instant I am doubting everything. "Just turned eighteen last month, in fact. But I'm finished with school. I come out here all the time to fish and to read. I think there's nothing better to clear the mind than some time on the open water."

I wait to see if this is what he wants to hear.

He scratches his mustache. Clearly my age means nothing to him. A white-winged bird flies low and cuts between us.

"I lived in Paris for a while."

The voice in my head speaks even though my lips stay sealed.

I know. I used to steal some coins from Maman's hosiery drawer so I could buy some candy when she was cross with me and refused to give me any. I ate it right across the street from your old building. The first one, remember? The apartment you lived in before you were a success, where you slept on a thin mattress on the floor.

He continues. "Who are your parents? Maybe we've met. There aren't very many Frenchmen here. Mostly the expats here are journalists. Americans." He wrinkles his nose a little. I can't tell if the distaste is for my people or his.

"I came here alone, I'm afraid."

I came here for you.

His eyes widen slightly. He has finally found something to hold his interest.

"Alone? All the way from Paris?"

"Yes."

He looks down and then back up. Has he realized? Could he? "Goodness. Well."

Ask me why.

"That's quite something."

Ask me why. Look at the name on the side of my boat and ask me why.

"Doesn't look like anything's biting out here," he sighs. He gets up, stretches out his arms. "I can't stay longer. You have a good day, Delphine."

I want to call out and beg him to stay, but I smile and wave as he packs up his fishing rod and his flask. In a few moments all I can see is the blurry outline of his boat as it fades away.

I close my eyes. I can hear Javier's footsteps approaching. In a moment the barrage of questions will start, and my tongue will unstick from the roof of my mouth.

In the end, that was far from perfect. Papa didn't claim me on sight; the heavens didn't part and angels didn't sing.

But I have met him.

I have met him, and he knows my name.

Chapter Ten

~~~~~~~~~~~~~~

Dancing Bears

Havana, Cuba
March 1947

I see Papa no less than once a week. Javier, clever, clever Javier, always finds a way to know where Papa will be.

Twice we've met on the water. Once he had his boys with him, and we exchanged a few words. They're handsome, well-mannered boys. Maybe it would be nice to have brothers. I was brought up as an only child and I have always been curious about what it would be like to quarrel over toys and squabble over petty nonsense, and yet still know at the end of the day that you are two halves of one whole for life. What would it be like to have someone to protect me?

I'll never know.

They seem like sons to be proud of, though I must say I don't see much of a resemblance. I still think I have Papa's eyes.

Usually, I see Papa at his favorite bar, La Bodeguita del Medio.

He has a table by the window that he likes, and he sits there with his notebook and drinks. Often he is talking to someone else—he is quite sociable, he is prone to slapping people on the back—and I lurk in the back of the room with Javier and watch him. In my fantasy, he should come to me, but so far he has not noticed me.

Javier is working on his second mojito. He is wearing the gold watch that I bought him as a present. I saw it in the window of a jewelry shop and just knew he'd like it. His grandfather always wore a watch. Right now, he is helping me look for a house of my own, to be purchased with the money I stole in New York. I keep waiting for the guilt to come as I spend it, but so far there is none. Louise would be horrified with me, but when I think of watching that mansion go up in flames, all I want to do is smile.

I hope to be moved out of his stepgrandmother's boarding-house by the end of next month.

I never thought that I would settle in a place so quickly, but it makes a kind of sense. Papa's here, of course. But it's becoming more than that. The warm weather is good for my disposition, and I like watching the boats go in and out of port. I like the Cuban Spanish better than the version from Spain, with their "ico" instead of "ito" to denote something small or to indicate affection. My Spanish is improving faster than I'd thought it would.

I like hearing the chickens squawk on the side of the road when Javier takes me for drives. I like iguanas, which I had never seen before but now look for all the time. They're so ugly they're cute, with their beady, pensive-looking eyes.

I see why Papa is so happy in this city, why he first started with winters and then decided to make a full life here. I feel an eerie sort of peace when I am near the sea.

So much so that when I finally receive a reply from Louise, I don't want to read it. I have been keeping it in my pocket for the past three days. Even without reading it, I can see the disapproving owl-like gaze, the set of her head, her thick blonde hair that she sometimes uncovered and let me brush in private when I was a little girl. I don't want to think about her.

I'm happy here and if it is a sinner's happiness I don't mind it. That's all I have left.

Javier shakes out his newspaper.

"I think I found a place that may work for you."

"Did you?"

"It's two bedrooms. You could use one as an office. But do you know how to keep house? Are you going to burn down the neighborhood?"

I poke my tongue out at him. "I'll have you know I'm quite handy. And I can cook."

"So you'll have me over for dinner?"

"I didn't say I could cook *well*."

The only thing I can make decently is stew. Stew from leeks, canned anchovies, or sardines, sometimes a bit of whatever meat could be found as a rare treat—that's what I made day in and day out when I was a little girl.

Before the Germans came, I would make a lot of cassoulet or onion soup. On her good days Maman would socialize and come back with some fresh vegetables donated by an elderly male neighbor who was sweet on her, and she'd help me chop the ingredients to make pistou or ratatouille. On holidays, I made coq au vin, which I always burned.

Mostly Maman charmed our way into restaurants or cafés for

free meals. There was always a friend of a friend, a friend of her mother's who knew the chef . . . somehow she found a way.

I realize now that she was possessed of a singular intelligence. I wonder what she could have done with it had she not wasted her life falling in love: first with a man, and then with a bottle of Chardonnay.

Javier barges into my thoughts. "You don't have to do this, you know. You're welcome to a room at my home. I could put you in the chicken coop if you don't want too much of my hospitality."

I respond, but my eyes are on Papa. He is scribbling something in his notebook. I wonder how it works for him, the stories. Do they pour out perfectly in one go? Does he stop and start, roil with existential dread between each chapter? Or is he like me? Does he struggle to pin down the details but keep pushing on, driven by a feeling too powerful to ignore? I have been writing nearly every night since I saw him for the first time, but I still feel like I am chasing after leaves scattered in the wind.

"That's very generous and I'm grateful. But I need a place of my own. It's the best thing for me."

"If you're sure."

"Certain."

I need a place that I can cling to. I want a place where I can paint the walls a bright, eye-watering yellow and plant marigolds in the green space that is all mine. I'd like a writing room, a special place where I can forget my life for hours at a time and fall into someone else's.

Papa starts speaking to a man at the neighboring table. I will have to be vigilant to catch a moment with him today.

I keep one eye on him and one eye on Javier.

"I'd like a garden too."

"In the city?"

"Outside the city is also fine. I'd like a cottage. Near Papa."

He folds his lips in. "Hm."

"What?"

"I'd prefer you live near me. Somewhere I could keep an eye on you."

His teasing tone betrays genuine concern. He tweaks his growing mustache.

I manage a smile. "I'll be fine. I'm used to taking care of myself."

"So I gather. I'm waiting for the day I come to pick you up and find you brawling in the street."

"I don't do that anymore," I say primly. I wish I hadn't told him that part of my past. Fighting with my schoolmates or anyone else who mocked me was not my finest hour. "I'm reformed."

Javier flips the page in the newspaper, trying to appear nonchalant. "So you're staying, then? A permanent resident of my fair city?"

Papa lights a cigar. I feel a little whirl of disappointment in my belly. I hate smoke. Maman smoked like a chimney when she was stressed. The smell seeps into everything. How many hours did I spend scrubbing the walls, the curtains, the couch with a wet rag trying to get that damned smell out? I want a house that smells like lemon and lavender, to erase the memories of smoke and shame, of liquor and pettiness and death.

I glance back at Javier. "A semipermanent resident."

Technically this is all any of us ever are.

"Your Spanish has improved. You learn quickly, probably because you spend most of your time talking to me. But your pronunciation . . ." He chuckles. "Very French."

"That will change."

He clucks his tongue. "Don't change too much. I won't be able to mock you with such regularity and that would be a shame."

"I have no doubt that you'll find a way."

Papa laughs loudly and we both look. He's standing now, one foot on the chair, talking to an attractive young woman in a green dress and matching high-heeled shoes. I am immediately irritated, and mad at myself for not going over earlier. He draws people to him like a sticky web. This could take all day.

Better late than never. Javier doesn't even try to stop me as I push my chair back. He reaches across the table and starts in on my unfinished lemonade.

"I thought you were going for the subtle approach?"

My patience has deserted me. I'm not getting any braver. "Change of plans."

"Per usual."

I give him a dirty look, but he's already turned his attention back to his newspaper.

I try to walk over to Papa as naturally as possible. The woman in the green dress turns her head for a moment when something outside the window catches her eye, and I slide in between them. Bump, more like, but it does the job.

Papa's bushy eyebrows shoot up. "Oh, hello."

I know that I'm flushing. "We've met."

He smiles. "Yes, we did. On the water. You're Delphine."

He *remembers*. I dare to go one step further.

"I'm Delphine Auber."

His smile does not waver but there is no spark of recognition behind his eyes. I push through the fear and keep going.

"Was there something you wanted?" he asks.

My mouth is suddenly dry. I swallow hard gulps of air. "I . . . I wanted . . ."

He nods and produces a pen from his pocket. His expression is gentle. "A signed copy, perhaps?"

This is the second worst thing that could have happened after him looking at me with disgust. He thinks I am a common admirer. Or worse, the lowliest of creatures: a critic.

"What? No, no. I don't read."

He guffaws and I could melt between the floorboards. I'm such a fool. I've already told him that I go out onto the water to read. The woman from before gives me a nasty look when she sees I have taken her place and goes off to speak to another gentleman.

"You don't read at all? Or just not my books? It's all right. You won't offend me."

I've read them all, but I fear this makes me sound even worse.

"I do, I do! But what I wanted . . . I wanted to ask . . ."

I grip tight onto my nerve, dig my heels in, and blurt it out.

"Did you know a woman named Sylvie when you lived in Paris? She lived on the rue des Écoles."

His smile drops. He frowns, scratches his chin. Then I see it. The memory dances across his face, but I can't tell whether it's good or bad.

The tension is unbearable. If I believed in such nonsense as fainting, I would be on the ground already.

Then he speaks, and his tone is hard to read. "I'll be damned. The suffragette, right? The one who wanted to be a poet."

Then he smiles again, an altogether different smile. The years scrub away from his face. I see the handsome young man that my mother swore she loved with a passion. "The one with the hair like autumn leaves."

It's true. It's really true, everything Maman told me. It's all true. My coming here, everything I have done, all of the suffering I have received and doled out in equal measure—all of it was meant to be. My fingertips are tingling.

"The very same. She . . . she's my mother. She said you two knew each other."

This part is a bit more delicate. He'll get my meaning well enough. I wish to God I could read his face.

I press onwards. It is eerie to say the words out loud that I have practiced in my head for so long. "When I found out you lived here, I wanted to ask you . . . I was hoping . . ."

For everything. Everything, everything. My eyes are opened wide; if they could speak they would be howling, a primal shriek from another world. I want to tell him so badly, but I cannot bring myself to speak such precious words in such a common place. I wish myself alone with him, perhaps in his study where Maman told me that he writes standing up.

I see one of his cats curled up in my lap, the afternoon light catching her dark gray fur. I see the look of surprise on Papa's face, the gentle raise of his brow, the slow droop of his lower lip. Then the pieces clinking together, the mercifully brief hesitation, and open arms.

I don't need him to take me in; I don't want to be a burden to him. But we could take meals together and he could teach me to write as he does. He could tell me stories and show me how to catch fish. I could grow to tolerate his wife and love his sons.

And I would see him every week. At least every week. Everyone would know I was his, and no one could ever overlook me again.

Someone bumps between us, sloshing their drink on my shoes, and the moment shatters.

Papa glances at his watch. "I'm afraid I have an engagement in a while. I can't stay. But maybe we'll run into each other again?" He shakes his head. "Sylvie's daughter. Small world. I haven't thought about her in ages."

She thought about you every day. More often than she thought about me. But all of your women fall together, one to the next, and you forget. Will you forget me too the second I am out of your sight?

I reach for my composure, find it scattered to the wind, and settle for weak nonchalance.

"Of course. I didn't mean to keep you." This next part pains me but I force it out. "It's not urgent. I was just curious. She told me a lot of stories about those days."

He smiles that secretive smile again. "Those were good days. Take care now."

And then he's gone again. I watch him wind through the throng of people and vanish. How many more times do I have to watch him walk away from me?

Javier comes to my shoulder, and I allow myself to lean against him and absorb the comfort of his warmth. I feel as bereaved as an orphan child. My mother is gone, my father is ignorant of my existence, and I am alone.

"You look like you're going to cry."

"I am absolutely not going to cry."

He takes hold of my elbow and guides me out of the bar and into the darkening street.

"What did he say to you?"

I shake my head. He offers me a stick of chewing gum as we walk over to his car. I take it and chew on it very determinedly so that I don't have to talk.

"Did you tell him?" he presses. "Delphine, really. It's never going to be easy, or right, but you can't dance around it forever."

"Soon," I promise. "I just need to get him alone."

He throws his hands in the air. "Ay, no. Not again with this. You're being ridiculous. I can't take it anymore. If you don't tell him by next month, I swear I'm going to tell him myself. Really I will. I'll leave a letter pinned to his door. I'll take my guitar and serenade him the truth from outside his window."

I let him open the car door for me, go around to his side, and drive off before I respond.

"I care for you," I say awkwardly. "This is new . . . for me. I am grateful for your friendship and your advice. But really, Javier, if you do anything to interfere with my plans, I'll feed you to a pack of dogs."

He honks at someone driving too slowly and speeds around them. I feel my half a glass of lemonade coming back up.

"If you keep talking like that you'll end up with no husband to love you. Alone in that house you want to buy so badly, surrounded by books and cats."

I snort and cast my eyes on the steeple of a cathedral that reminds me of home. He may think this is some great threat to me, but I've seen enough from people not to fear comfortable solitude. There are worse things.

I see him looking at me out of the corner of his eye, and I turn to him and give him a bright smile.

"Love is fickle. Books are eternal."

Chapter Eleven

~~~~~~~~~~~~~~~~~~~

Pas de Deux

Havana, Cuba
April 1947

I give in. Of course I do. I was never going to be able to resist. I wake up in my room at the boardinghouse, sweating in the night despite having thrown the window open. All that has done is get me mosquito bites all over my calves.

It's the damn letter. It's burning me up from the inside of my bones. Louise and her conscience have stalked me across the ocean. Her arrow always seems to find my heart.

I fling off the covers and go rifling through the stack of papers beside my typewriter. I have typed up page after page of scenic descriptions, of beautiful sentences, of names for characters whose faces I still can't see clearly in my mind. But it's not a book. Even I lack enough capacity for denial to call it a book. Right now, *The House of Pristine Sorrows* is nothing more than a collection of thoughts. Though I'm certain that even when it's finished and polished and I have poured five years of sweat and tears into it, someone reading it will miss every single point I make, and since people never recognize that in themselves, I will be blamed—so what's the point in bothering? I like writing, I do. I like the freedom it gives me to control a narrative, because it is the only control I've ever had. But the idea of it is far grander than the reality.

I wish again that I could do something different to make Papa love me. Pottery, maybe.

I find Louise's letter buried at the bottom, half stuck underneath a paperweight shaped like the Eiffel Tower that Delia bought me from a trinket shop. My hands tremble as I open it. A sliver of moonlight covers the page and a cat yowls from a nearby rooftop.

Dear Delphine,

I am so happy that you are alive and well. I suppose I never really believed that you would pursue this course for so long and that it would take you so far from safety and from me.

For years I have waited for you to move away from this obsession. After the death of your dear mother, I did not want to distress you further. I thought this was part of your grief. But I have coddled you for too long. You are eighteen now.

Forgive me, child, but it's time you know the truth.

Your mother, God rest her soul, was not a woman unfamiliar with the company of men. She told me herself that she had many lovers near the time of your birth. Her own inner circle knew that her personal account of her lovers, and even her friends, was not reliable. She was not well. And she had a great deal of vanity.

Your mother always thought she was more to some people than she was. So much genuine love was offered to her, but she refused it.

That was her greatest failure: her inability to love what she had.

I don't want to see you make the same mistake.

You are smarter than she was. I do not say this lightly. You have a fine, sharp mind and a keen insight into the human condition. You'd be happier if you didn't, but since you do, I beg you do not waste it.

If you want to write, write, but do it because you want to. You're talented. Truly. Your stories in school were always fascinating. I hope you will allow that to be enough.

Please understand that your mother wanted you to be proud of yourself, and so she gave you a famous and accomplished father to worship from afar. I am sure if she had lived, she would have told you the truth eventually. But she is dead. And so it falls to me, as the one your mother entrusted you to when you were just a baby, to do the hardest thing a parent can do: to destroy their child's innocence for their own good.

The man that you are chasing is nothing to you. He is not your father. Your father is most likely a wastrel, or dead, like so many of your mother's acquaintances. He will never know your name and you will never know his.

Your mother is dead. You are an orphan.

You must learn to live with these truths, just as we must all learn to live with the immutable realities of life.

You have always said that there is no such thing as a lie, and that truth is only what some other people happened to agree on before you arrived. But the world doesn't see it that way. It will not bend to your wishes. You have no choice.

You are who you are in the eyes of the world the day you are born. All that you get to decide is what to do with your one, brief life.

I know you will probably never forgive your mother. I know that you will probably never forgive me. But you must forgive yourself.

I pray that you will, one day. Qui vivra verra.

Live, goddaughter. Live and see.

I will be waiting for you here when you come home.

All my love,

Louise

. . .

My skin is cold. The sun can do nothing to warm it. I help Javier rig the sails on the *Tournesol* in complete silence and stare out at the sunlight rippling over the water, illuminating different shades of blue and green. Louise once told me that the gentle waves we see on the surface are just a glimpse, that deep beneath the water there are forces beyond our understanding.

If I sink down to the bottom of the sea, what will I understand in that last moment between life and death?

Javier frowns at me. I haven't seen him in a week; he has been off performing with his friend's band. I really do wonder why his parents don't make him get a real job. But I guess that's what happens when you're rich.

"What's wrong?"

He doesn't pretend not to know that something has happened. Ever since I confessed to him the truth about how and why I came to Cuba, there is a refreshing lack of pretense between us.

I consider denying it. Then I consider lying, saying that I had some bad fish. But in the end, I let him place a calloused hand on my shoulder and draw me closer.

"Rita Hayworth," he teases, and it forces me to laugh. "Don't tell me you are leaving empty-handed."

Wordlessly I take the letter from the pocket of my sundress and hand it to him.

"You can read French, no? Do you want me to read it?"

He places a hand over his heart as if I have mortally wounded him. I walk to the other end of the deck and let him read alone.

I grip the metal railing tightly. It's windy today. Maybe Papa won't come.

He didn't come yesterday, but we caught several fish and Javier showed me how to clean them properly. We knelt over old newspapers, took small knives and slit open their bellies, pushed out the guts and gills, and chopped off the heads. He laughed at my green face and told me about his grandfather making him do this when he was barely old enough to hold a knife. He actually enjoys this.

Javier's cook made us the most delicious sea bass last night. I had the smallest sip of wine with it. It tasted like horse piss, but I felt brave.

It was a nice day, a great day even without Papa's presence.

Why couldn't I have let it be? Why did I have to read that damn letter?

I don't feel brave now. I feel like one of the fish oozing blood and gray juice onto a slab.

Javier appears at my elbow. The air around us pulses and swells with the effort it takes him not to say *I told you so.*

This is what he warned me about. This is what everyone tried to warn me about. I lorded my certainty over them, and now I am a joke. A fool dancing to music that only I can hear. If Louise is right, then I have been stumbling around in the dark all this time. If by some miracle she is wrong, she has poured gas on the flame of my doubt. I will never be free of it now.

The tears come easily. Javier has the grace to look away.

"I'm sorry, Delphine. Are you still going to tell him?"

"I won't play the coward anymore," I spit bitterly. "I'll do it when I next see him. And then once he has cast me off, I suppose I'll run to some small corner of this island where he'll never have to see my face again. But I will never go back to Paris."

That is my punishment. For what happened to Maman.

He reaches for me, and I shirk away.

"Please don't. I'd rather you just laugh than have pity on me. Go on, laugh. I deserve it."

"I'm not a judge. I'm not here to decide what you deserve. I'm here to be your friend."

I wipe the tears away with the back of my hand and look at him through my stinging eyes.

"Why do you want to be my friend?"

"I told you—"

"You're not telling me everything. It's obvious you're holding back. I know your stepgrandmother owns the boardinghouse and asked you to look after me. But you've done quite a bit more than that. And don't tell me you just like helping lost souls, you're not a saint. So what is it? Do your other rich friends bore you so much?"

He takes the slightest step away from me.

"Are you in love with me, is that it?"

His face springs alive with denial, but it is not as vehement as it was before. I don't give him a chance to tell me no.

He's getting angry now, I can see it in the set of his jaw. The light in his eyes dims.

"Nobody could ever love you. You'd scare off anyone who tried."

I slap him. It feels sweet to lash out again, the way it did the night I set that fire. I felt powerful then, perhaps for the first time, and I feel it now. It is an immense relief to focus my rage and grief on someone else. I understand wars now; I understand why people burn foreign cities to the ground to avoid tending their own gardens.

But the pleasure is brief.

Javier crumples away from me; I slapped him hard enough to make him stagger. He puts his palm to the place where I struck him and looks at me with surly resentment.

"You're a spiteful harpy."

The anger surges back but I hold still and do not reply. I am in the wrong. And I can't afford to lose anyone else. I don't want to be alone. I take two heaving breaths like Louise taught me.

"I'm so sorry. Please forgive me."

He looks as if he's going to curse at me, and I lower my eyes so I don't have to see the crude words escape his mouth. Because I *do* love him, in whatever way someone like me can understand love. I love his company and his sweet spirit. I don't want him to turn his back on me, yet I give him no reasons to stay.

He sighs and turns to look out at the water.

"I had a little sister. Elisa. She was thirteen when she drowned."

I clamp my hand over my mouth to stifle a gasp. This is the furthest thing from what I was expecting. Not from a young man who bounces around like he has sunshine in his pockets.

"I wasn't there," he says quietly. "I was never there back then. I was serious. Always studying or helping my father with business. She asked me to go fishing with her, like Grandpa used to do, and I told her . . ." His voice cracks. "I told her I didn't have time for stupid things like that and to go alone."

I want to touch him, but I can't. I have never seen such a stricken impression on a human face before. It paralyzes me.

He is quiet for a long while. Ours is the only boat in sight. There is no sound but the wind, the waves, and the birds screeching after each other above.

When he speaks again his voice is steady.

"She was a good swimmer. I taught her myself. But the currents were too strong. Her body washed up on shore a week later. She still had one of her shoes on."

I can see the gruesome picture before me. A young girl with Javier's willful curls, her body twisted, her face bloated, her eyes bulging and sightless. One pink slipper clinging to her stiff left foot. A white bird picking at her lips.

"If I had gone with her, she would be alive. My parents would still be able to look at each other."

This time I do go to him. I stand behind him and wrap my arms tight around his waist. I lay my head against the soft fabric of his linen shirt.

"Don't. Don't. This is no good. Trust me. Trust me of all the fools on this earth. This is no good."

He shakes and I can't tell if he's weeping or not. I hold him tighter.

"I just wanted to help you. You've got nobody here. You were drowning, that's what my stepgrandmother said, those were her exact words. I didn't . . . I thought maybe doing something good for someone could be my penance."

Teddy's face flashes across my mind. A bubble of insane laughter rises in my throat. I can't stand to watch another person embark on the same doomed path.

"You don't have to tell me any more. I'm sorry. I'm so sorry. And this guilt, you have to let go of it. Do you understand? You have to."

"I failed her! I failed her completely and now there will never be another chance."

I move around to his side, seize his face, and force him to look into my eyes. His are dry, mine are not.

"I *do* understand."

Something cracks inside me. Maybe it is the fact that out here it feels like we are the only two people on earth. Maybe the lock on my chest of secrets has finally rusted. I swore I would take it to my grave, but if my damnation can save him, I have to break that vow. What's another vow broken?

I have to tell him.

"You want to know what it's like to truly have blood on your hands? I'll tell you what happened to my mother."

Chapter Twelve

~~~~~~~~~~~~~~~

Aubade

Paris, France
September 1945

I am home again. In Paris, on the narrow street near my apartment building.

The shoemaker's boy rides by me on his bicycle and splashes dirty puddle water on my school shoes. The orange tabby that I feed is not in the cardboard house I built for him, in the alley where we keep our own bicycles chained up. I lean against the wall and wait. A few minutes later he appears. He comes and rubs against my stockings, and I scratch him behind the ears and feed him the two sardines I saved him from my lunch. It took him two months to let me feed him from my palm, but now my reward is the pleasantly rough feel of his tongue and his loud purring.

When I'm finished, I make sure that no one has taken the blanket I put in the box for him, and I pour some fresh water from my cantine into a small chipped bowl Maman dropped when she was drunk.

"I'm sorry I don't have any milk for you, mon ami. Soon. I'm sorry it's been so long."

He looks up at me with his big green eyes like he understands my words and will hold me to them.

Begrudgingly I tear myself away and go inside.

We live in a three-bedroom flat on the top floor, up five long narrow flights of stairs. I don't know most of the neighbors, only the old widow on the fourth floor whose son died in the Great War. She carries a lock of his baby hair in a locket around her neck. Sometimes if she leaves her window open, I can hear her playing the piano.

When I get to our front door I find it unlocked. I push it open, take off my wet shoes, and place them on the mat.

The apartment is bigger than the others in this building. Grandfather bought it outright in 1915.

You can tell it was nice once, but the furniture has gone shabby and the walls are in desperate need of a fresh coat of paint. The eggshell-colored walls are stained with fingerprints and the taint of smoke from cigarettes and charred meals.

Maman calls me from the kitchen. That's not usual. She's usually in her bedroom, or sprawled out on the couch with a book.

When I find her she is rifling through the top cabinets. She turns around when she sees me and smiles. Like she does every day, she opens her arms and wiggles her fingers to beckon me into a hug.

She's tall for a woman, with a high, firm bosom, and long dancer's legs. Her eyes are blue as cornflowers and sparkle against her creamy complexion and auburn hair. It is pure luck that she is still as pretty as she is after the careless way she has treated herself. She's wearing a navy dress today, belted at the waist.

I allow her to hug me and then pull back to look at her face.

"Maman, what are you doing?"

The ever-present stench of wine is on her breath, but she's not drunk. This is just maintenance.

"Oh, my darling, I'm just looking for the real coffee."

"I think you used the last of it."

She pouts for a split second before it morphs into an easy smile.

"Listen, I have a friend I can borrow some money from. Let's go to the picture show this weekend. They're still open, right?"

"Maman, I need to ask you something."

She must see the urgency on my face because she falls away from my touch, slick as oil.

"Not now, my darling. Maman's tired."

"Henriette told me something today."

She sniffs. "Henriette? That little slut from your class? They'll shave her head and march her through the streets if she's not careful."

Henriette's entire family are known Nazi collaborators. She was crying into her books today because her uncle has been arrested on suspicion of treason and since she's tormented me for a decade, I could not help but relish in her misery.

"I called her a stupid whore and a traitor today."

Maman giggles. "Delphine, language. But it's true."

"But then she told me something too."

"Oh?"

"She told me that Papa was here, in Paris, and that you knew about it."

Henriette was the first person I told about my real father, back when I was no more than six. It was the first week of school and she swore that we would be the closest of friends and that I could tell her anything. She promptly told the rest of the class within a day and they've been laughing at me ever since.

I see it then. After years of watching my mother, I know what it looks like when she is preparing to lie. She fiddles with her earrings.

"And how would she know what I know?"

"She was sent to Mother Bernadette's office. While she was waiting outside, she said she heard the two of you talking. When you came to my school to discuss my last suspension for fighting."

I put Brigitte Russo's head through some shrubbery in the courtyard because she mocked a patch on my skirt.

Maman scoffs. "When?"

"It doesn't matter when!" I snap. The numbness I have felt since Henriette told me is melting away. I didn't want to believe it. When the liberation happened I wanted to believe that it would change everything, that everything could be brand-new.

"Don't yell, Delphine," Maman says meekly. "Really. You don't even like that girl."

But a stopped clock is still right twice a day.

"It doesn't matter! It's true, isn't it?"

She backs up against the sink. "You're too young to understand everything. I didn't see a point in telling you. He's got his own life. He didn't want us, you know that."

"He didn't want *you*," I spit at her. "He doesn't even know about me. You kept it from him."

Her ears are pink. "To protect you. I've told you this. Since you were a little girl, I've told you all the stories about before because I wanted you to know. But this is our life now. We can't go back-wards."

My voice is shaking with rage. "You're a liar. You've always been a liar. You aren't protecting anyone but yourself. You're pa-thetic."

She winces but tries to show a stern face. "Stop this, Delphine. I'm your mother."

This is too much. My self-restraint collapses. I have spent years feeding her, rolling her on her side after she passes out, changing her clothes when her bladder lets go. I have stolen for her, endured the humiliation of being whispered about. A million little indig-nities that I have endured without a whisper of protest.

"Oh, *now* you want to be my mother?"

She takes a tiny step towards me. "I have always been your mother. I will always be your mother. I gave birth to you."

I have no interest at all in being bound to this woman for life. It's still baffling to me that simply because someone comes out of your body that you're allowed to hold them hostage for the better part of twenty years.

"Congratulations," I say, as nastily as I can. "On your ability to open your legs twice, then. Certainly no one else has ever man-aged it."

Her mouth drops open. I have never spoken to her this way. I've never spoken to anyone this way. Years of barbs traded across the schoolyard still come nowhere close to this.

She props herself up against the counter. Beads of sweat appear on her forehead, on her nose, quivering on her chin. "You can't speak to me this way. I could have thrown you in a ditch the day you were born. I've done my best with you."

Three months, six days, and nine hours. The longest I have ever seen her go without a drink. That, apparently, is her best.

I puff myself up. "I would probably have been better in the ditch than with you. Why even tell me? Why even tell me who my father was if you were going to keep me from him my entire life?"

Her face has lost its color. She looks at me in silence, her eyes imploring me to stop this line of questioning, these things that we have both tiptoed about in silence for our entire lives together.

Even in my rage and despair, I am willing—hoping even—to hear some plausible explanation. If she could tell me anything, anything at all, that would explain why she would keep me here, locked away from the life I could have had, the two of us barricaded in this flat like Rapunzel's tower, or like Persephone in the kingdom of the dead.

My father was here in August of last year. He liberated the bar at the Ritz Hotel, just a stone's throw away, and she didn't even tell me. I cannot forgive her for this.

But I am waiting for a reason to try. I look at her imploringly.

All she does is blink away tears.

All my sympathy withers away. I am so sick of seeing her cry. I never get to cry, I'm too busy watching her do it.

"I'm finished. I'm finished with this, I'm finished with you. The war is ending. I have some money saved up. I have nothing left here. I have no friends in school and never will, I have no sweetheart willing to marry me and rescue me from this life. I can't do it for one more day. I'm wasting away here. I'm meant for more and I intend to do something with it. I'm going to find Papa. I'm going to America."

This spurs her into action. She flies at me, digging her nails into my shoulder blades. "You can't go! I didn't tell you about him so that you would seek him out. I won't allow it."

I start to turn away, but she holds me tight.

"Get off me!" I snap.

"What would he want with you, anyway?" she shrieks.

I yank away and shove her back. She hits the wall, and it sounds like dropping a sack of flour. Down she goes, sliding to her knees. Her face is contorted but I don't see regret and even if I did, one cannot jump off a high tower and stop when halfway down. I have to go. I have to go, and I cannot stop and consider that I am breaking her heart.

And maybe my own.

"I'll take my chances because I'm not a coward like you! I won't shut myself away from life. What does he want with me? What do *I* want with *you*? What does anyone want with you?"

She doesn't look up. If I were a predator, this would be the time to deliver the final blow. Instead I turn my back on her and walk to my bedroom.

She never really wanted me. This is easy to believe and it assuages the tiny pinpricks of guilt that I feel as I take my pre-packed suitcase from underneath the bed. It's been packed for more than three weeks, ever since I found out that Papa had been here and she hadn't told me. I can't waste my life as her consolation prize.

I worry that she will try to stop me as I come back down the hall, but she is still slumped over where I left her. She has drawn her knees up to her chest, and her head is slung between them.

I don't know what else to say to her. I have salted the earth between us.

"Feed the cats in the alley for me, will you?"

She doesn't reply. Probably for the best.

I place my hand on the door handle and finally, I hear her voice. It comes out in a raspy little chirp.

"Delphine, please."

Please.

My chest tightens. I feel such a contradiction of love and hate that I despise myself, and I despise her for bringing us to this moment. All I ever wanted was for her to choose me first.

But she didn't, and now I must. I choose myself forevermore.

"I can't."

I don't say goodbye. I go out and lock the door behind me.

. . .

I sleep on the rooftop. Well, I try to. But I toss and turn, and the anger drains out of me and is replaced by fear.

By the time the sun comes up, I have lost my nerve. I still want to leave, but I just . . . can't. I may have enough money saved up from all my petty theft to get me out of the city—my wealthy schoolmates have served one purpose at least, and they really should keep a better eye on the collection plate in the chapel—but how far could I really go? I don't have a real plan. I let my temper get the best of me once again.

I have to go back to her. I can't leave her like this. She is still Maman. Maybe it is possible to make her understand. Maybe we can write letters to each other when I'm in New York with Papa, because surely all writers live in New York? And perhaps when I am settled she can visit us?

As my key turns in the lock, I prepare myself to look penitent. I have never been very good at it, but I will try anyway.

"Maman?" I call softly as I shut the door behind me and slip into the cocoon of familiar surroundings.

I think I hear her response, but it is muffled, faraway sounding.

I scan the living room. There's an empty wineglass on the table with her lipstick stain on it, and an open bottle of nail polish on the table.

She's not here.

I check the kitchen then.

She's not here either.

I check her bedroom, which in contrast to the kitchen is completely spotless. I think she must have washed all of the clothes in the apartment, hers and mine. They are folded in neat stacks all over the room.

Her antique jewelry box is out from beneath the bed and placed in front of her fluffed pillows.

Her collection of poetry books is stacked beside it. She's usually not that neat. The hairs on the back of my neck lift ever so slightly.

I check the bathroom. Nothing.

I check the dining room that we never used. Nothing.

I think how many times I have done this. Which room is she passed out in today?

"Maman?" I call again. "Maman, it's Delphine. I've come home to . . ."

I let my voice trail off. My cheeks are burning at the thought of looking her in the eye again.

Maybe she's not here. Maybe she's gone to seek solace in the arms of one of her old friends.

But then, as I trot down the hall, I see her silhouette out on the balcony. She is sitting with her long legs outstretched and with her face turned away from me.

I spy a bottle of wine by her side and I only hope that she's had just the right amount to put her in a talking mood.

I go towards her, and smile when I see that she is wearing the bright yellow dress again, the one that puts so much color in her skin, that she wore the day that we went out to cheer the liberation.

I open the balcony doors.

"Maman?"

I feel it instantly. Now that I am this close to her, I feel that this is not our familiar ritual, as I had thought.

This is different.

I hear a squelch beneath my feet, and when I look down and red fills my vision, I think that I must have stepped in some spilled wine.

"Maman," I whimper. "Maman, wake up. It's Delphine. I came back."

But she is not sleeping.

And that is not wine.

I move forward to stand over her, despite every nerve in my body crying out for me to run away.

There are two deep, hideous gashes on each of her wrists. She has sliced nearly to the bone. Longways. For results.

I snap my eyes shut, but I have already seen. The sight is burned into me. Even if I plucked my eyes out, I would still see it.

I fall to my knees and cover my head, as if that will help me. As if anything can help me now. The breath rattles out of my body for a long time before I finally scream.

When I run out of air, all that's left is a pitiful whine. I don't want to be here. I want to hide underneath the covers until this all just goes away.

But I don't.

I force myself to look at her. At what I have done.

Without the blood, she could be sleeping. Her auburn curls are smoothed over one shoulder to form a pillow for her cheek to rest on.

I curl up beside her, wrapping her frail body in my arms. Her blood soaks through my dress, soaks through my skin, soaks through me.

She is cold in my arms, but still soft. I can still smell her perfume.

I know that I will have to call someone. But once I do that, they will take her away from me. They will take her somewhere that I cannot follow, somewhere she will be all alone.

She never wanted to be alone.

I keep her pressed against me and the tears cascade down my face, but I don't sob. I don't want to move her. I kiss her cold cheeks.

I want us to stay like this, just this way, until we turn to stone.

I want her forgiveness, but she is no longer able to grant it. Her lips are as blue as her silent eyes.

I want to tell her that I forgive her too, worthless though it is, but she is no longer able to hear me. I whisper to her that I am sorry. That I came back. Over and over again, I tell her, but it's too late.

Maman is gone.

Look. Look what you've done.

. . .

Havana, Cuba
April 1947

The water looks different at night. There are no tones. It is a flat, black expanse that the moonlight cannot penetrate, only sit on top of in broken fragments. The wind has died down, but there is an all-encompassing chill. I have never told anyone the full story of how my mother died before today, and I doubt that I shall ever repeat it again. Not even Louise, who found me holding Maman's corpse, who called the police, who washed me and tucked me into bed at the convent, knows everything that I said to her when we fought. I couldn't bring myself to look into the eyes of the one person who has always believed in me and tell her what I truly am.

Javier says we should go below, where there is canned food and blankets, but I couldn't move if I wanted to. My hands have frozen to this railing. My back and knees protest the injustice of being made to stand for so long.

Javier tugs at me. "Please. You'll catch a cold. Go below and let me take us back."

It's the first thing he's said since "Dios mío," in a barely audible gasp.

"How can you look at me after what I just told you?"

"It wasn't your fault."

I hear a crack. I think it comes from deep in my bones. "Didn't you hear me? How can you even say that?"

"Delphine, people don't commit suicide over one argument. It's never just *one* thing. She was probably unhappy for a long time."

"And I didn't do anything to make her happier," I whisper brokenly. "I was a stupid child. I was so certain that Papa was my father, that he'd give me a life that was a thousand times better than what I had with Maman. I never appreciated her."

"She wasn't well."

"She was fine before I was born."

"That's not your fault. And probably not true either."

I look down at the water. "I've thought about it, you know."

In darker hours. It seems such a simple thing. A moment of pain, and then nothing.

No need to ask what. He follows my gaze and, firmly but gently, pries my fingers loose from the rail. He tugs me backwards, back towards the warmth of the cabin, and the lights to ward off ghosts.

His tone is urgent. "Don't. Don't you ever think about doing something like that."

"Of course I think about it. But I'll never do it."

He doesn't look convinced. "Good. It's a mortal sin."

I manage a small shrug. "Oh, I don't care about that. I'm just not going to have a bunch of men writing my obituary and calling me crazy. That's how they win, you know. Maman always warned me that a crazy woman is a man's greatest escape."

His grip on my arms tightens. "It's not about winning or losing! You should *want* to live."

I don't see what wanting to live has to do with anything. But there's work to be done.

There's nothing glamorous about death. I've seen enough to know. We all die alone. There is no beauty in that. The poets and their love of martyrs do not interest me.

I have to live long enough for things to change.

"The winner tells the story," I mumble. My eyelids are drooping. I want to fall asleep to the sound of the waves and wake up clean. "That's the most lasting victory on earth. If that's not a battle worth winning, what is?"

PART III

~~~~~~~~~~~~~~~

Chapter Thirteen

Carnival of the Animals

Havana, Cuba
July 1948

I don't give up. Every day I go on the water and wait for my North Star. So far I have not seen him again. For three weeks, I have come here at dawn and left at dusk. It is weary work, waiting for hours, clinging to the mast like a haunted mermaid, staring out at the sea hoping that meaning will sail back into my life. I could go mad doing that, so I've started bringing my typewriter in its traveling case instead. Every time I touch the keyboard of Blue and Delia's gift I feel the guilt curdle in my belly. I have started a dozen more letters to them and ripped every single one of them to pieces. I'm afraid to tell the truth about Maman. I'm certain that my apologies will never be enough. And, if I am being honest, I am afraid that they may try to come and fetch me if they know exactly where I am. And what if they find out about the fire I set? The money I stole? They are much closer at hand than Louise.

I rub my temples. I have to stay focused on why they gave me the typewriter to begin with. I think I may actually be getting somewhere.

I have written more than one hundred fifty pages, and I have actually managed to come up with a solid plotline that I don't change my mind about every two days.

I've renamed the main character Louise. I will make her an irreverent atheist who wears skirts up to her thigh, who swears and drinks and lights things on fire. That is the writer's petty revenge. I am the tyrant of my own little world of white paper and black ink.

Teddy would be proud of me.

I can see faces now too. Freckles, crooked noses, weepy, red-rimmed eyes. I can see gangly limbs and bushy eyebrows, chipped fingernails and anxious expressions. They are becoming real to me, realer in fact than the world around me, because they can never leave me. I am their keeper, even though they will long outlive me.

Javier lets me go on the boat alone some of the time now. He's signed up to teach a dance class to young children three times a week. I don't like to admit it, but I usually get more done when he's with me. His chatter keeps me from taking myself too seriously. It's not helpful to feel like every word I put on the page is life or death.

"So what's it about?" he asks, with his mouth half full of a pastelito.

I hate this question. Why do people insist on asking this question? *What's it about?* What an unnecessary personal attack.

"It's about a girl named Louise. She's Belgian. She has two loving parents and a puppy, but she wants to run away and join the circus."

"Belgian? Why not French?"

I start a fresh page. I am starting to get a little tingle down my spine every time I do this.

"Why should she be French?"

"Because you're French, silly."

I stop typing to look at him. "It's a novel. It's not real. Do I look like a circus clown to you? She could be from the moon and have green horns if I say so."

"Still, some people will expect it."

I snort. "Oh, be still my beating heart. In that case I'll rewrite the entire thing."

He sits beside me on the bench. "You're in a good mood."

"I am, actually."

The melancholy that threatened to descend on me when I read the real Louise's letter has lifted. I was so afraid that I would turn into my mother, give in to my inheritance of despair and death, but I feel oddly . . . "peaceful" isn't the right word. But I have accepted that nothing I do now will change anything about the past. I cannot pour my passion into a sieve. I have no choice but to go forward. Ever since I told Javier the truth about my mother, the weight of a gigantic boulder has shifted off me. I hope that now I'll be able to move faster.

Javier intrudes on my thoughts. "What will you do . . . if the letter is true? If he's not who you thought? You seem better equipped to handle that than when I met you."

I look out at the water, glimmering in the noon sunlight. All of the voices in my head urging me to dive its depths are quiet today.

"I won't do what my mother did."

He scratches underneath the thin gold chain around his neck. "That's . . . an awfully low bar, Delphine."

"I don't know. I won't know. Until after I tell him."

"And how are you going to do that?"

I have thought about this. In the long nights I do not sleep, I have realized there is only one way.

"I'm going to write it down. All of it. I'm just waiting for the right words. It's not something I can force, but I'll be ready soon."

He looks doubtful. "Just like that?"

"Just like that. Writing is the only thing I've ever been decent at. If I have to hang my fate on something, I want it to be this."

"Well, I'm proud of you for finally making up your mind to do it. For not being afraid anymore."

I can't help but giggle. "Oh, I'm absolutely terrified. But either way I'm starting to think that everything worth having in life lies on the other side of fear."

He looks doubtful. "But what lies on the other side of rejection?"

I wince. "Something. And if I never bleed a little I'll never grow up."

"Something beautiful?" he asks hopefully. "Maybe you'll write a bestseller."

I snort. "Don't get carried away. I said something, not a miracle."

We eat our cold packed lunches and I ask him to tell me more about his sister. How she liked to steal shiny objects from strangers' gardens, how more than once he'd had to intercede to get her out of trouble. She was afraid of dogs. She played the clarinet. She was truly musical, not like him.

"She played wonderfully well." He always beams when he speaks of her. "She could have gone to a conservatory here, maybe even to Paris or Rome. Her favorite piece was Mozart's Clarinet Concerto in A Major. Adagio."

I nod vigorously, though really, who listens to that kind of thing? Old people maybe. Hard to imagine a girl younger than me devoting her precious hours to something so stuffy.

"Have you heard it?"

"I don't think so. Maman only played music with words."

"Well, you'll come over to dinner tonight and I'll put the record on."

It's both a command and an invitation, but I allow it. Javier has found me a two-bedroom apartment of my own in the Vedado neighborhood just west of Old Havana. It has a balcony, and a private rooftop just for me. He knows the landlord—of course he does, it's his stepgrandmother again—and I can paint the walls whatever color I want. I am thinking yellow.

But most nights I still eat with him. His cook has put an additional ten pounds on me, but I have reached a point where I would refuse him almost nothing. He has listened to the worst thing that I have ever done and he has not turned his face away. He looks at me with compassion.

I am his for life if he will have me.

"Will your new girlfriend be there?"

"Not tonight, she made me promise to take her to the beach this weekend. I can't spend all my time with her."

Javier *always* has a girlfriend. They are always very pretty and none of them last long. They are usually uneasy when they hear about me, but they always seem to relax when they see me. I am currently seeing a young man named Ramón. He works at a bread factory and doesn't strike me as the sharpest tool in the box. But

then, it's not his mind I'm interested in. I could laugh when I remember that I was worried I'd never turn a man's head. I sense that
Javier both quietly and hypocritically disapproves of my casual dal-
liances with men, but he never says so to me.

"What's this one's name again?" I ask him.

"Julissa. She wants to be an actress."

I hesitate for just a second before telling him about Teddy. "My
friend from New York wanted to be an actress. Teddy. I guess it's
a cliché, a farm girl wanting to be an actress. It was a silly dream."

He scoffs. "Dreams are dreams. They aren't meant to make
sense to everyone. You'll waste your life worrying what other people
think of them. If people can't do a thing themselves, it makes them
feel better to think that nobody else can do it either. Life is full of
bitter people who want everyone else to fail just because they did."

"You mean like art critics?" I ask dryly, and this earns me a
guffaw.

Maman was always deeply skeptical of critics. She was adamant that most of them had a sense of arrogance that they'd done
nothing to earn. It's one of the things we actually agreed on.

"I mean like those old men on their barstools raging about the
lives they could have lived if they were brave."

I shiver. "I'd rather humiliate myself a thousand times than end
up like that."

"You won't end up like that, Delphine," he promises. "You
might end up dead in a roadside ditch, but you won't end up like
that."

I don't reward his barb with a reaction. "I think my book will
be finished by the end of this year. I'm aiming for three hundred
pages."

He takes a sip of his beer. "That's so long. I don't like long books, but I was always lazy in school. Why don't you make it shorter?"

"People will like it, or they won't," I say curtly. "And as you just said, I'm not spending my life worrying about people like my mother did. She never published any of her poetry, partly because her parents didn't approve and partly because some in her circle didn't like it. I'm going to say what I want to, and let the chips fall."

"What happened to wanting to be adored?" he teases. "Wasn't that your reason for starting this?"

I give him a level look. "Children require adoration. Some of them actually get it. The rest of us find something else to need."

I put down my sandwich and wipe my hands on a napkin. "Give me the binoculars, please. I think I see something."

There's a boat coming. A very familiar-looking boat. I blink twice to make sure it's not a mirage conjured by a desperate fool.

His hands don't move but he follows my gaze. "You're right. Is it him?"

My heart soars, as it always does. "It is."

He squeezes my hand and makes himself scarce without another word. I love that I don't have to tell him when to stay and when to go. It feels like I've known him much longer than I really have.

I stand up and wave, hopping up and down like a little girl. Then I run to the wheel and move the *Tournesol* starboard so I can pull up beside Hemingway. He's alone. Thank God he's alone. I can speak freely.

Who knows, this may be the last time I see him before he breaks my heart.

He doesn't look like his usual cheerful self today. His beard is unkempt, his clothes are wrinkled. He looks tired.

He fiddles with his fishing equipment for a long while, mumbling to himself as he opens his tackle box. When he finally looks up, his small eyes do not spark when they see me.

"Oh. The young woman from Paris."

I quash my disappointment that he does not remember my name. He has met thousands of people, many of them famous and important. I can't expect him to remember me yet. But one day soon, he will never forget.

"Delphine. Sylvie's daughter," I prompt.

He just nods. His eyes rove over my boat.

"You're always out here alone."

I suddenly feel pathetic. "Erm, yes."

"And you never catch a damn thing."

I wince. "Yes, well, I'm not much of a fisherman. I just like the quiet out here."

He doesn't respond for a moment. Then he digs into his pocket and pulls out a flask. He takes a long drink, mumbles some more, and wipes his red-rimmed eyes. His tan skin seems to have more wrinkles than before.

"How old are you anyway?"

Again, I push down the sting. "I'm nineteen."

He shakes his head. "And out here alone? Don't you have any friends?"

My mouth unzips itself before I realize who I'm talking to. "You're out here. Don't you?"

At once I'm horrified, but the words are already out. He stares at me blankly and then his bushy eyebrows rise and he bursts into raucous laughter. His entire face turns red and the loose skin around his jawline shakes.

"I guess I deserved that."

"Forgive me, I'm so—"

He waves away my apology. "Oh, no, no. Don't ever apologize for being clever."

I look down to gather myself. I'm such an idiot.

"I don't have too many friends."

His tone softens. "You don't need many."

I glance up at him again and seize the chance to ask the question that is scalding my tongue. "Do you remember her? My mother? Sylvie Auber?"

He frowns and smiles at the same time. "Well, it was a long time ago. But you never forget a face like that."

"What else do you remember?"

His eyes leave mine. "She was Zelda's confidante at one point, until they had a falling-out. I only met Sylvie a few times. She wrote bad poetry."

I swallow this insult. It bothers me that she is not here to defend herself to him, to reply with a barb about his horrendous female characters or his emerging bald spots.

"It wasn't so bad."

We are all
Briefly golden
Like flickering candles
In a patient dark

He doesn't push the issue. "She was a nice woman, your mother. How is she?"

Don't you know? Can't you feel it? When someone who loved you with all of her tremulous passion took her last breath, did it touch you at all? Or did you drink your morning coffee, kiss your wife, and admire your precious sons like it was any other morning?

My hands shake. "Dead."

He looks genuinely shocked.

"Oh. Oh, my. I'm sorry to hear."

Empty and useless words. I don't want to hear it. All I want are answers.

"She spoke of you often."

"Did she?"

"Yes. All of you. And those days. They meant a lot to her."

I remember her smile when she spoke of her old friends. God, I miss that smile. She smiled with her entire face, like a child seeing the sunrise. I will never see anything like it again.

He lights a cigar. "They were good days."

I watch him blow out the smoke. The weight of the words I'm holding back makes it difficult for my lungs to expand.

What else can I tell him?

"I'm a writer."

This has his attention now. His ears perk up like an old hunting dog. He leans over the railing.

"Are you? And what have you written?"

My ears flame. "Um. Well, nothing yet. I'm working on something now."

His tone is indulgent. "Is that a fact? And what's it about?"

It bothers me that I don't have a more polished answer for him. I wish I felt comfortable enough to ask what his own creative process is like. I am filled with such fiery curiosity that it makes me want to dance on the spot.

"It's a bildungsroman."

He looks bemused. "How can you write a coming-of-age story when you haven't done it yourself yet?"

I am mildly offended by this. "I may be young, but I come of age every day. And I pay attention."

If I didn't know better, I could swear he looks impressed.

"I think that's an admirable way to look at it."

"I have to write," I confess. I feel like he might understand me. If not as my father, then as the legend he has made himself into. "The thoughts won't leave me alone. But when I go to put them down they feel so jumbled. It's actually quite maddening."

"That will sort itself out. Don't think of every sentence as existing on its own. Think of it all melding together. Ask yourself, how does this help push the story where it needs to be?" He pauses. "Does writing make you happy?" he asks as if it does not matter either way.

I shuffle my feet. "When it's not making me sick, it makes me happy."

"Well, I'm sure your book will turn out. They always do in the end. I promise."

I am emboldened by this sudden advice, but I no longer feel like I should fall to my knees and thank him for it. My frost towards my mother has finally thawed, and now for the first time I can see him through her eyes. I can hear the superficial charm in his voice, the self-assured tone that borders on arrogance. I have ample proof that his promises to women are all but meaningless. He is no friend to my sex, and for all his intellect and charisma, I am keenly aware of that now.

I will never again be able to look at him quite the same.

But still, I lean forward. I so badly want to understand him, this man that I have paid such a high price to know.

"Why do you do it?"

He goes rigid and I worry that I've overstepped. I'm not even a real writer, and I know that this is the most personal question one can ever ask.

He raises his cigar to his lips but doesn't draw on it.

"There's a lot unsaid in this world of ours. It's probably better that way. But it's got to be said in the end."

I dare further. I can't help myself, I always want to hug the flame. "And you think you're the one to say it?"

He laughs and shrugs a broad shoulder. "Why the hell not?"

This is not the earth-shattering philosophy I expected from the man I've idolized all my life, but it makes me laugh.

When he excuses himself and sails on to deeper water and more enthusiastic fish, Javier emerges. Clearly he's been straining his ears trying to eavesdrop.

"He's awfully talkative, the American. Did you make any progress?"

I sigh. "I never make any progress with him. He slides through my fingers like mercury; every time I think I understand what to feel or do, it changes."

"Sounds like family."

"Oh, well. I wouldn't know."

He leans in. "Did you hear? There are some rumors of another divorce. I have it straight from a friend of mine who attended one of his parties at the Finca that there's trouble between him and his wife. Do you really think he'd dare? *Four* divorces. If he does do it, I'll bet you good money that he'll have a new wife soon."

There's a sinking sensation inside me. I don't take any joy in this. I don't feel victorious as Maman may have. All I see is another woman, another domino, falling down. I wonder if he ever loved my mother at all, or even if she loved him and not just a fantasy she created to make life bearable.

"I won't give him the letter yet," I decide aloud, though I have finally finished it. "For if I tell him I love him he might leave me too and I'm still getting to know him. I can bear that, of course, but I'd prefer to delay. Right now I'm having fun."

Javier looks like he wants to throw me overboard. "So when?"

"When I'm ready to lose him."

. . .

That night I step out onto my balcony. Every time I do this now, I think of finding my mother's body.

I pinch my palms. Enough of this.

I am too stubborn and vindictive to die. I cannot stomach the idea of leaving the earth to the many degenerates who never have such dark thoughts, because they never feel bad about anything.

I feel sick to my stomach at the thought of what Maman was thinking in her final moments.

I sit down and pull out my notebook. This is what I do now, when I get these unhelpful thoughts. I write. I chase them away with my pen on paper.

I have so many people to write to, so many people who deserve to hear from me. Blue, Delia, Louise. Papa.

But instead I find myself writing to her. It's the only way I can talk to her now. It's the first time that I've even tried.

Dear Maman,

I feel selfish even writing this. I have no right to assuage my guilt. I deserve to carry it with me forever.

I see your face everywhere. I want to tell you all that I am learning about the world, but then I remember you are dead.

I don't hate you anymore. I did, I think. Because you drank, and because you were so beautiful and I am not. Because I never felt like your first choice in life. Because you made me worship a stranger. Because I was always alone, even with you.

So many reasons to hate you, but now I only miss you.

I think I understand now why you didn't tell Papa about me, why you didn't hunt him down after he abandoned you and demand that he claim me. You were trying to protect me, weren't you? He is very clever, and very gifted, but he is not the best man. I don't even know if he is a good man. But you let me blame you for everything and you gave me the idea of Papa as a gift to keep me sane.

But you were there and he was not. He was never there. Perhaps I should write a poem about it, but I have no talent for such things.

I hope wherever you are, you are happy.
Goodbye, Maman.

I stop writing and close my eyes. I tip my head back. I am crying, but not from rage or pain.

"I love you," I whisper, to the silent sky.

Chapter Fourteen

~~~~~~~~~~

Fair Winds

July 1954

Dear Louise,

I'm sorry. I know that is a worthless thing to say. There is nothing I can say to make up for ignoring your letters. The truth is, I didn't even open them. I threw them into the fire, or drowned them on a fishing line. I resented you for what you told me as you expected that I would.

*You stole whatever was left of my innocence. I have finished one novel—*The House of Pristine Sorrows*—and started on a second. I think I am finally in control of my plotting, so I hope this one will be easier than the last. I'm going to call it* Tocororo, *after my favorite of the birds here. They are common, and absurdly colorful, but still beautiful to me.*

I have enrolled in university and will start this autumn. I'm going to study literature. Can you believe it? Javier's family has been very helpful getting me admitted,

*but I have every intention of working as hard as I can.
I am nearly fluent in Spanish now and I think it's the
right time.*

*Of course I miss you, and Paris. But this is my home
now. It is the first place that I have carved out a space for
myself. Sometimes I lie on my balcony on a January
night, and I think of the horrible winters during the war
when there was never enough coal to keep warm
properly. It is so comforting to think that I may never
be cold again.*

*I am out of words for today. I hope you write back so
I can think of more.*

I love you.
Your goddaughter,
Delphine

. . .

Havana, Cuba
September 1954

Universidad de La Habana was built in 1728. Since 1902, it's been in the Vedado district, where the wealthy businessmen in finely tailored suits walk around with their faces buried in newspapers. I've gotten used to peering over my balcony at all of the action bustling below.

We've walked La Rampa many times, Javier and I, but I never thought that he would actually enroll in school. I never thought that I would join him.

"My father wouldn't give up," Javier grumbles as we march up the imposing set of wide steps. "He studied business here, years ago, and he wanted me to follow after him. But I was always a terrible student."

"It's because you're so lazy," I say gleefully. "You are completely idle by nature. He had to threaten to cut off your allowance to motivate you. Your family's hardworking nature must have skipped over you."

I adore teasing him. I never lamented being an only child, but I realize now that I was deprived both of a confidant and a sparring partner.

"Maybe so," he says, not bothering to deny my accusation. "My sister, Elisa, was always the ambitious one. She got top marks in school, and she could practice the clarinet for ten hours a day. I love music, but I want to enjoy my life more."

"Your sister seems like she got all the sense."

He grunts. "Oh, please. And you're the hardest worker in the world. I haven't seen you banging down doors to find a job."

I elbow him sharply in the ribs and he laughs and skips away from me, joyfully racing up the steps. I take my time going after him. We have thirty minutes before our first class of the day.

The terrible rush of my teenage years, when I always felt like I had to be moving or speaking, is thank God at an end. It is a tremendous relief not to give so much of a damn. There is comfort in being still.

"I've started a new novel."

Javier gives me a sideways glance. "Oh? So that means you're finally happy with the first one?"

I shrug. I am exhausted with it. Three hundred pages, printed and bound with ribbon, sit in the bottom drawer of my desk. If I read them again, I will probably rip them up and eat them out of frustration.

But I know I have done my best.

"As happy as I'm likely going to get."

"Are you ever going to let me read it?"

We settle into a shady spot on the grass. Javier wipes his hair back from his sweaty forehead.

"I don't even know if I want anyone to read it," I confess. "Besides, I wrote it in English. That's part of why it took so damn long. Right now I'm working up the nerve to tell Papa that I've finished it the next time I see him. He has been rather elusive lately."

I've only been able to find him twice in the past six months. I suppose he is busy.

He looks exasperated. "You've got to be kidding me. I would never write a song and not sing it."

"That's because singers are peacocks. You live for glory."

He rolls his eyes at me. "So do you, whether you admit it or not. All you have ever wanted was to be Delphine Hemingway. You have been fighting since the schoolyard for people to see you."

I consider what he's just said for a while.

"I thought so too. But I think now that what I really wanted was to be listened to, and that is not the same thing."

I take my books from him and glance at my watch. I'm excited for class today. We're going to be discussing los cuadernos of José Martí. His fight to keep Cuba from Spanish rule seems especially relevant now.

He shakes his head. "So tedious. Just publish the damn thing already."

"It's not that easy."

"It could be that easy, if you told the American who you were already. Though I've said this until I'm blue in the face and should probably save my breath. But don't you think he'd help you? His own daughter? A writer herself?"

"He may," I concede. "But he may also have me committed to an asylum."

He locks his fingers together and stretches out his arms in front of him. "I think you'd do well in an asylum, Rita Hayworth. You could meet your true soul mate at long last."

I give him a sugary smile and don't rise to his teasing. "I could do well anywhere as long as I have my books, pen and paper, and a view of the sea. I am very adaptable."

"I'd go insane if I had nothing to do but read all day."

"I have an author you might like."

"Oh?"

I keep my expression completely bland.

"Paul Lafargue. He's French-Cuban. He wrote an entire book defending laziness. He's perfect for you."

He looks like he's about to respond but then someone catches his eye from across the square. I glance over and see a young man in a red shirt who looks about twenty. He and Javier nod at one another.

Javier glances back at me. "Excuse me, Delphine."

I start. He sounds serious for once.

"Who is that?"

It's not usual for him not to offer an introduction. Often on our walks we will run into a friend, or a cousin—I didn't know it was possible to have so many cousins—and he always stops to hug and chat.

"Just a friend. I'll catch up with you later. Come to my house for dinner, the cook is making vaca frita."

Something in his voice disquiets me. "Javier, who is that man?"

"It's better if you don't know," he says softly. "Go on to class." He kisses me swiftly on the cheek and runs off.

. . .

October 1954

My dearest Delphine,

I am overjoyed to hear from you. I have prayed to God every night for you. I still pray for your return, but it comforts me to know that you are happy where you are.

There is no need to apologize to me. I am a sinner myself. You are always forgiven.

Though I cannot see you, I can tell that you have grown.

Tell me more about these novels of yours. I want to know everything. I have so many questions for you but I am confident that we will have time.

There are reports of some disquiet in Cuba. I hope they are exaggerated?

Yours,

Louise

. . .

December 1954

Louise,

I am so glad you are well. I have missed our conversations.

I don't like discussing my work very much but I will make an exception for you, my earliest supporter. Besides, it is much easier for me to explain it if I write it down.

The House of Pristine Sorrows is about a young Belgian girl named Louise. She runs away from home to be a circus clown, but they won't let her do it because she's a girl. She is tasked to tend the animals instead and ends up taming one of the lions. I won't spoil the rest for you. Hopefully you will read it one day.

Tocororo is about a wealthy Cuban girl named Elisa. She wants to sail all seven seas.

That's all I have so far.

I have an idea for another book too, but I don't know if I dare to attempt a third. I would call it Gossamer. *I can't say more yet. It's the kind of thing I'd like to ask Papa about if I could find him.*

I haven't seen him much at all lately. I wonder if he is still in Sweden. Did you know that he won the Nobel Prize in Literature? That's the most incredible thing that anyone could ever do. Though I am guessing the selection committee is staffed entirely with men.

I have reread his books several times now and I still greatly admire him as a writer, but his female characters

seem somewhat less convincing than his male ones.
Though what do I know?

Papa is the cleverest man I've ever met. I can't deny
that, though I think I hear him more and more now with
the ears of an adult. He is boastful. He can be arrogant.
He talks more than he listens.

But I suspect most geniuses are like that.

I've just started reading a book by Gertrudis Gómez
de Avellaneda. She was considered a scandalous woman
for her views on abolition and interracial love. I think
I'll like it.

As for what you heard, it is true that things here are
uneasy. President Batista dissolved parliament earlier
this year. No one can challenge him now. But Javier
says he should be afraid now more than ever.

There's an upstart causing problems, but it will
probably come to nothing. Last year he staged a failed
attack on a military barracks and was thrown into
prison. Some people call him El Caballo, The Horse.

His name is Fidel Castro.

Yours,

Delphine

· · ·

February 1955

Dear Delphine,

I am so glad that your writing is going so well and
that you are pursuing your education once again. Your

mother would be so happy to see it. She always hoped that you would be part of the new wave of women who could do absolutely anything.

As for your Monsieur Hemingway, I am sure that he will return soon. I am glad he is a comfort to you. But I am even happier that you are coming to accept that you never needed him in the first place.

The situation in Cuba is worrying. I'm not sure it will blow over as quickly as you hope. I implore you once again to consider coming home.

Sadly, there is an outbreak of tuberculosis in some of the city's poorer neighborhoods. Too many people, I'm afraid, living in too little space, without even proper toilets or bathing facilities. I am sure there were not so many people in the city when I was a girl.

Though I shouldn't indulge, I have some local gossip for you. Your classmate Henriette, with whom you were so often at odds? She married shortly after graduation— a wealthy shop owner.

Anyway, he has been arrested for fraud. The government has seized all of their assets. She has been left quite destitute with her two children. I have them all in my prayers.

But you see how your predictions fail? Things are always changing.

I hope you will not consider staying in a country in upheaval just because you are afraid to come home. You have seen enough conflict for one lifetime. You're a woman now.

*Be hopeful for your future instead of fearful of your
past. Plant your seeds, and pray to a merciful God that
you will live long enough to watch them bloom.*
    Love,
    Louise

. . .

April 1955

Dear Louise,

    *It may surprise you to learn that I have grown weary
of my rivalries with other women. I think the world has
set things up this way, like the Romans would take
starving animals and throw them into a pit to fight
over meat.*

    *I take no pleasure at all in Henriette's misfortune, or
the misfortune of any other girl who does what she is
told, or who values things different than myself and
merely wishes to be happy.*

    *My mother was right about many things—God
knows I wish I could tell her that—but she was also the
architect of her own misery. I'm not afraid of Paris
because of her. I know that I don't have to be like her.
I have started something here in Havana and I know in
my bones that it isn't finished. I think that perhaps Paris
was intended to be the home of my childhood, but
not the home to whatever it is that I am becoming. We
are not all destined to grow in our native soil, you told
me that yourself. So now I am blooming under a
different sun.*

251

Perhaps I will return to Paris one day, find love and have a family, as I know you hope for me.

But I am saving my hopes for smaller matters. I live in hopes of growing my hair out past my shoulders because I think it suits me better, or writing a prettier paragraph tomorrow than I did yesterday. I've had lovers here—I know, I know—and I live in hopes of finding more.

If I could speak to the Delphine that you last saw, I would tell her that it gets easier when you realize that no one is coming to save you.

That she is not one of the girls whose lives come easily to them. The pretty ones from the nice families, with the right interests, and the right friends, and the decent men lining up to marry them. The ones who check all the right boxes at exactly the right moments, who never miss a step in the routine. The ones nobody ever worries about. If they do fall, someone will catch them, and they know it.

Once I accepted that I was not born underneath those stars, I stopped torturing myself by expecting things to be like that. I stopped comparing myself to others. It is not about being better, or worse. We all play our cards as best we can.

Things will always be harder for some people. But that doesn't mean there's no way. There is always a way.

I am sure that the political situation will right itself. I will make a way for myself here, in Havana. I now have

what you've always tried to teach me—faith. It's in
myself instead of God, but we'll have to make do.
  Love,
  Delphine

. . .

Havana, Cuba
July 1955

I am waiting for Javier as he leaves his summer class. I knew something was wrong immediately when he willingly signed up to do extra work. He sees me at once and attempts to pivot, but I swoop in on him before he can escape. I haven't seen him in nearly a week.

"We can't talk here," he says instantly. "Too many ears."

He grabs me by the crook of my arm and leads me into the courtyard, where he promptly stashes us both behind a large bust.

"You're hiding something," I accuse him. "For months now you've been acting differently."

He has the grace to look uncomfortable. "Delphine, please. I have to go."

"Yes, yes, you always have to go," I say irritably. "To places unknown. I know that I'm a foreigner, and there are things that I don't understand, but I'm not deaf. People gossip, you know. I know that you've been going to protests and meetings in back rooms. You're pro-Castro and you don't even try to hide it. You're going to get yourself arrested."

"I believe in this," he says simply. "True, that this conflict is not about race. It's about what Cuba is and what it will become, and who will have access to it. But you know how I feel about my grandfather. And Castro has promised to enact equality for all Cubans and end Batista's corruption. He's a monster. He's killed thousands, Delphine, no one can even say how many for certain. I won't live in a police state anymore. I don't care if I get arrested for helping Castro's men. Besides, there are people I can bribe for my freedom."

I give him a hard look. "Are you going to a protest right now?"

I've seen them, of course. They seem to grow more massive with every passing month. And I've seen how the police handle them. They are ruthless. On my walk home yesterday I saw a young man with an obviously broken jaw being dragged into the back of a van by two officers. If he is still aboveground, I wonder how much it will cost to get him out of a cell.

Javier nods and glances around us, but nobody is paying us any mind. I don't know why he's so nervous. Most of the students here appear to share his sympathies. The youth are nearly united in their distaste for the current regime. I want the same things that Javier does for this country, but I have difficulty trusting any politicians.

"So then I'm coming with you," I say promptly. "We can go right now."

He does not even pretend to consider it. "No."

We have done nearly everything together for all these years. It's been a long time since I have felt the urge to throttle someone, but I feel it now.

"Since when do we have secrets between us? I thought I was your friend."

He must hear the pain in my voice because he puts his hands on my shoulders. "You are more than my friend. And I won't do anything to put you in harm's way."

I am not soothed by this. "I don't require your protection."

"For God's sake, Delphine, I know that. But you have it anyway."

"If you think you're flattering me by telling me what to do—"

He lets me go and rubs his temples. "Can't you just listen to me for once?"

Surely he knows me too well to expect this.

"I want to know why I can't come with you."

He starts to walk away from me. "Delphine, just go home. Finish your book."

I match my stride to his without a second thought. I expect him to give up and let me trail after him, but instead he rounds on me and picks me up, slinging me over his shoulder like a potato sack. He ignores my furious yelps and marches me over to the green.

"Put me down!"

"Are you going to go home now?"

"I don't have to go anywhere!"

He sets me down and catches my hands before I can push him. His face is dark.

"You don't know what could happen. *I* don't know what could happen. This isn't your fight. You don't need to distress yourself over it."

I could laugh if I weren't so annoyed. Life threw me into the pit without an ounce of ceremony the day I was born, and Javier is behaving as if I am some maiden in a tower who needs guarding.

I have rarely been proud of anything about myself, but I am proud of the fact that I don't need looking after. I probably have more practice throwing a right hook than he does.

"I can help," I insist. "I can be useful, you'll see. Your fight is my fight."

He groans. "I cannot do this with you here. Don't you understand? I can't think clearly if you're in danger. Please."

I feel the resistance leak out of my bones and I drop to my knees. "You have done so much for me. I owe you a debt that I can never repay. All I wanted was to do something for you."

He sinks onto the grass beside me. "You *have*."

I dig my nails into the damp earth. "I've been nothing but trouble for you since the day we met."

He looks at me with the softest expression I have ever seen on a human face.

"When I met you, I was drowning. Every single day. You gave me peace . . . it is I who can never repay you. You have always been useful, Delphine, but now you are valued. So please. Stop fighting me."

I am left speechless by this. I have never thought of Javier as melancholy. I've never met a more boisterous person. I've never even seen him cry.

"So will you do me the favor of going home now?"

I draw my knees up to my chest. "I think I'll go out on the boat."

"Not too far," he cautions me with a small smile. "And don't swim alone."

"I won't swim alone if you promise not to get your skull cracked open by one of Batista's goons. I'm serious, Javier. I'll stay away if I must, but you have to tell me everything that's happening. I will keep my head down and my mouth shut, but I can't be left in the dark."

"There are rumors," he says in a low voice, switching from Spanish to French so that no one can eavesdrop. "I've heard from an old friend in Ciego de Ávila. His whole family wants to join Castro's forces. I'd join up myself if it wouldn't kill my mother. I think it's high time."

"Castro was ousted," I caution. "He's lucky Mexico was willing to shelter him. I know you think he'll come back with a vengeance, but Batista has the support of the Americans."

Javier puffs out his chest. I know he has more secrets than he will share. I just pray that he has nothing to do with the bombings or the more violent kinds of protests.

"You can't deny the will of the people forever!" he exclaims. "You're a Frenchwoman, you should know that. We want change."

"Not everyone," I point out. "The rich seem pretty happy with the way things are. So does President Batista."

He scowls at me. "Batista! He was turned away from a social club himself, you know, for not being white enough. But still he does nothing to change anything. Comemierda! You know there are still beaches I can't go to? Because I'm mulato? And it's worse outside of the city. When my father's father moved here, he was guajiro trash. When they hired him to clean for the rich people, they acted like they were doing him a favor. He had to beg for the loan to start his business, and I suspect he did some things that were not entirely legal too."

"But he did it," I soothe, knowing that Javier idolizes his grandfather. "He was a clever man."

Javier is not mollified. If anything, he raises his voice. "By some miracle. He died wealthy, and my father was wealthy, but half my mother's family still disowned her when she married him. Her sister speaks to us, but even she has told me to pick the 'right' wife . . . so I can mejorar la raza. Fix my mother's mistakes. Elisa,

God rest her soul, was lighter than I was. She was my aunt's great hope for the future."

He makes a disgusted face. "For all we say 'we're all Cuban,' that's never been true."

I have met Javier's parents. His father is brown skinned and dark haired. His mother has blue eyes, nearly blonde hair, and is paler than me. I've observed, of course, that most of the people with money seem whiter looking, but it's never really talked about openly. At least, not around me. It's not quite as obvious as it was in America that there were two worlds, one for the whites and one for everyone else.

"Your mother has sugarcane money too, right?"

"Loads of it," he says, sounding a bit guilty. "She has mostly Spanish blood. But she's not like most of them."

"So what will you do?" I ask simply. "If this keeps up? If communism becomes the law of the land? You're a businessman, after all. What if Castro wins?"

"I will survive," he says stubbornly. "I'm not afraid of change. I have the heart of Antonio Maceo himself. I won't deny my African and Indio blood. I'll wait and see what happens."

And what will happen to me? Will I be able to stay in school? Will I be able to stay here at all? Would the new regime tolerate foreigners or cast me out?

What about Papa? What will happen to Papa?

I thought I was past this. But once again, I feel the fear of the unknown crawling across my skin like a spider, wrapping me thread by thread in its web.

Chapter Fifteen

Revolución

Havana, Cuba
January 8, 1959

We don't have to wait very long. Fidel Castro returns from Mexico after a mere eighteen months in exile. In response to growing dissent, Batista shut down the university in 1956. Javier and I barely finished in time.

Despite Batista having the police, the military, and American money on his side, he is beaten by the rebels after years of fighting. He flees to the Dominican Republic just after the New Year, much to Javier's delight, but I feel uneasy. Cuba is not my country, but it has been my home for so long, and I am fearful of change, even if I am told it is a good change.

Javier assures me that my doubt is unfounded. And maybe he is right. For years we have lived through uncertainty and oppression, of having the rights to free speech and assembly dismantled before our very eyes. The terror of not knowing who one should speak to, whether they are on Castro's side or the side of Batista's faltering regime. The rigged elections, the people being arrested and tortured. I'd heard rumors that in the bohío areas outside the city, people were simply disappearing and their families were too afraid to ask after them. Were they jailed? Or did they run off to join the revolution? I've seen armed men roaming the streets in uniform looking for skulls to crack, or defiant tongues to rip out. Just before they closed the university, one of my professors disappeared without a trace. I'll never forget the frantic look on his wife's face when she asked me, asked everyone she could lay her hands on, where her husband had gone.

Now that is all over. We can breathe and smile once more.

And so I find myself in the streets again, celebrating the coming of a liberator. A hero. A man who promises that everything will change, and every Cuban will be equal—heavens, even women.

I'll believe it when I see it.

This time my hand is tight in Javier's instead of Maman's. He holds me close as we wade through crowds of people. The tanks with Castro and his men on top, still in their military uniforms, their guns at the ready, make their way through packed streets.

People are shouting and crying and waving flags and it is all too much like what has come before. If I close my eyes, I can see de Gaulle's victory procession as clear as day. But I am not as trusting as I was then. I don't believe in saviors. Whenever I see someone stoking a great fire, I always wonder whose house will burn.

Javier is beaming. He's going to throw a party, he shouts at me, he's going to invite his best musician friends to come and serenade us all underneath the moonlight. This is a time for miracles.

At one point the pushing and shoving from the crowd gets so intense that I think I'm going to drown, and Javier pulls me up onto a staircase so that I can snatch a breath of air above the sweaty foreheads and stench of strangers' cologne and smoke. He bursts into song and the people around us join in.

I tilt my face to the sun and let it warm me through.

But no matter how hard I smile, I feel an utter absence of joy.

.   .   .

Havana, Cuba
June 1959

Javier's garden—or should I say, his mother's garden—is in full bloom. Someone has strung up lights on the magnolia trees. Her dogs are running after each other, barking like mad. The musicians strike a lively tune, and men in uniform walk amongst the guests offering hors d'oeuvres. This is the second party his parents have thrown in two months to fraternize with officials from the new regime. Every detail has been attended to. This is, ostensibly, a happy occasion.

But I cannot help but notice that his mother is white as a corpse, washed out by her red lipstick as she moves amongst the uniformed officials with a strained smile.

They are trying to get on the right side of things. The government is seizing property left and right. In exchange, they promise to take care of all citizens, to provide free housing, education, and medical care. The rumored six hundred people already covertly executed for being tied to the Batista government will not get to enjoy those things, but Javier says that people always die when things change, and that Batista probably killed more people than that anyway.

Javier is mingling, smiling and chatting, but I can feel him keeping a strict watch on me out of the corner of his eye.

After an hour or so he excuses himself and comes over to me.

"Don't talk to anyone," he says flatly, as if I need to be reminded again. He parked me on a stone bench the second I arrived with strict instructions not to call attention to myself. I'm glad I brought a book.

I sip my papaya nectar. "Why did you bring me here, anyway? Surely you could have brought a proper date? One of those nice, pale girls your mother keeps shoving under your nose?"

He grunts and I chuckle. His mother is desperate for grandchildren. Or at least, she was before.

He switches to French and sits beside me, leaning in close. "I wanted to speak with you. You've been busy."

"I've been working a lot on my book," I confess. It feels more important now than ever with the world outside spinning further out of my control. "And I've been looking for Papa. I can't seem to run into him anywhere."

I've had liquor-free mojitos at the bar at La Bodeguita del Medio, I've had dinner at La Terraza, I've been to the cabaret shows at the Tropicana, but I haven't seen him once. So far, I haven't noticed much change in these places that have become so familiar to me. I wonder how long that will last.

"He'll turn up. Anyway, I need you to promise me something."

His face is difficult for me to read. He has been unusually quiet lately. I haven't seen him look as happy as he did the day we marched in the street.

"Tell me what it is first," I insist, but he just sucks his teeth.

"Promise first."

There is an urgency in his tone that compels me to relent.

"I promise."

He places his hand over mine. "You have to swear to me that if your Papa leaves Cuba, you'll leave too."

I bite back my refusal. After all, I have just sworn.

"Why?"

"Because if he goes, that means it's not safe for Americans anymore."

My hand pulls away from him and flies to my heart. "I am *not* American."

"I know, but if things continue . . . The United States won't tolerate us being allied with the Soviets. Father says things will only get worse. Diplomatic relations are becoming a thing of the past."

"What does that have to do with me?"

Someone walks by and he goes silent until they pass.

"It has to do with the tide. You're a sailor now. You should understand."

"I understand that there is nothing for me in Paris anymore but Louise. I want to stay here."

"I want you to stay also, but I need you to be safe. My mother and my aunts already want to leave."

"Flee?" I ask incredulously. "Already?"

"Mother says communism is the devil, but my father will never agree," he says stoutly. "Never. He says America is nice and Europe is grand, but Cuba is home. He says we'll have to find a way to make it work."

"'We' should mean us too. You and I."

"You're not Cuban," he says, overruling me. He grins to appease me and reaches into his pocket and pulls out a cerulean fountain pen, marbled and sparkling. It reminds me of the sea on a calm day.

"It was my grandfather's," he explains. "He gave it to me, and now I am giving it to you."

I almost recoil from its beauty. "I can't take that."

For several reasons. It is far too important an heirloom, and besides, this is starting to feel like a goodbye. I don't want anything to remember Javier by. I want Javier.

"Please," he says, so quietly that I know he really means it. I hold out my hands and he presses it into them. "I'm not a writer. You are. You'll do something with it. My grandfather was the hardest-working man I ever knew, and he would want someone to do something useful with it."

"I'm . . . honored. I will put this in Maman's jewelry box."

He nods. "And you'll take it with you when you go?"

"*If* I go. But it won't come to that," I say firmly.

He looks up. "Let's pray, flaca. The two of us together, and your nun too. Let's all pray."

Javier has never once suggested praying. I realize that he is afraid, and the terror of the realization makes me shiver.

. . .

Havana, Cuba
June 1960

For once fate is on my side. I'm not even looking for Papa when he walks into El Floridita, a bar painted the world's most obnoxious shade of pink. I'm sitting at a corner table reading and drinking

mango juice. I haven't seen him in months and though the old desperate longing is gone, it's still a relief to lay eyes on him.

But he's not alone. There are two men with him, and they take
a corner table and look very grave about something. Certainly, they
huddle together with their serious old-man faces and speak in low
voices, and I am much too far to eavesdrop.

They're journalists from the looks of them. Probably American
from how badly they are dressed. British journalists are rarer but
I can always spot them because they walk like they own the pave-
ment. I order another drink, keep one eye on them and one eye on
my paper, and wait.

Three hours go by. He keeps ordering more drinks—I count
five—and his voice grows ever louder.

When they finally leave, Papa lays his head on the table and is
still for a while. I glance at the barkeep. He's starting to look impatient to close up shop. We are the only people left in here.

I shove my newspaper into my purse and approach the table
tentatively, as one might approach a sleeping beast in the menagerie.
I poke him gently and he jerks up, his eyes bloodshot.

"Papa?" I whisper. I realize too late that I've never called him
this to his face before. "Are you okay?"

"Damn FBI," he grunts. "They want to know what I know
about the situation here. I'm not a politician. I don't know Fidel's
pant size, I said. I spoke to the man once. About *fishing*. And now
they want to know if I have state secrets to sell them."

"Let me hail you a taxi. Come on, let's go outside."

He sighs. "I don't want to go home yet," he says piteously. "I
just want to rest here for a while."

I sit across from him. "I'm sure your wife is expecting you."

"Mary will wait," he says dismissively. "She knows how."

I hesitate. "Are you okay?"

He laughs. "Oh, sure, kid."

He burps loudly. His face is beet red, and I think that I have never seen him looking so old. His beard needs trimming and the lines in his face look deeper. At once I feel an immense pity for him, poor man.

We all put too much on him.

"Can I do anything for you?"

His gaze sharpens. "What does a young girl want with me anyway? I've always wondered. You've been sniffing around me for years."

I have no idea how to respond. I am partially shocked and partially surprised it took him so long to ask me this. I know he must have suspicions, but I can only assume that he's held his peace because he is as terrified of the real answer as I once was.

I try to divert his attention. "My mother . . ."

"Yes, yes, I know about your mother. But I'm asking about you."

I hesitate. Is this the moment, after all these years? But then I think, *God, not like this*. Not with him too drunk to stand. When my mother was in this state I used to stay up all night beside her to make sure that her skin wasn't turning blue. I loathe drunks. I pity them, certainly, but I hate being around them. I hate their stench. I hate their ridiculous slurring. I can no longer ignore that so many of the things I despised about Maman are present in Papa too.

I have the tortuous and simultaneously wonderful thought that if the man in front of me is *not* my father, then maybe both of my parents were not drunks. Maybe at least one of them smelled like clean linen and freshly baked bread, and not like liquor and smoke and disappointment.

"I admire you," I say, because it is true, and safe. "I have always admired you."

"Because I'm a writer?" he asks casually, as if he is just some pencil scratcher and not someone who will live forever.

I used to sleep with your books beneath my pillow; I used to sneak them behind my textbooks in school. And now I have come to understand a little of your mind and the way you see the world, your willingness to share your knowledge, and I respect you even more. I am grateful to share a lifetime with you; I am blessed to be born even in a time that contains so much unrest if it means that you are here too.

"At first" is all I say out loud. I try very hard not to blush. I am too old to blush, surely. "But I have enjoyed knowing you."

He smiles sleepily, and I have a sudden glimpse of him as a little boy, not a great writer at all, but just a child scribbling furiously in the margins of his schoolbooks. It's hard to imagine that such greatness could emerge from such fragility.

"And how is your writing?"

The change of subject is a relief. "It's going well. I think. I never really know for certain. But I'm doing my best. I've actually finished some things."

He slumps onto the table. "Good for you. That's the hardest part done."

"I want to write something else too. But I'm not sure . . . it's . . . personal."

He blinks slowly. I recognize the look in his eye as one that tells me he will not remember a word of this conversation tomorrow. "Oh, you have to write it in that case. Tell me about it."

I can hear Javier's voice in my head, urging me to be bold: *Oyeeee! Esa muchacha tiene chispa!*

"It's called *Gossamer*. I'm about halfway through. It's moving along much faster than anything else I've written. It's about a young woman from Orléans. Her name is Daphne."

He's still listening. "What is she like and what does she want?"

I am very nearly breathless telling him about this character who has come to feel so real. "She wants to get away from her mother and find the man she believes to be her father. She runs away to be with him, but it doesn't go the way she planned."

He keeps his drooping eyes on me. There's a strange brightness in them even as they are nearly shut.

"What happens?"

"The girl's mother throws herself from the balcony."

He is silent for a moment. He clears his throat before speaking again.

"Sounds interesting. I would read that myself."

Even his praise is not enough to quash my fear.

I gesture helplessly with my hands. "It's too close to home. It's too . . . I can't stand the thought of anyone judging it."

The fog lifts from his gaze and for a minute he is stone-cold sober. He rears up and slaps the table with his palm.

"I can guarantee you that you will be judged harshly, and by people without enough talent to fill a puddle, or enough courage to try to do anything themselves. That's the lot of anyone who has ever dared to do anything outside of the absolute ordinary. If it's important enough, you'll do it anyway."

And with that, he collapses face first into the table, shaking it so hard that a glass slides off and shatters.

I turn my head to speak to the impatient barkeep. "Please call a taxi for the gentleman. I will wait with him."

I cross the table and raise Papa's head as gently as I can to place my pocketbook beneath it. Absently, I stroke his thinning hair, just as I used to do to Maman's.

I do not melt. I am not transformed, there is no chorus of angels. I am still just Delphine—perhaps Delphine Auber, perhaps Delphine Hemingway. But still Delphine.

I kiss his damp forehead.

"Merci beaucoup, Papa."

I have touched the sun now.

.   .   .

July 24, 1960

"Delphine, levántate."

The voice creeps into the sanctuary of my dreams. I am somewhere in a great library, with endless rows of books. It has that wonderful, indescribable smell that only libraries can have. But it all recedes in an instant as I open my eyes.

"He's leaving. Hemingway. He's going back to America."

Javier stands in my bedroom doorway and drops the words into my lap like a sack of hot coals.

I haven't even had my morning coffee. The sunlight streams through my cracked window and bathes the room in soft white light. In it, I can see that he looks weary. Even his curls look flatter.

I pull my blanket up to my chin. "No."

He comes and sits beside me. I don't even scold him for sitting on my bed in his street clothes or letting himself in instead of knocking. I just look at him and shake my head.

He crushes my denial without pretense. "Yes. I have it on excellent authority. I've been keeping my ear to the ground for you because I knew you'd want a chance to say goodbye."

I don't want to say goodbye. I don't want everything to change *again* just as I am finally happy. I pull the covers even further up and bury my face in them.

"You'll have to go too," he says in a joyless monotone. "That was our deal."

Stop talking. Please stop talking.

"But for now, we should go if you want a chance to speak with him. The car's outside."

I pitch forward and he holds me tightly to his chest.

"I'm not ready," I groan. "I told myself that I was grown up now, that I didn't need him or care if I lost him. In my mind I let him go, but there was a place inside me that wanted to believe that someday . . . by some miracle the lights I wished on as a little girl in Paris had heard my pleas, and that one day, if I could just be good enough, he would see me and love me. Against all common sense, I let myself hope. I know better. I've learned better. And I did it anyway."

"No one is ever ready to let go of hope, Delphine. It can die a thousand deaths and never leave us."

I bow my head in resignation to the fact that I will apparently never be finished growing up.

"I had better get dressed, then."

He pats my shoulder. "I'll be just outside the door."

When he's gone, I stand up so quickly that it makes me sway. If I don't get up now I may never. Part of me wants to cling to my pillow and weep, but that's never solved anything.

Instead I move blindly, doing things I have done a million times. I fumble through my closet and snatch a dress. I go to the bathroom to brush my teeth and splash water on my face. In the end, I comb my hair out in front of the mirror and barely feel my hand move. For the first time in a while, I take the time to really look at myself.

My hair is nearly as long as Maman's was. It's a tad thicker now that I don't put any heat on it, and I like the way it frames my face.

My skin is still unblemished, lightly bronzed from all my time in the sun, and I have developed a scattering of freckles across my nose that suits me just fine. I have finally grown into my limbs and though I am still woefully flat chested, I have nice legs and good teeth. I have learned that I look better in higher hemlines and clothes that cinch at the waist rather than below the bust. Red is my color.

I am no Rita Hayworth, but I think that my eyes look brighter than they used to. I give myself a little smile.

Javier knocks and pokes his head in with his eyes tastefully on the floor.

"Ready?"

"Yes," I lie. So many things in my life started as lies and are true now. Maybe this can be the same.

"All right, then. Let's go."

. . .

I just knock. After all these years of carefully placing myself in his path, I just walk right up the steps to Papa's front door and knock on it. His wife answers. She looks like every old woman you'd ever see at the market on a Sunday morning, but she has a nice smile. Her hair is pulled back with a scarf, and she looks tired. In the background I can hear shouting and banging.

"Yes?" she asks pleasantly enough.

I tuck my hair behind my ear. "I'm sorry to intrude. My name is Delphine Auber. I'm a friend of . . . well . . . I'm here to see—"

"I know who you're here to see," she says with a chuckle. "No one is ever here for anyone else. One moment."

She shuts the door and goes away. I take a moment to imagine that this farmhouse is my home. I close my eyes and see my tiny handprints staining the wallpaper. I see pencil marks on the wall to measure my growth, skinned knees from wrestling with three brothers, arguments over who gets the last piece of dessert. I see myself holding up a marlin bigger than me with Papa standing behind me and beaming, just beaming as if he never needed a Nobel Prize or four wives to be happy. All he ever needed was me.

The door opens again, and Papa is standing there looking harried, with his thinning hair standing up. He does not smile to see me.

"Oh, Delphine."

I nod and swallow a few times before I can speak.

"I'm sorry to call on you like this. I heard you were leaving tomorrow. I just wanted to say my goodbyes."

He looks down. "Well, yes. Mary wants to go and everyone seems to think it's for the best."

I wish I could hug him. "Everyone always thinks they know what's best for everyone else."

This wins me a smile and my heart lifts.

"Things will calm down," he says with certainty. "They always do. I've seen worse than this. I'll be back before long. I've never been able to stay away."

I can't stand here for too long. If I do, I will cry, and I will never cry in front of him.

I pull the letter out of my pocket. "I have something to give you."

His bushy eyebrows shoot up. "Is it your latest work?"

"No, it's just . . . just some things I've been meaning to tell you."

I have finally run out of time. I want to sit down with him on a park bench and tell him the story of my life. All these years. All those years I wasted being afraid, and now there is no time left.

He takes it from me and turns it around in his thick hands. "Should I read it now?"

"Please don't," I croak. A coward until the end. "Just whenever you're settled. When you're safe . . . when you're happy again."

His eyes are dull, but he is smiling. The laugh lines around his mouth twitch. "Happy again?"

Yes. May the day come soon when we are both happy again.

"I have to go now," I say. "Safe travels."

"And you. What will you do?"

"I want to stay. But if I can't, I'll go back to Paris."

He looks at me intently. I am wearing a blue dress today, with my hair long and loose around my shoulders. I am barefaced and red-eyed before him.

"You look a little like her after all," he says with the lilt of surprise in his voice. "More as you age."

"You still remember?" I ask, struggling to keep my tone bland when my heart is throbbing.

"Oh, always."

Always.

My eyes fill with tears.

His wife calls his name, and he turns away from me to shout back at her. No, he doesn't know where the green journal is. Check the study. Maybe one of the cats knocked it over.

When he turns back around, I am gone.

.   .   .

Dear Papa,

I am your daughter.

I am sorry for the lack of a preamble but I think there has been enough of that. For years, I have wanted to tell you who I am, and perhaps in some ways I have.

But please allow me to leave no doubt. I was born on the eleventh of January, 1929. My mother was Sylvie Auber. She told me that the two of you were lovers while you were married to your first wife, and before you married your second.

She told me that she knew with absolute certainty that you were my father. She filled me with so many stories about your time in Paris together, with all of the

274

great artists and thinkers. You were my first bedtime story.

I have admired you all my life. I left Paris to find you. I became a writer because of you. Every journey I have ever started on was to reach you.

Of course, I didn't know you then.

This was before fishing, and conversations about writing, and the mojitos. You have given me the confidence to fight for a dream, as you have. You have made me as close to fearless as I could ever be.

I have come to know you over the course of my life and I can say, without any shadow of doubt:

I have loved you. I do love you. I always will.

For whatever that is worth.

Yours,

Delphine

~~~~~~~~~~~~~~~~

Chapter Sixteen

An Old Friend

Havana, Cuba
July 25, 1960

Here I am again: in exile.

A lifetime ago, when I was just a girl, and not the thirty-one-year-old woman that I am now, I remembered thinking that the world had learned its lesson after two great wars in less than fifty years. That people had seen enough bloodshed and death, and that there would be no more of it.

What a stupid child I was.

Javier's grip is firm. He is practically dragging me towards the marina, one of my three suitcases clutched in his left hand. I try to dig my heels in but it's useless, he is unstoppable.

"I won't go," I shout at the back of his dark, curly head.

"You will. Your own father left yesterday, there's nothing keeping you here now."

"I can't leave you!"

"Fine, I'll leave you, then. However, you want to think about it, you do that, but you're getting on that boat and sailing into Key West. Today. This very afternoon."

"No!"

"Yes, Delphine."

He will not change his mind. I know this, I've known him for over a decade, I know he will not change his mind. When he showed up at my front door this morning and told me to get my suitcase from underneath my bed, I knew I had already lost. He was waiting, I realize now, for Papa to leave. He planned the entire thing in the gentlest way possible and I both love and hate him for it.

But still I plead with him, the entire time. I make promises and then threats. My anger roars to life but there is no one that I can fight to make this stop. I rage, I cry. I beg, I bargain. I do everything but fall to my knees.

But he just shakes his head.

"I can't go! This is my home!"

"Paris is your home."

"*You* are my home. I can't leave you alone here, not with what's happening. This regime could take your property, they could arrest you, they could kill you!"

He finally stops walking. The *Tournesol* sits to our right, rocking gently, oblivious to the fact that there will be no pleasure cruise on this day.

He lets me go. I think I may have found an opening, but quick as lightning he climbs up and starts unmooring her.

"Did you hear a word I said?"

He nods. "I did. And you can't stop them from doing any of that, Delphine. Neither can I. The only thing I can do is get you out of here. Here. I've got the nautical maps to Key West, it's not a difficult sail and I know you can do it. I've put some money in your suitcase."

He extends his hand to me, and I let him pull me onto the deck without a word of protest.

"Come with me," I plead.

He doesn't hesitate. "I can't do that."

"Of course you can."

He shakes his head, like a parent to a well-meaning but misguided child. His voice is gentle.

"No, I can't. I'm Cuban. This is my home, and I'd rather be Cuban than safe, popular, or anything else."

"You can be Cuban in France!"

He smiles but it doesn't reach his eyes. "Like you were French in Cuba? Oh, the songs I could write."

I cling to him like a child. "Please. I'll go if you come with me. We'll leave right now."

"There's nothing you can say that will change my mind, Delphine. I'm truly sorry. I don't like this any more than you do."

Tears of rage pour down my face.

"I don't need your sorry, I need you. All these years you have been my favorite person in the world. And now I'm standing here in front of you asking you not to leave me like all the others, and all you can tell me is no."

He looks down and does not deny it.

"I love you, Delphine."

He has never said this to me before. It is beyond cruel for him to say it now, the day he decides to let me go.

I am flooded with bitterness. "I have no use for love."

"You do. We all do. I hope you have lots of it in your life."

I whimper and he pulls me close to him.

"You know this is how it has to be. The people who haven't left already will be wishing they had in a few years. I can feel it. I can feel a change in the beating of this country's heart. But I have to see this through. This country is going to need people who can try to guide her down the right path."

"What about you?" I ask piteously. "What will happen to you? I will see you again, won't I?"

"Only God knows that. But this isn't your fight. Go back to Paris. Get those novels of yours published. Say what you need to, make them listen. That can be your fight."

He kisses my cheek. Then, before I am ready, before I am anywhere close to ready, he hops back down to the dock.

His face is contorted. I have never seen Javier cry once. I wonder if this is what it looks like when he's about to.

"You have to go now, Delphine."

My voice is shaking. "I'll write to you. You have to write back. You have to promise."

He manages a smile. "Of course I'll write back."

I'm stalling. I want to hold this moment in my hands but it's already slipping away. He's already gone. I can tell by the look on his face that he has made his peace with never seeing me again.

This is more painful than I had thought possible.

"I have to watch you go," he says gently. "I'll stand here until I can't see you anymore."

I don't move to take the wheel. I just sob. I cry more than I have since Teddy died, or when I held my dead mother in my arms.

But my brokenness changes nothing. There is no cosmic scorekeeper; Louise is wrong. There is no fairness in this world. There is no one up there watching who will say, *Oh, yes, she can have this one. We can rewrite the story, just this one time.*

There is only this cruel reality and my submission to it. Again.

I bow my head and start for the wheel.

"Try to be happy, Delphine," he shouts after me. "You don't get extra points for being miserable. You just get to be miserable."

I spread the maps out. Start the engine. Place my hands on the wheel. And then I look at him.

I try to tell him that I love him, but the words don't come out. I lose my voice and try again.

"You changed my life."

He touches his heart. "Ah, well. There's nothing better. Dedicate a book to me someday so I can live forever."

There's nothing left to say. There is no collection of beautiful words that can ever make these moments better. These are ugly moments. They feel like bones breaking and jutting out of torn flesh. They feel like salt rubbed into eyes, and hearts twisted up like towels.

They are excruciating and an unavoidable symptom of being alive.

I cast off.

He smiles and waves, with both hands like a child, as if he is sending me off on a glorious adventure.

"Safe travels, Delphine! Write to me!"

I don't turn my head again until I am several yards from shore.

But when I glance back one final time, I see that he has stopped waving. He is a little speck sitting on the dock with his feet dangling over the water and his head fixed in my direction.

I feel the loss of him at once. My skin is hot, itchy, pulling at me to turn back.

But I don't turn back.

I go forward into the known and unknown.

. . .

Key West, Florida
August 1960

I languish in Florida for only three weeks. The people are ghastly.

It's sunny here too, but in a way that seems counterfeit. I can't explain it but I don't like it. The entire place feels gaudy. Most mornings I walk down to the water and cry silently for an hour before starting my day. In the afternoons, the humidity is unbearable and I hide inside my hotel room. I have felt sick since I got here. This heat is different from the Cuban heat. It's leeching life from my bones instead of putting it in.

I don't read the papers or listen to the radio. I don't want to hear about the world.

The day I sell the boat is the hardest. I don't need the money, but I can hardly take her with me all the way back to France.

I buy my plane ticket back to Paris and my face is so pale that the travel agent who sells it to me asks if I'm ill.

"You'll love Paris," she says enthusiastically. I wonder if she is deaf to my accent. As she nods her solid, shiny beehive hairdo stays firmly in place. I wonder how much hair spray it takes to achieve that. She risks both of our lives when she lights a cigarette. "Oh, yes siree. Who doesn't love the City of Love? It's impossible to be unhappy in a place like that."

I manage a dull smile. Americans have this bizarre notion that Paris will solve all of their problems. I don't argue with them. We all need something.

I wonder if Papa has read my letter yet. It appears that the thought of him caring about what I have to say is the thing that I need.

It's easy enough to get the address for his home here, though I am told he is not currently staying here. When I creep in one night to look around, and it is easy enough, I find the cats. They have free rein of the courtyard and I sit amongst them and feed the brave ones from my palm.

Apparently there's a custodian who comes to take care of them when the family is not in residence.

There are so many of them that I am confident he won't notice I have stolen one.

I choose a fluffy white polydactyl girl who reminds me of a snowball and name her Minette. She submits meekly to capture without so much as a meow.

She likes to climb onto my shoulder and sit there. It makes me feel like a pirate, and I feed her bits of tuna fish instead of crackers. She sleeps curled up on the pillow beside my face.

She also chews on everything: clothes, shoes, the blinds in my hotel room. I am convinced she is part wolf. When she is in a temper, she will fling her tiny body at the meat of my arm and dig all of her claws in. She doesn't listen to a word I say and steals the food from my plate.

She is the cat I deserve and I love her for it.

There's no question of me leaving her behind. She nips my ankles while I gather up my courage and fish my address book from my suitcase.

I pick up the phone and have the operator put me through to New York.

My hands are shaking. I am half hoping she won't answer the call. I really don't have any right, calling after all these years. It's appallingly selfish.

But she does answer. Her voice sounds just the same and then I am blubbering, and she is shouting, and then Blue's voice is there too and they are both telling me in one voice to get my narrow behind on a flight and come home.

. . .

Harlem, New York
September 1960

I step out of the taxi in front of the brownstone. They are both waiting for me, along with a heavyset woman in a maid's uniform. Business must be good.

I can barely crack the door open before Delia all but drags me out of the car. She greets me in French, and it is wonderful to hear again. I haven't spoken my mother tongue since I parted with Javier and half the time we spoke in Spanish. "Delphine! Delphine!"

She presses me up against her and I bury my face in the warmth of her arm like I am still a little girl.

I feel the prickle of tears but I know that I don't deserve them. "I'm sorry."

"Hush," Delia soothes.

The guilt is too much for me. I can barely catch a breath underneath the weight of it. "No, please. I understand how much I hurt you and I'm just . . . so truly sorry. For all of it."

"I said hush, sweetheart. There's no need for this."

Blue stands to her left, beaming at us both. He is as sharply dressed as ever in a dark blue suit. Neither of them look like they've aged more than a week. The street also looks exactly as I remember it.

I resist the urge to mumble. I stand up straight and look him in the eye, like he taught me. I speak to him in English.

"Hi, Blue."

He nods at me. "Seems you've had quite the adventure."

I crack a tiny grin. "Yes, sir."

"Maybe you've learned it's not easy to make it on your own in this life."

"Yes, sir. That's a fact."

He shakes his head. "You aren't even my daughter. And I know you're more than thirty. But I still feel I ought to paint your back porch red for not writing more often. That last letter of yours scared us half to death. And telling me about your mama's death that way . . ."

He could melt an icicle with that tone. His face is hard now.

But I don't lower my eyes.

I speak clearly. "I was wrong to handle things the way I did. I should have told you the truth about my mother the second I arrived in New York. I should never have forged letters or lied to you. I felt responsible for Maman's death. It was a suicide but I thought . . . I thought you'd blame me as much as I blamed myself. I was so ashamed. I only hope that you will grant me the grace to earn your trust again."

He nods. "That's going to take some time."

"Yes, sir. God willing I have time."

He rests a hand on my shoulder. "You know that I loved your mother. But her death wasn't your fault, Delphine. It was never your fault."

I wipe a falling tear. "Yes. I know that now."

He hugs me tightly. Delia is already counting off the list of what she's made for my welcome dinner: gumbo, blackberry cobbler. She runs her fingers through my long hair and tells me how well it suits me.

If these two had been my parents, I would never have had my adventures, or seen Havana, or felt such a burning need to write. It's really much better that they were not my parents.

The tears that soak into the freshly starched fabric of Blue's shirt call me the liar I buried long ago.

. . .

I realize immediately that I can't stay here too long or I will never leave. It's too safe.

I sleep in my old room above the restaurant. Minette likes to sit in the window and emit perturbed shrieks at passersby.

In my absence, Blue and Delia have opened a dry cleaner's, another restaurant, and a car wash.

Delia told me that she wants to open an orphanage for non-white children.

They have a color television in the living room, a live-in maid, and another girl who comes twice a week to help with whatever else needs doing.

I help Delia in the kitchen, and she compliments my skillful butchering of the fish.

I tell her about Maman. About Javier and the boat. About Louise's letters. About Papa. I tell her everything with my eyes fixed firmly on the slab in front of me.

She is quiet for a long while. The only sound is the radio and the honk of a car horn from outside.

"He stayed here, you know. Fidel. When he came to New York, he stayed right here in Harlem, with the coloreds and Latins. He says he's a man of the people."

"Funny how they all say that and nothing ever gets any better."

She chuckles. "You're just the same."

"I'm not," I say simply. I could never be the same again. "But as dumb as I was, I think I found my way to the simplest conclusion."

"And that is?"

"Better not rely on anyone's promises."

"Generally speaking, you're not wrong, my dear. But tell me more about this boy, this Javier. He meant a great deal to you."

"I didn't say that."

"You didn't have to. It's all over your face. All those years you spent with him . . . sounds like you two were family."

"I don't have any family."

She shoots me a sidelong glance. "You're going to insult me in my own house?"

I give a shamefaced blush. "That's not what I meant. I love you two. I love Javier and Louise. I loved Teddy. But we aren't blood."

She scoffs. "So? You think I give a damn?"

I push the gills out of another fish. "He wouldn't come with me. I begged him to—and I have never begged for anything—I tore my heart out in front of him and all he could say was no."

"You can't take that personally, Delphine. He loves his country."

Just once I would like someone to choose me first. It's a selfish, stupid thought but I can't make it go away. It is my secret desire from childhood that may never leave me.

I don't speak it aloud, and push it down.

"I know that."

"And have you had a reply to the letter you gave your father?"

I wash my hands and then squeeze her arm. Her indulgence is touching.

"I put Maman's address on it. If he has replied, it will be waiting for me in Paris."

She nods approvingly. "You must be so excited to go back."

I close my eyes. She pulls me close and kisses my forehead.

"I am so proud of you, Delphine. You brave, smart girl."

"I have done nothing for you to be proud of," I mumble. "I was too much of a coward to tell Papa to his face who I am. Or who I *think* I am. Some days I don't even know."

"You grew up."

"I have," I concede. "But what have I really done?"

"You walk with your head held high now. That's not nothing. And you wrote three books."

"That I'm afraid to share with anyone! My mother always insisted that she wanted me to be braver than her."

She looks at me sternly. "Look. Joseph has a new contact at Random House. He's a patron at the restaurant. If you're certain about this, we could possibly set up a meeting."

My jaw nearly hits the floor. "What?"

"If you are serious about this?"

"I . . . I've never been more serious about anything. It's all I've ever wanted."

"Well, then, give me your manuscript—probably just one to start, whichever one you think is the strongest—and I'll have it dropped off at his office."

I am near to tears. "You would do that for me?"

"I can't guarantee anything," she warns.

I throw my arms around her neck. "I don't deserve you two."

"We're here for you. Whenever you need us," she says simply. "You don't have to keep acting surprised. It will never change."

I love you be damned. That just may be the most beautiful thing anyone has ever said to me.

"Thank you, Delia."

. . .

I choose my first love—*The House of Pristine Sorrows*. Besides being the most polished, something in my gut tells me to choose this one.

If the editor despises it, it will feel like someone telling me that my newborn baby is ugly. But that is the risk. And now is my moment to be brave.

Three weeks pass with no reply from the editor. I am useless the entire time. Now I have *two* things to wait on and make myself sick over. Papa's letter is either waiting for me in Paris or it is not. I know that. But still, I cannot stop my hands from shaking all the time.

I try to help in the restaurant, but I get the orders wrong and finally Blue gives me some money—like I'm still a teenager—and tells me to go see a movie.

"No sense in worrying. He's going to say what he's going to say. Now, get out of here before you wear a hole in my floor."

So I do get out. I walk, miles and miles, the way I used to with Javier. But now I am alone.

That does seem to be the natural state of things.

I stop to get a hot dog from a cart. It's disgusting but oddly satisfying.

I see Teddy everywhere in this city. I see her glowing brown eyes and her dyed blonde curls that never went limp, no matter how long we stayed out. I see her batting her lashes to get her way. I see the steely determination to make a dream come true that was often barely detectable beneath her coy façade. She had grit. No one else might have seen it, but I did.

I wonder where they buried her. I just realized that I don't know. When I left New York they were trying to call her mother. The scab flies off the wound when I think I cannot even lay flowers on her grave, and I have to stop walking and sit on a park bench. Watch children run by in disregard of their nanny calling after them.

Teddy has been gone for such a long time, but today it is almost as if she is sitting here beside me, smoking a cigarette.

Theodora, I can hear her lamenting. *What kind of name is that? Not a name for an actress. Not a name for an actress at all. Can't you just see me with my milk pails in the field?*

I have a quick, wild, dangerous thought to find Harlan and set something else he owns on fire, but I don't allow it to take root. I stay away from the Upper East Side entirely and I wear my hat pulled low over my face.

I don't know if they're still looking for me, if they ever were.

I still don't regret the fire.

I make sure I'm home before dark. I'm too miserable to make an appearance at dinner, and instead I head straight to my room.

I don't know what I will do if getting published doesn't work out. Really. I have no idea what else I will be in this life if I'm not a writer. The only good thing about being mostly useless is that you know exactly what it is that you *can* do, and you give it everything you've got.

I would pray if I thought I had any credibility left.

When I make it back, I go straight to my room above the restaurant. Minette rubs herself against my legs and graciously allows me to rub her belly for a full ten seconds.

I kneel down and hold myself very still. I take two deep breaths.

There is no scale, I remind myself. *There is no justice in this world, and perhaps you should be glad of that after all. There is nothing you can do about the outcome of this. There is no point in anger, or fear, or bargaining. There is only acceptance. You know this. This is written in your blood, you have learned this so many times.*

I place my face in my hands.

Oh, but please.

Please.

Please, just this once, let it be my turn.

Let me be that girl.

That night as I am helping Delia make dinner, the phone rings.

. . .

I sit across from him in my best lady day suit, with my hair teased into a sleek updo and crammed beneath one of Delia's pillbox hats so that he will not see I've grown my hair long like a revolutionary. My hands are neatly folded in my lap. Not a hint of a tremor. My ankles, on the other hand, are shaking uncontrollably but are safely hidden by the desk. Bertrand Mullins is forty-eight, with a sad patch of salt-and-pepper hair clinging to the back of his head. Other than that he is completely bald. He has on oversized spectacles that cover watery blue eyes and a poorly fitted suit that is only half ironed. He looks like he doesn't get enough sleep.

And right now, he holds my life in his hands.

He sips his coffee slowly.

"So, Miss Auber. Joseph passed your manuscript on to me. I have some thoughts."

I suppose we are cutting right to the chase. "Such as?" I try to keep my voice even.

"First, what was your inspiration for this novel?"

Oh, no. Not this again. It's actually *worse* than "What's it about?" and I didn't think that was possible.

I plaster on a smile. "I wanted to write a coming-of-age story centering on a female protagonist. The rest sort of fell into place."

"The main character is from Belgium and eventually lands in Havana. Why did you choose those settings?"

I force myself not to avert my gaze. I wish to God that Javier were here. "I've never lived in Belgium. But I lived in Havana for a long time."

"But you're French, correct?"

"Yes. But I can write in English with no trouble, as you can see, and I could write in Spanish too if that would help. I studied literature at the university in Havana."

He is awfully grim looking. I'm guessing he is about to tell me no. I look down at the ugly tweed carpet. I expected this but it still feels like someone is ripping apart my seams.

"I enjoyed it," he says, and I have to grip the bottom of my chair to stop myself from jumping for joy. "It needs some work, but I enjoyed it immensely. I don't know how much of an audience it would have, and I should warn you the advance would likely be very small but . . ."

I look him in the eye. They could give me two quarters for it, and I wouldn't give a damn. I could kiss him.

"Are you saying that you'll publish it?"

At last, he cracks a wry smile. "That is what I'm saying, yes."

"Oh, *thank you*."

It's happening. It's really happening. I never thought . . . I never truly believed until this moment. I am grinning from ear to ear.

"Well, yes. But thank yourself. You wrote it. It reminded me a bit of *A Tree Grows in Brooklyn*. The main character, Louise, has a lot of spunk to her. She made me laugh out loud almost as often as I wanted to throttle her. You have a lot of talent, Miss Auber, quite a lot of talent indeed."

And now I am bawling. There is no higher compliment for me. I am a grown woman, on the most important day of my life, crying like a damn fool.

But my cup runneth over after a lifetime of drought, real or imagined, and I couldn't stop if I wanted to.

I am seen.

I am listened to.

I am *real*.

He looks uncomfortable but says nothing while the flood passes. I dab my eyes with tissues from my purse.

"I'm sorry," I say weakly. How many women get this opportunity? I had better pull it together before I shame my entire sex.

He smiles faintly. "Not a problem. I was a war correspondent, you know, before I became an editor. I've seen grown men faint. Anyway, Miss Auber, we have some details to discuss. My secretary, Ruth, will give you your contract on the way out if you'd like to have your attorney review it."

I sit up straight and clear my throat. "Yes, of course."

The rest is a blur. He asks me if I have any other novels and I tell him that I do. He says he'd like to see them but makes no promises. The contract is for *The House of Pristine Sorrows* only. It's a one-book deal and he'll do what he can with marketing, but . . . do I intend to keep writing in English? Good, good. I should get an agent, he can give me a list of names.

"Any questions?"

"No, sir. But I have a request."

"Oh?"

"I was hoping to publish anonymously."

He looks at me as if I've asked to run naked through the streets of New York.

"You want to do what?"

"I would like to publish without anyone knowing who I am. I suppose I'd also be open to using a pseudonym. Lots of women have done that. But I wouldn't want any photographs of me released, or any information about me available to the public."

The flabbergasted look does not leave his face; if anything, he leans forward a bit.

"Miss Auber, why on earth would you want to do that? Why would you want to refuse credit?"

I understand his confusion. When I started on this road, all I wanted was acclaim and recognition. Now I just want the words to stand on their own, pure as a nightingale's song. Fly or fail, so long as they do it without me in the way.

I try to sound confident. "I think it is better this way. I don't want anything muddying the water. In my experience, people really can't help themselves."

He scratches his chin. "I'm not sure that's going to work. I'd have to inquire."

"Please do."

"Joseph said you were a bit of an odd bird. But I wasn't expecting this."

I flush. I don't want him to think that I'm going to be difficult and change his mind.

"I promise I'll be a good author. I'll hit all my deadlines. I'll work harder than anyone, I promise."

He runs his hand over the shiny top of his head. "Miss Auber . . ."

"Delphine, please."

He looks down at the stack of papers on his desk. "I really can't understand this choice."

I make the split-second decision to lay myself bare in front of this strange man who is offering me salvation.

"I used to be ashamed. All the time. Because I'm a girl, because I'm a bastard and my mother was . . . a lot of things. I wanted admiration. Respect. Something to prove that my life was more than just a pitiable accident. I chased after someone . . ." I break off and squeeze my hands together to gather myself. "I don't have a prominent family name, or really any kind of traditional family at all. I'm not beautiful, I'm not even particularly charming. All I have ever had is my stubbornness and my talent. I wrote my way out of hell. And so now I am proud. I am proud, because I did that, and no one can ever take it from me. Even if I am the only one who ever knows it, that is enough."

He stands up and I have a moment of blinding terror that he is going to throw me out onto the street and ask the next girl with a dream to come in and take my place. A girl with a biddable manner and no demands.

Instead he extends his hand and smiles.

"Welcome to the Random House family, Delphine."

I stand up too and take it. I think this is the proudest moment of my life. I wish my mother were here.

"Thank you."

. . .

I stay with Blue and Delia for another few weeks. They take me to a restaurant downtown that they're allowed in now to celebrate my book contract, and we all pointedly ignore the stares we get from other patrons.

Out of the corner of my eye, I see an empty booth at the far end of the dining room. And just for a moment, it is not empty at all. Teddy raises a glass of champagne to me and gives me a cheeky wink.

Well done, Delphine. I always knew you were the clever one. Maybe they'll turn it into a film! A major Hollywood production. That would be just perfect.

You be the voice, and I'll be the star.

I meet with the agent I chose, the only woman on the entire list Mr. Mullins gave me—a German immigrant named Irma Wagner. She meets twice with my editor, and my one book deal turns into three. All three of my novels will be published. I can use my name or not as I please. She likes my idea of using my middle name as my nom de plume.

I bawl in front of her as well, and she pats me on the head and makes me promise to come to New York four times a year to meet with her.

As soon as I get home from the meeting, I write a letter to Javier telling him everything that's happened. I am grinning from ear to ear thinking of the dance he will break into when he finds out. He will peacock as if it's his own triumph. *Mira! I knew I kept you alive for a reason.*

On my last night, I sit in the living room with Blue and Delia drinking lemonade and listening to the radio.

"We sure will miss you, sugar," Delia says, dabbing at her eyes. "I'm glad your work will be bringing you back around soon."

"Me too," I say, and I mean it.

Blue smiles like the cat who ate the canary. "I'm so proud of you."

"I couldn't have done it without you."

He shrugs. "Your mother would haunt me for eternity if I didn't help you. And I didn't do the hard part—you did."

"Are you sure you won't put your own name on it?" Delia asks for the hundredth time.

"Violette is my middle name."

Delia tuts. "You know that's not what I mean."

Blue rolls his eyes. "Delia, don't start on her again."

"Well, excuse me, but I'm going to. It is nineteen sixty. It's time for women to get some credit for things. Lately I've been trying to get more people from the community registered to vote and I couldn't help but think . . . Delphine, I didn't know your mama personally, but her being a suffragette, I know she'd want you to put your full name on your work. She'd want you to be bold about this thing."

"It's her book," Blue says, in the way that lets us all know it's final. "Not yours, not her mama's. Leave her be."

Delia huffs.

"Well, what about the next one? And the one after that?"

"I don't know, Delia."

But I do know. I don't think I'll ever change my mind on this.

I hesitate before telling her the reason I think she'll understand the most. I feel like I need to give her something at least.

"I don't want people talking about me," I admit. "It reminds me of childhood. How they used to bully and laugh at me. Mock me, misrepresent me. Try to tell me who I am when they couldn't even be bothered to speak to me. People take one look at you and decide that they know your story. I don't want to open myself up to that all over again."

Delia pats my hand. "You've had the wind in your face for so long that you don't trust it to be at your back. Sweetheart, everything in life has a price. Absolutely everything, even the good things. All you can do is decide which ones are worth paying."

．　．　．

Paris, France
October 1960

Home at last.

There are no trumpets. Paris has clearly not noticed my absence, but then, that is the irreverence I love about her. She is an eternal dance; what does she care if one graceless girl steps out of line and then gets back in?

I am happy to be home, but it is not an easy happiness. It is not happiness without a cost.

Of course, there is only one place for me to go. Though I am dog-tired from the plane, I take a car straight to Sainte Geneviève and to my loving, inescapable godmother: Louise.

I wrote to her a few weeks before I left Cuba but received no reply.

Though I swore a thousand times that I would never come back here, I return to her now like a sinner summoned on Judgment Day. How nice it must be for her to always be proven right.

I step into the cool darkness of the cathedral, just as noon mass is ending. I consider it a good start when I don't burst into flames. Maybe God is not in the mood for a spectacle.

I walk down the long aisle, past the altar, to the back of the cathedral. I recognize her even with her back to me and her habit on. There's a change in the air around her; everything is a few degrees warmer.

She's chatting with a young rosy-cheeked girl, maybe sixteen. I stare at her for a moment. God, she is so *young*. Was I that young? When I thought I had everyone outsmarted? When I thought I had gone too far to be saved?

It seems so laughable that I could have been so certain then and so unsure now.

The girl walks away, with a spring in her step that I don't think I ever had.

It is then that Louise spots me. There are lines on her face that I don't remember, but her large green eyes open wide and her arms open wider still. A little wisp of graying blonde hair has slipped out from underneath her habit.

I fall into her easily, and she mumbles a prayer into my hair.

"Thank God," she says simply. "I haven't had a letter from you since you told me how bad things were getting in Havana. I was so afraid for you. Thank the Lord for his mercy that you have come home."

"Thank Pan Am and Fidel Castro," I say dryly. "They're the reasons I'm here."

She pulls back and smiles at me, that mischievous smile that seems so out of place on a nun.

"Delphine. Look at you. You're a woman now."

Lucky me. I feel like a woman—there is far too much to do all the damn time. I could sleep for a thousand years.

"I was hoping you could escort me home."

She looks surprised. "Now?"

"Before I lose my nerve."

"Well . . . if you think you're ready. I've kept the place clean for you, but it needs some work. I wish you'd given me more notice that you were returning."

I give her another squeeze. I have missed her more than I have let myself realize.

"You have done more than enough. Thank you."

Tears spring up in her eyes and I am struck with the realization that my departure was a genuine loss to her. She didn't chide me in her letters for her own amusement—she was missing me, and terrified for me because I was a stupid, willful child halfway across the world. She grieved my mother's death and my absence all together and never once complained to me.

She is a better woman than I could ever be.

Outside, we hail a taxi, even though it is only a short walk to my flat.

Louise looks at me out of the corner of her eye as I cling to Minette's carrier in my lap.

"Are you sure?" she asks quietly. "You can stay with the sisters tonight. Or a hotel. You don't have to do this yet."

I lean my head against the window. "I have to do it now" is all I say, and she nods.

I glance out the window. I see some new housing developments halfway through construction. A candy shop I remember from when I was a little girl is boarded up. I spot a group of women pass by in short, sleeveless floral dresses and tall white boots, and I smile at the realization that there are young people here too who will not bow down to social conventions. Maybe I will find my own artistic crowd to run with; maybe my parties will be the talk of the town. Maybe this time next year I'll be having lunch with Simone de Beauvoir. Maman would adore that. It's a nice distraction to think this way.

But the ride is still over too quickly.

My building looks a little worse for wear, but otherwise it is the same as it was in my memory. I wonder if anyone from my childhood still lives here, or if they've all moved away or died. I find myself hoping that I will see a familiar face.

We climb the steps to the top floor and the closer we get, the heavier I feel. Today I am Sisyphus again, and the boulder is about to squash me for good. I hear a faint, insane giggle and realize that it's coming from me.

Louise looks at me with alarm.

"Delphine . . ."

"I'm fine."

I'm lying, and she knows it, but she does not press me. There is no way to make this easier.

Finally, we reach the top. The paint on the door is flaked and cracking. I can fix that.

The door handle will need replacing. That too I can fix.

When Louise hands me the key and I turn it in the lock, I hear the groan of a hinge that is rarely used, and I get a whiff of stale air.

That's okay. I can open the windows.

We step inside and I place down Minette's carrier and my luggage before turning on the lights.

The wallpaper will need to be switched out. It looks oily, like it has seen too many burnt dinners.

The kitchen too will need to be refurbished. I run my fingers over the counters and look at the tacky linoleum beneath my feet.

In the living room, the old record player is still standing, and I can almost hear it croon a ghostly tune.

> There's a somebody I'm longin' to see
> I hope that he turns out to be
> Someone who'll watch over me

There is no question of me going into Maman's bedroom or mine. Not today.

There is really only one place for me to go.

As I walk down the hallway, I expect . . . something. More. Some sort of event.

It feels so wrong to me that it can feel so absolutely ordinary walking to the balcony where my mother died.

As I open the doors and step out, I wish myself far away. I long for my home in Havana, for my little garden, for the freedom of the open sea, for Papa's ribald stories shouted across a crowded bar. Most of all, I long for Javier, and I hope he knows that I am checking all the news I can get hold of and praying that he is safe.

I can't believe I mourned Paris so much that I called it Eden, the perfect place. I don't want a cold winter and a rainy, gray summer.

I don't want to be here anymore. I want to be anywhere but here, in the place of my beginning, at the root of all my shame.

Louise comes out to stand beside me.

This is where she found us both a lifetime ago. Here, in this very spot. I can't look her in the eye.

"I thought she'd be here," I whisper brokenly. "Not really, of course. But I thought that I would feel her—a living, breathing presence—but she isn't here. She's not like a genie in a bottle from one of the stories she used to read me, she's not clinging to her old things. She's just gone."

Louise takes my face in her hands and wipes away the tears.

"She's not part of her things, or this place. She's part of *you*. Hers is the voice inside you telling you to be wild, as she was, but stronger, and wiser. Hers is the whisper telling you to seize every chance at happiness that you will ever get, and that she will love you always. Your mother would be so proud of you. Be proud of yourself, Delphine."

The old guilt rises up from some deep place inside me and I pull away, lean forward, and grip the railing. "How can I be proud of who I am now? After who I was before?"

"The girl you were before kept you alive long enough to become the woman you are now," Louise says firmly. "Never forget that. Let her go now, Delphine. She has been dead for a long time. Let her go find your mother, and rest beside her in peace."

.   .   .

The next morning, I find a letter, waiting for me amongst the mail that Louise has been collecting on my behalf, piled onto the kitchen table.

> *Delphine,*
>
> *This letter will find you back in Paris, and I hope it serves as a warm welcome. I'm not much for letters, so forgive me for not knowing what to say. I got terrible marks in literature all my life, except in university where you did my work for me.*
>
> *We can't all be wordsmiths like you, flaca. Congratulations on your book. I knew you'd do it.*
>
> *Things here are difficult. My father is under investigation. I don't want to say more, though my hope is that no one but you is reading this.*
>
> *I still have people who can get my letters to you safely, so don't worry about not hearing from me, and don't you dare think about coming back here. I will invite you myself when it's safe again. In the meantime, don't forget all your Spanish after I took the trouble to teach you.*
>
> *I know things must be hard for you right now, but they will improve once you settle in. Don't be so glum. And make sure you go outside.*

How is your Papa Hemingway? Did he reply to your letter?
He'd be a fool not to.
Tell me about what your publisher is planning?
Your friend always,
Javier

I hold it to my lips and kiss the paper. He's safe. Thank God he is safe. I can bear anything if he is all right.

I go through the rest of the mail, but there is nothing from Papa. I groan a little and sink into a chair.

I have to give him up. I know that I do. The silence is the answer.

He doesn't want to claim me.

And perhaps that is fair.

I am a grown woman in need of neither mother nor father.

Perhaps I am strong enough now to endure this very predictable outcome with grace.

Tomorrow, I will consider all of those things.

But tonight, I want to lie down on the balcony and wish on the lights for a world that doesn't break the dreams of little girls every day.

Chapter Seventeen

~~~~~~~~~~~~~~~~

Papa

Paris, France
May 1961

I am having the walls of the apartment painted the palest yellow, like sweet butter. I'm also having the chandelier replaced and filled with brighter bulbs. The windows I've already had redone with obscenely expensive Venetian glass. But this is the best use I can think of for my first advance check. I want to capture sunshine and fill my world with it. I want to drive away any ghosts or cobwebs lurking in the corners. I am taking Maman's big bedroom for myself, and my own bedroom will become a place to keep books. I'm having bookshelves custom-made in the shape of ceiba trees. Louise says that I already have plenty of bookshelves in the study, but I tell her that one can never have too many books.

Minette has her own corner in the living room, with a plush burgundy bed filled with goose feathers. She has already started nibbling holes in it. I intend to spoil her rotten.

I am determined to be happy here, in this home that has been in my family for generations but seen precious little joy. Who knows if I will ever find a husband to stand by me? Or have children whose plump little feet will toddle up and down these halls?

I cannot say.

But there will be joy.

Today, of all days, there is joy.

My book is here. *My* book, which will outlive every child ever born.

The package is waiting for me on my doorstep when I arrive home from the market. As soon as I see it, I know.

I've been working directly through my French publisher on edits, but this is the first time I've seen the finished product. The English version will be released next month and then the foreign editions—French of course, Spanish, Italian, German, Russian so far. Random House is confident there will be more.

I am surprised that my hands don't tremble as I unwrap the package, but in the back of my mind I know that this is a moment I will look back on for the rest of my life. I hold myself with the poise of a ballerina, and as the wrapping falls away I can see a peacock blue cover with gilded golden letters proclaiming to the world that *The House of Pristine Sorrows* is a novel. A real novel.

I run my fingers over it. I take in the contrasting textures: the letters rough, the rest smooth. I hold it up to my face and inhale deeply, adoring the scent of the pages.

I am aware that I am weeping but I am beaming also, the laughter pealing out of my body like a tolling bell.

Someday soon, there will be critics, informed and otherwise, jockeying for the opportunity to rip this novel to pieces. I know this.

But I really don't give a damn.

Because today, there is no fear. No doubt. No shame.

Today I am victorious. Today, I am born again.

.   .   .

Paris, France
July 1961

In the end, it is Louise who tells me that he is dead. She arrives at my flat so early that I am still in my nightgown, with my hair in curlers, debating whether to get out of bed for the day.

She uses her key instead of knocking and rouses me from my half sleep in her gentle way. She comes to me dressed like an ordinary woman, not like a nun, with her graying blonde hair hanging in her face.

"Wake up, child."

I sit up and blink at her and she cups my face in her smooth hands.

"He's gone to God," she says quietly. "I wanted you to hear it from me first and not the papers. I'm so sorry, Delphine. He's dead."

She does not say who because she does not need to. The tears are instant, pouring from my wide eyes through the cracks of her fingers. I accept it without question. Somehow I know.

"How?"

She looks very much like she does not want to tell me. Her voice drops low. "The papers say that it was an accident but . . . I have it from a reliable source that he shot himself."

I close my eyes. Quick as a flash I can see it before I can force myself not to. I see the blood. I'm sure it was everywhere. Just like Maman's.

I feel my body heave forward and she holds me like that for a while, neither of us speaking.

But then I slide out of her grasp and clear my throat. "Thank you for telling me. Would you like some coffee?"

I pad down the hallway to the kitchen and she follows, buzzing with concern.

"We should talk about this."

I feel an insane laugh rise up in my throat. "Why? Will it bring him back? Will it bring my mother back?"

"Well, we should pray, then."

I cannot keep the disdain from my voice. "Because *that* has been so effective."

She knows me better than to push me when I am seething. She lets me make two cups of coffee in silence.

But as she takes hers, she pins me down with that owl-like gaze of hers.

"I told you what I did about your parentage all those years ago to spare you this pain. I didn't want you clinging to a phantom."

But he *wasn't* a phantom. I believe that I knew him. He was real to me.

I put my hand to my forehead.

I know she means well, I really do, but I don't need her mothering. My skin has turned from enamel to steel.

I already know, even as I sob quietly into my cup, that I will be okay.

That really, on a starkly practical level, this changes nothing for me. He was never really mine. I owned him as much as one owns the birdsong in the trees.

I have my own life, and much to look forward to. And anyway, I have been through far worse than this.

So I will be fine, in the end.

But not today.

. . .

I have never been to the grave site before.

I didn't go to the funeral. Louise was there but they buried Maman without me. I was in no state to get out of bed and I also had it in my mind that if I turned up, she might come flying out of her grave, shroud flapping, to accuse me of her murder.

Walking into the cemetery now just as the dawn breaks, I have a distinct sense that she is watching me.

I kneel in front of her tombstone and lay down the single sun-flower I have brought with me.

"Bonjour, Maman."

A blackbird answers me, but she does not.

I swallow. "I've come to tell you that he died. Hemingway. Papa."

I feel oddly numb telling her this. After all, she's been dead for more than fifteen years. Perhaps she is past such silly troubles. I should hope so.

"I wrote him a letter, telling him everything that you told me, and everything that happened to you. Everything that I did to find him. But I don't know if he read it or not. I suppose I never will now."

I take a breath. I am forced to accept the obvious but somehow astonishing truth that she will never answer me again.

"I defended your poetry to him. And he remembered you, how radiant you were. I don't think he was ever capable of loving a woman . . . not just you. I know you always felt you weren't good enough. But I don't think it was that. You were perfectly lovable. Truly.

"I wanted to tell you that I have three novels published and they've all done so well. I'm a wealthy woman in my own right. And lately I've decided that maybe it's possible for someone to love me and it not be a waste. I won't chase it, but I won't run from it either. I'm hopeful. For so many things. I have made it further than I ever thought possible. I think I will see how far the current can carry me. I'm not afraid of the storms now, for I have learned how to sail. I think you would be proud of me.

"Women can vote now too. I knew you'd want to know. I vote in every election. Every single one, Maman. And I fixed up the apartment, hired a contractor and everything. It looks beautiful. I have a cat, Minette, and I'm thinking of getting another one."

I place my hand on the polished stone. In a more merciful life, this stone would disappear beneath my touch, and Maman would get up from her grave refreshed from an afternoon nap, take my hand, and lead me on some wild adventure.

Fix your hair, Delphine, this isn't a farm. I have to live here, you know. Oh, look, there's Remy. I used to know him! Come on, let's see if he'll buy us an ice cream.

But not in this one.

I kiss the headstone. I see myself sitting at her feet as she tells me stories of when she was young and her world burned bright. I hear her voice singing in my ear, clear as ever.

The Wildest Sun

No one here can love or understand me
What hard luck stories they all hand me
Pack up all my cares and woe, here I go, winging low
Bye, bye, blackbird

The pain washes over me and I don't fight it. I let it toss me in its depths and I feel tiny, gasping breaths leave my body.

"Oh, Maman. Tu me manques. I wish we'd had more time. All three of us. I think we could have managed if we'd just had a little more time."

. . .

Antibes, France
September 1964

"Are you sure you want to buy this?" Monsieur Satie asks again. He is an anxious little man with a thin ginger-colored mustache. He rifles through the sheaf of papers in his hand. I know you aren't meant to judge books by their covers, but you would never take him for anything other than an accountant.

I have been contemplating it for years. "Yes."

"Mademoiselle Auber, this is a very expensive property."

I gesture to our ornate surroundings. Six bedrooms, four baths. A kitchen that I could fit my entire Paris flat into. Gigantic windows with a view of the cliff and the bright blue sea beyond. The mid-morning sunlight has made everything look vaguely orange.

"It's a chateau in the Côte d'Azur with a view of the ocean. I expect it would be expensive. It was my grandmother's when she was a girl. She sold it to pay off debts and I want it back in the family."

He dabs at his face with a handkerchief. "But, mademoiselle, you don't have children. This is a house for a family, surely? An heirloom to be passed down through the generations. You don't even have a husband, though I'm sure one will arrive presently."

I grin. Now that I am approaching thirty-six and still unmarried, people constantly feel the need to conciliate me on my poisonous bad luck. I am currently entertaining two gentlemen and I think one is rather taken by me, but I don't feel the need to mention it.

"I am significantly less sure, but I appreciate the sentiment."

"It's a valuable investment for certain. And you can afford it, with your books having done so well, but . . ."

"Good, that's settled. I'll sign the papers."

"But, mademoiselle, you have always been so conservative before. Why spend so much now?"

I stroll over to the banister and run my hands along the fine mahogany. "Because, Monsieur Satie, as you've said, I have saved most of my money. I'll buy this house and then I'll buy a sailboat to keep in the dock."

He shifts his weight from one foot to the other. Clearly, he is realizing that I am serious.

"Why not start with something smaller? And then when you find a husband—"

I cut him off as gently as I can. "Have you been advised of some new financial policy that allows me to take my money with me when I die?"

"Well, no."

I take my checkbook out of my handbag. The cerulean fountain pen that Javier gave me is safely tucked away inside.

"So then, why not?"

. . .

As soon as I have the keys, I write a letter to Blue and Delia and invite them to come next summer, as soon as I am settled. I feel a rush of pride inviting them to a home of my own.

> *You will be the first and most honored guests in my*
> *new home. I am practicing my cooking especially for*
> *you. Maybe we can visit Paris also so that you can finally*
> *meet Louise.*
> *I can't wait to see you both.*
> *Love,*
> *Delphine*

I pass the first few weeks picking out furniture from catalogs and watching the workers bring it in from my perch on the balcony—oh, the balcony. It is the stuff of dreams. I could live the rest of my days out here.

My assistant, Adeline, arrives a few days after I do and brings the cats with her. Simone and Minette chase each other through the long hallways, and I hear the occasional crash as they go tumbling down the stairwells.

Adeline pops her head out onto the balcony, where she finds me curled up in a folding chair with a poetry book and a glass of Chardonnay.

"The desk and typewriter are set up in the upstairs room you picked out, the one that gets all the sunlight in the morning. And your bed is ready too." She looks down at her feet and coughs. "So you can stop sleeping out here, madame. Someone may see you and people will talk."

People will talk. A prequel to endless wasted lives.

I glance up at her. "You can look at me when you speak."

She raises her eyes. They are the color of cornflowers, like Maman's.

"Monsieur Martin phoned to congratulate you on your lovely new home."

The editor for my French publisher. A boys' club member if ever there was one. My hairstylist is his latest mistress. He's not my favorite.

I stifle a laugh. "And?"

"And he has asked again if you will put your real name on your fourth book."

I flip a page. "No."

"Or if you will at least explain yourself."

"I told him I have my reasons. The English publisher, Spanish publisher, and all the rest are fine with my decision."

"And those reasons are . . . ?"

She is nearly stammering in her exasperation. Obviously, she has been persuaded to wear me down. Perhaps even paid to.

"Mademoiselle, please. If you are afraid of the reception you will get, you shouldn't be. Almost all of the reactions to your work have been positive. The harshest critics praise you to the sky. They won't mind that you're a woman, if that's what you're afraid of."

"I am running out of ways to say no. Tell him to come here and beg himself if he wants to hear me say it again before I get back to Paris next month. He's a grown man, you don't need to do his dirty work."

She flushes. "Mademoiselle, he has offered to negotiate an increase in your pay if you will relent. Won't you at least consider it?"

I am not even irritated with her, poor girl. She is twenty-two, very pretty, blissfully unaware of said fact, and desperate to please everyone who blinks in her direction. She is no match for a man like that. Not yet, at least.

"I *have* considered it, that's what seems lost on him and his cohorts, and I am saying no. If you learn nothing else from working for me, learn that 'No' can be a complete sentence. Now, is that everything?"

She is beaten. She digs into her pocketbook. "I have some letters for you. I picked them up from the publisher."

I jump up and snatch them from her outstretched hands. "Is it Javier?"

She shakes her head gently and I tilt my head away so she won't see how crushed I am. But I am sure that my voice must have given away my hope.

It's been three months since his last letter. I may write to him again tomorrow in case my reply was lost. I am so afraid for him that some days it leeches all of the joy out of my world, even though I know he would not want it to.

"They look like they're from readers. The New York publisher sent them on."

I open the first envelope. I read the letter twice.

Dear Violette,

I really enjoyed your novel Gossamer. *Actually, I stole it from the bookstore when no one was looking. I read it three times. Once I was late for school reading it. I'm in grade nine.*

I wanted to write a letter to you, and I took a job painting fences to get the money for postage. It was hard to get since everyone prefers to hire boys for that kind of work. I live in a small town in a place called Ohio. You have probably never heard of it. Nothing ever happens here. It's just my mom and I. She drinks as much as the mother in the book. Sometimes I want to run away too.

I have never been to France but I felt like you took me there. I went to the library and looked up some photographs. Very pretty.

Thank you for writing this book. I look forward to anything else you write next.

Yours Truly,

Suzanne Logan

I fold the letter up and put it into my pocket.

"You said my desk is set up?"

"Yes."

"I'll reply to this one later, then. Can you mail it in the morning?"

"Yes, of course."

I already know what I will say. The answer unfolds in my mind with no effort at all.

Dear Suzanne,

Thank you for writing to me. I'm very glad you liked the book.

I am certain that one day not too long from now you will be able to go wherever you like. Don't run away. Finish school, and then find something to walk towards instead. Something that will make you happy.

I have attached ten dollars. Save half, and use the other half to buy more books. They help.

If you ever want to write to me again I will reimburse you for the postage.

Sincerely,

Violette

The rosy glow of the setting sun cascades over us. Adeline holds up a hand to shield her face.

It's going to be a beautiful evening. I make a quick decision.

"I think I'll go for a sail. Would you mind feeding the cats their dinner?"

She looks aghast. "Mademoiselle, you can't go sailing in the evening! It will be dark soon, it's dangerous!"

"I won't go far from shore. The lights will guide me. I'll be fine."

"You should take someone with you."

I am already winding my hair into a quick bun to keep it back from my face.

"I'll scour the house for volunteers. In the meantime, please don't wait for me to have dinner. There's some ham in the kitchen."

I breeze by her and give her a swift pat on the shoulder on the way out.

It is a short walk down the hill and to the pier. My as-of-yet-nameless boat is moored right where I left her.

I feel the familiar rocking as I climb onto the deck, and I have no issue shortening the sail in the dimming light. Though really, I don't need my eyes to do it anymore. The running rig is marked already so it will be easy to adjust if I need to.

Javier and I always used to argue over whether the sunset was orange or red. Today both of us are wrong. It's pink as cotton candy.

I sail over calm water into thick clouds, farther out than I said I would. Still, there is always that voice inside me urging me on, daring me to take one more step towards the edge.

"A wild spirit," Maman always called me, with a rueful shake of the head. "But," she'd add, "better wild than weak."

Louise would tell me that there is no changing some parts of my baser nature, and that channeling it into something useful is the best way to make sure I live a meaningful life. Blue and Delia would tell me to endure and to trust in myself.

Javier would tell me not to outsmart my common sense and to be grateful for every day aboveground.

And Papa . . .

I have to lean against the wheel when I think about Papa. It's astonishing how much I can miss a being that I could only catch in glimpses, like light filtered through pieces of glass.

And even though I stopped worshipping him in the end, I never stopped loving him. I never stopped loving everything that he gave me the courage to do.

Whether he was truly my father I will never know, but it has been many years since I have truly cared. He failed me, inspired me, crushed me, and built me back up. He was my North Star, and I will always be grateful.

I wonder what he thought of me, in the end? If he saw a young woman living a life worthy of remembrance?

I never fully let them go. Not any of them. Teddy. Louise. Maman. Papa.

Maybe even Javier is lost to me. Maybe I will never again receive a reply to my letters, or see his beam as he bounces up the path to my door. I can hope. But my constant vigil will not bring him back.

I thought I was honoring their memories by wrapping myself up in them, trying to stop them from becoming faceless, nameless leaves lost on the ever-flowing tide.

And maybe I was.

But I was also just as afraid to decide who I am without them.

The sun dips behind the clouds at last, and finally, I let them go.

I watch the ghosts of all who I have loved dance off into the pink mist, and I raise my hand and wish them well. I have their gifts, and memories, even if I don't have them anymore. Those are mine to keep.

The lights from the shore beckon. It's growing dark and I know it's time to go back to my beautiful home, and my cats curled up beneath my bedsheets, and the silence that I will soon fill with the clacking of fingers on typewriter keys.

I have only this fragile flesh, and a voice, and time. So little time.

Because I need to tell her. I need to tell that lonely girl on the rooftop in the too-small shoes that she is artfully made. I have to try.

This is who I am: Delphine, who will never be silent and who will die only once.

Look what you have done.

Here I am: chosen. Golden at last.

Acknowledgments

Writing my sophomore novel was a transformative experience for me. One riddled with fear, anxiety, joy, reckonings, growth, and in the end, a sense of peace.

As always, thank you to my fantastic literary agent, Rebecca Scherer, and everyone at JRA. Thank you so much to my amazing editor, Maya Ziv, and the entire team at Dutton. It's been a dream come true continuing to work with all of you.

A very special merci beaucoup to my favorite French auntie Cecile for your insight and assistance. And to mi prima Cubana, the incomparable Morgan Radford: Your invaluable knowledge has made this book possible. I am so grateful to you. Y con tumbao.

Lastly, my deepest gratitude to my supportive readers. I'd like to take a moment to acknowledge you.

Look how far we've come.

About the Author

Asha Lemmie is the *New York Times* bestselling author of *Fifty Words for Rain* and *The Wildest Sun*. She currently resides in New York City but can frequently be found wandering. Asha writes historical fiction that focuses on bringing unique perspectives to life.